About the Author

Ian Robert Bell was born in Newcastle-upon-Tyne, England, in 1955. He studied for an MA degree at York University in 1979 before working as a picture restorer for a number of art galleries and museums in the north of England, including those of the city of Sheffield where he now lives. Though a restorer of paintings by profession, he took up creative writing as his main occupation in 2002 and works primarily in the mystery/thriller end of the literary spectrum. He is also the author of two other books: *London Underground* and *The Beauty and the Blood.*

Resurrection Blues

Ian Robert Bell

Resurrection Blues

Olympia Publishers
London

www.olympiapublishers.com
OLYMPIA PAPERBACK EDITION

A CIP catalogue record for this title is
available from the British Library.

ISBN: 978-1-78830-308-8

This is a work of fiction.
Names, characters, places and incidents originate from the writer's
imagination. Any resemblance to actual persons, living or dead, is purely
coincidental.

First Published in 2019

Olympia Publishers
60 Cannon Street
London
EC4N 6NP

Printed in Great Britain

PROLOGUE

London Daily News
Police Raid in Harlow

By Charles Cooper
London Daily News
Following reports of a serious incident, police have raided a house in the town of Harlow, Essex, in the early hours of Saturday morning. A bulldozer had to be used to gain entry into the heavily barricaded building, thought to be the headquarters of a local gang of Hells Angels. The building was found to be deserted and no arrests were made, but some computers and other sensitive material were seized and a man was spotted running away from the scene, whom police wish to question. A spokesman for the Essex police has since confirmed that the building was being used as a clubhouse for the Hells Angels, and may even have formed their main headquarters in England. As such, the material found in the building, including a memory stick left in one of the computers, may provide authorities with much valuable information concerning the activities of other Hells Angels gangs in Britain and abroad.

One

Where was he?

Cassidy glanced at his watch for the tenth time in as many minutes. It was getting on for nine o'clock of a cold November evening and his contact hadn't shown up yet. He wanted to believe that everything was going according to plan and that whoever it was that was coming to pick him up had just been delayed in traffic, but that wasn't the way that Silver worked. Jimmy Silver enjoyed keeping his underlings waiting.

No. Not waiting—just playing with his mind.

Silver owned him heart and soul and there wasn't a damn thing he could do about it. He would just have to sit tight in this little corner of the London pub he'd been told to go to and wait.

That's what she was doing. The woman sitting opposite to him across the room in profile. She was waiting, he could tell. There was a clock on the wall and she kept looking at it every few minutes before getting up to put some coins in a slot machine and pulling the lever hard. Then, pocketing her winnings, she would sit back down and light up another cigarette, staring fixedly at the clock as if willing its hands to go round.

Strange, thought Cassidy, how she just sat there as cool as ice smoking her cigarette. Smoking had been banned in London pubs years ago but nobody took any notice in this place. It wasn't your usual sort of pub and the clientele weren't your usual sort of people.

Stranger still was the way she looked. Dressed in a black leather biker jacket and faded blue jeans, she looked more of a 1980's biker-chick than anything contemporary. The mirrored sunglasses concealing her eyes made it difficult to estimate her age. About twenty-three he guessed. Not more than twenty-five at most; black hair with a long, angular face and a firmly set jaw. Not a girl he would care to date, but fascinating all the same.

Before Cassidy could finish this thought, he was dazzled by the flash of her mirrored sunglasses as she momentarily turned her head towards him. Pale white skin with a small, five-pointed black star tattooed on her right cheek. An ornamental silver razor blade dangled on a short chain from one of her earlobes. Long nose, aquiline but broken at some point in the past and badly set. No, she was definitely not his type. Probably a dyke from up the road, he reasoned. Soho was full of them.

Satisfied with this assumption, Cassidy returned to the newspaper he'd been reading. There was an interesting article about some police activity up in Harlow which had caught his attention. Something about the Hells Angels and a police raid. He had a friend with Hells Angel connections and knew that his boss, Jimmy Silver sometimes did business with them. Funny to think that an organisation like the HA were still around in this day and age, but they were. Apparently, some computers had been seized by police during the raid and someone had left a memory stick in one of them containing some valuable information about Hells Angel's activities in the UK. *I bet he's popular,* thought Cassidy as he turned the page.

The woman got up and walked over to the slot machine, humming a tune softly to herself as she went. Cassidy noticed her boots. They were old black biker boots, scuffed at the toes and in a style well out of date. A fox's tail hung from a strap on her waist belt as if she was saying to anyone looking: "You got any problems with that?" She was truly a piece of work.

Kerchung! Kerchung! Kerchung! The ancient machine paid out immediately and the woman pawed her winnings out of its tray. Then she sat down once more at her table and resumed her lonely vigil with the clock. Cassidy shrugged and turned the pages of his newspaper. This time his attention was caught by news of a fatal shooting in the Kilburn district. Turned out the victim was an Italian guy called Lorenzo Molinari, believed to have had associations with a Neapolitan crime gang known as the Camorra. Cassidy knew the Neapolitans had a habit of resting their hitmen in England, keeping them out of sight long enough for the trail to go cold, at which point they could use them to launder some of their money in the London property market. Judging by the mess he'd been found in, it looked like someone had wanted this geezer real bad – shot twice in the chest and once in the head on his own doorstep, and he wasn't the first. Another bloke by the name of Francesco Bianchi had been found dead in an alleyway up in Maida Vale. Same pattern. Shot in the chest and head, and with a single black rose left near the body with a note bearing the phrase: "Kind Regards—Sterling". Clearly someone was sending a message to the Camorra to keep off their turf.

Dammit! Where was his ride?

He'd expected a car turning up around nine, and now it was nearly 9:30. They were late. Instinctively he checked his mobile but then remembered that Silver and his men never used mobiles in the capital if they could help it, preferring instead to keep their phone chatter to a minimum to avoid being tracked.

Stuart Cassidy was in a dilemma. He could get up now and walk away, but that would be inviting trouble. In his line of business you never crossed a crime boss without attracting some form of retribution sooner or later. Equally, he couldn't ring Silver because he'd been given strict instructions not to. In a quandary what best to do, Cassidy ordered another drink at the bar and sat back down in his seat waiting for the signal he'd been told to expect. Two short blasts on a car horn followed by one long one, then the sequence repeated – standard Morse Code.

Just then a stranger walked into the bar. Male, dressed casual-smart and around the same age as Cassidy – about thirty, give or take a couple of years. The place was almost empty with only Cassidy, a disinterested bartender and the woman in sunglasses taking up any space. The woman tapped three times on her table with a pound coin and the man walked over and sat down facing her.

Not a dyke then, thought Cassidy as the pair began talking. They kept their voices low, but he managed to catch a bit of what they were saying.

'I don't need anything special,' the woman said in a dark, husky voice, 'just so long as it's quiet.'

The man nodded. 'You returning?' he enquired, lifting a small package out of his coat pocket.

'No. It's a one-way trip.'

'Five hundred then,' the man replied, pushing the package across the table towards her.

The woman produced a wad of banknotes and handed them over in exchange. 'It had better work,' she said with a faux smile.

The man nodded again. Taking the money, he got up and left, glancing momentarily at the bartender as he reached for the door. The bartender looked away, pretending not to notice. Whatever had just taken place wasn't any of his business and he didn't own the pub so it didn't matter anyway.

Junkie, thought Cassidy. *She's probably about to take her last shot by the sound of it, poor lass...* For some reason the image of a long dead acquaintance came into his mind. Claude Dubois was his name. He'd been a heroin addict found dead in this very same bar back in 2003. It looked like the young woman in the mirrored sunglasses was going the same way. *Pity...*

The woman stubbed out her cigarette and got up from her seat. Sliding the package she'd been given into her inside jacket pocket, she walked towards the door and left the bar. Cassidy was glad when she'd gone. She'd given him the creeps. It was as if the whole room had suddenly become brighter the moment she left. Odd thing that.

He heard a sound. It was a car horn. Two short beeps and then a long one. He listened again. The sequence repeated. It was his signal. Folding up his newspaper, he swallowed the remains of his pint and walked out into the cold night air.

Lifting up his collar against the chill, Cassidy looked around. A graphite-grey BMW saloon was parked about thirty metres up the road. That was the car. He made towards it but as he did so, his attention was caught by something else. It was the woman in the sunglasses and she was about to climb into the saddle of the biggest low-rider muscle bike he'd ever seen. All black and chrome with swept back handlebars and twin exhausts, the machine roared into life as she kicked the starter down. Then she rode off in the direction of Lisle Street without looking back.

Not a junkie then, thought Cassidy as he went to meet his contact. But what was she up to he wondered?

Two

The Cumberland Arms Tavern
  Harlow, Essex, late evening, 23 November 2016

Joe Rackham sat tearing up the table mats in his favourite corner of the Cumberland Arms tavern. He was in a foul mood. As if the police raid hadn't been bad enough, his best mate, Gordon Dyer, had just got into an argument with his woman and slapped her hard across the face, prompting her to take a seat at another table nearer the bar just in case things got worse.

It was all getting out of hand, thought Joe as he started work on his fourth table mat of the evening. The problem with Gordon and Christine he knew he could solve, but the police raid on the Hells Angel's clubhouse was a different matter. He knew it wouldn't be long before the head honchos in California got wind of it and then there would be trouble. Pressure would be brought to bear and heads would roll. But what could he do? The police had the memory stick and all the hard drives. Names and addresses of every Hells Angel member in England and the Netherlands. It was nothing short of a complete disaster, and all because of that stupid cunt he'd left in charge of the place. As for Gordon Dyer, he would have a quiet word with him later and tell him the facts of life. Gordon wasn't a full-patch member of the Angels yet and if he wanted his colours then he would have to clean up his act fast. It wasn't the done thing to go round beating up your girlfriend in a public place. It got the Angels a bad name.

Around 9.30, a few more people drifted into the bar from the fog-bound street outside. Most of them were regulars, and of these the majority were Blue Boars – the name of the Harlow chapter of the Hells Angels that Joe ran at the behest of his overlords in America. The gang had all but commandeered the Cumberland Arms since the police raid and were now settling in nicely.

About 9:45, Ray Dixon arrived and gave a nod in the direction of Joe's table before going over to order a drink at the bar. Then he went to have a chat with Gordon, glancing first at Christine sitting at her table near the counter. He could tell they'd had a row.

Across the room sat Whiskey Pete and Ronnie Frinton playing cards. They were both former blaggers and getting on in years, as was their leader, Joe. Most of the Angels had had some form of involvement with the police in the past but no one ever talked about it. The Hells Angels were a motorcycle club when all was said and done.

Bored with demolishing table mats, Joe got up and ordered a pint of Carling at the bar. As Ruth the barmaid poured him his pint, he turned and looked around the room. Everyone was behaving themselves. Good. That was the way he liked it. Joe ran a tight ship and wasn't going to stand for any nonsense from his subordinates.

Handing a fiver over the bar, he took his pint and waited for his change. Just then his mobile rang causing him to spill some of the amber liquid down his shirt collar. Muttering an oath, he reached for his phone and took the call.

'Yeah?' he said in a thick, estuary accent.

'It's me—Sterling,' came a husky, female voice on the other end of the line.

'Where are you calling from?' enquired Joe, picking up his change from the counter.

'London! Where do you think?'

Joe creased his brow. The phone reception was poor near the counter so he moved across the room to where he knew it was better.

'You still got my gear?' he asked gruffly.

'Course I have,' the woman replied. 'It's in the old warehouse near Tower Bridge. Safe as houses it is.'

'It had better be. How's the bike performing by the way?'

'Brilliant! Thanks for the loan of it. Jerry Skinner brought it round for me a few days ago. Drives like a dream it does.'

Joe's brow creased again. 'Tell that stupid cunt, Skinner he'd better stay away from Harlow if he knows what's good for him. I've got half of California breathing down my neck on account of him.'

The woman laughed. 'Just like the old days, eh, Joe? When Jerry fucks up he really does it big time.'

'Not funny, Sterling. The Essex coppers will have handed the memory stick over to the Metropolitan Police by now. This thing is massive.'

'Never mind, Joe. There's always a way to sort things out.'

'What do you mean…?'

'Just leave it with me. I'll think of something.'

'Like what?'

'Getting your memory stick and hard drives back, that's what.'

'Impossible—'

'Nothing's impossible, Joe. Both you and Skinner never thought you'd ever see me again but you did. Anyway, it's not the reason I rang.'

'Oh... and why did you ring then?'

Joe heard the woman take a breath. As she paused, he heard the sound of road traffic in the background. Then she spoke:

'You haven't seen any strangers in the Cumberland today by any chance, have you?'

'Hmm, not really,' replied Joe, switching his mobile to his left ear. 'Why do you ask?'

'Well, it's just that I've had one of my premonitions, that's all. Now, think hard Joe. Has anyone you wouldn't normally see in a shit-hole like the Cumberland Arms paid the place a visit in the last few hours?'

Joe thought hard. He knew that Sterling's *premonitions* were usually quite a lot more than just vague hunches and wondered what on earth she could be driving at.

'Come to think of it, Sterl,' I did see someone earlier on. Tall, black guy. Smartly dressed in an expensive coat and wearing a trilby hat. He had a patch over one eye. Didn't stay long though.'

'Sounds like one of Silver's men,' the woman replied. 'I remember him from way back.'

'What's Silver doing sticking his nose in here for?' exclaimed Joe angrily.

'It's possibly got something to do with that lethal batch of ecstasy tablets you sold him. The ones you traded so you could buy all that A-grade cocaine you've got stashed away in my warehouse ready for distribution.'

'How did you know about the tablets?' said Rackham, his voice suddenly hardening.

'There's not much you can keep from beings like me, Joe. You should know that by now.'

Joe shrugged. 'So, what is it with the black guy then?'

Again, the woman took a breath. 'Think, Joe. Where exactly was the black guy sitting when he was in the bar?'

Rackham glanced around the room trying to recall where the man had been seated. The massive joint he'd smoked earlier in the day wasn't helping. Then he remembered.

'He was over by the radiator sitting next to the window...'

Joe's voice trailed off when he spotted the bag. A large, navy blue holdall had been wedged under the bench where the black guy had been seated. There were some wires sticking out of it.

'Sterling, I think Silver's left his calling card. It's a bomb—!'

Joe Rackham stood with the others about fifty metres up the road waiting for the blast. The Cumberland Arms was a typical Essex pub with a small forecourt patio and wooden benches outside. There was a blinding flash followed by a deafening roar as the bomb exploded blowing all the windows out across the street. With his ears still ringing, Joe reached for his phone to check if it was still connected. It wasn't. The woman had rung off, presumably having some business of her own to attend to. She'd done her job and the gang had been lucky that evening. But for how long?

Three

'You can take the blindfold off now, Mr Cassidy.'

Stuart recognised the voice. It belonged to the black guy with the eye patch sitting next to him in the passenger seat.

'Where are we?' said Cassidy staring out of the tinted windows of the BMW.

'That's classified,' replied the man. 'Step out of the car and we'll go and meet Sir James.'

The door clicked open allowing Cassidy to step out. It was still dark and the air was cold with a distinct maritime feel to it. He guessed he must be somewhere near the sea.

'This way,' said his companion, putting on the trilby hat he'd kept rested on his knees for most of the journey. 'My name is Tarrou by the way. I'm Nigerian.'

Together, they walked up the gravel drive towards a spacious Victorian mansion with neatly trimmed lawns and concealed lights. More of a castle than a country house, the place oozed with malevolent charm and eerie shadows. As they reached the front entrance, one of the shadows detached itself from the wall and blocked their path.

The shadow was another of Silver's henchmen. One big son of a bitch, he towered above Cassidy with shoulders wide enough to block the doorway. Growling some words at the black man, the minder eyed Cassidy suspiciously.

'It's all right, Fetch. He's been cleared,' replied Tarrou. 'You can let him through.'

The guard nodded and resumed his position near the doorway, allowing them both to pass. Cassidy could feel the man's eyes on his back as they entered the house.

The entrance hall was like something out of an Addams Family movie and the living room wasn't much better, with a high, plaster ceiling and a few pieces of antique furniture scattered about the place. It was evident that nobody spent much time there.

'Follow me.'

Tarrou led Cassidy down a narrow corridor towards the rear of the house. He halted outside a door at the end of the corridor and knocked softly.

'Show him in, Tarrou,' came a voice from within.

The room's only light came from a table lamp set atop a huge Renaissance-style desk. Behind the desk sat a middle-aged man with dark hair turning grey at the temples. Evidently the room functioned as some kind of study, but Cassidy could have sworn it more resembled the lair of some arch-predator than any comfortable office space. In spite of the central heating, the room felt cold with a definite chill to the air.

'Ah, Mr Cassidy! Pleased to make your acquaintance at last.' The man rose from his seat and extended his hand in greeting. Although Cassidy had never met his boss in the flesh before, he was surprised by how accurately he had pictured him to be. Suave and elegant, and wearing a crimson smoking jacket with a black velvet collar, he seemed like a creature from another time. And he had a faintly sinister upper-class accent to go with it.

'Sir James,' Cassidy heard himself say as he accepted Silver's hand. It was cold to the touch with a grip like steel.

'Call me, Jimmy,' said the man, putting his hand on Cassidy's left shoulder and leading him over to a leather upholstered wing-back chair. 'Sit down here and make yourself comfortable.'

'Uh, all right…'

Silver motioned for Cassidy to be seated, then glanced at Tarrou who was still standing by the door.

'Sorry we were late, boss,' said the Nigerian. 'That job up in Harlow took a bit longer than I expected. We were held up in traffic on the way back to London. It's foggy up in Essex.'

'I quite understand, Tarrou. That will be all for now.'

Tarrou nodded and left the room leaving both men alone.

'You must forgive me for having summoned you here at such an ungodly hour,' Silver smiled. 'Can I offer you a drink?' He produced a bottle of vintage brandy from one of the desk drawers along with two glasses. 'Oh, and do help yourself to the cigars,' he added, pointing to an ornate lacquered box on the table next to where Cassidy was seated. 'They're the finest Cuban. Only the best for my main man, eh Stuart?'

Cassidy lit his cigar with a lighter that had been placed near the box and took a sip of brandy. *He's calling me by my first name. He's after something… but what?*

'I hope the brandy is to your satisfaction, Stuart. My cellar is quite old and extensive. Goes all the way to the Vatican one might say. I'm only joking of course. We wouldn't want that now, would we?'

There was something in the way Silver was looking at him that made his flesh crawl. Narrow eyes. Always with a smile. The elderly patrician was in control and there wasn't a damn thing Cassidy could do about it.

'I expect you're wondering why I brought you here tonight, Stuart?'

Cassidy nodded and took another sip of brandy.

'Of course you are,' continued Silver, 'and you have a perfectly legitimate right to know. But before I tell you, might I enquire if you are in possession of a current passport?'

Cassidy nodded again. 'Yes I am, Mr Silver.'

'Good. Then we can get down to business. The fact of the matter is, I am in dire need of your services.'

Cassidy thought for a moment. What would a man like Jimmy Silver need him so desperately for? He'd run lots of errands for his boss in his time. Most of them in London and mostly to do with collecting rent from Silver's tenants. People who rented tiny basement flats and bedsits in the capital and who paid a fortune for the privilege. Whenever they got behind with their payments, Stuart would be sent round to have a quiet word with them. If they still didn't cough up then a different bloke would be sent to deal with the situation. It was how Silver worked.

'Look, Jimmy,' said Cassidy finishing his drink. 'It's all very interesting, but what exactly do you want me to do? Are you having problems with a difficult tenant?'

'I want you to go to Venice for me, Stuart.'

'Why?'

'Because there is someone there I would like you to check on for me. It's a woman. One of my former acquaintances in fact. Her name is Caroline Westvale… Lady Caroline Westvale to be precise. She looks after certain interests I have in Italy and I would like you to establish if she is running things to my satisfaction.'

'That's awfully flattering boss, but there are hundreds of perfectly good private investigators in this country. Why not let one of them go instead?'

Silver smiled and poured Cassidy another drink. Then he sat down opposite in a matching chair and fixed him with his gaze.

'Because you have all the right credentials, Mr Cassidy— *and because you work for me.*'

Cassidy sipped his brandy. It had been a long while since he had tasted anything this good.

'So what is it you want me to do exactly?'

Silver paused before answering. 'I want you to visit a cemetery for me and search for a corpse.'

Cassidy nearly choked on his drink. 'You want me to do what?!'

'I'll pay you two thousand pounds a day plus expenses,' Silver went on. 'Don't worry, Stuart; the body you will be investigating is interred in a tomb, not a burial pit. Lady Westvale holds the key to the door of the tomb. I will give you a letter of introduction to show to her. She knows who I am and there should be no problem in carrying out your task.'

Silver produced an envelope from deep inside his jacket pocket and handed it to Cassidy.

'I don't know, Mr Silver. I mean, it's an awfully weird thing to do.'

'There will be a twenty-thousand-pound bonus in it for you when you return to England. What do you say?'

Again, Cassidy gagged on his brandy.

'What do I do when I enter the tomb?'

'Simple. You go over to the coffin and open the lid.'

'Why?'

'To ascertain if there is still a body inside.'

'A body? The body of whom exactly?' Cassidy was aware his boss had dealings with Italian gangsters and wasn't sure what he was getting himself into.

'The body of a young woman,' Silver replied. 'Her name is Julie Kent.'

Cassidy thought hard. There was nothing intrinsically wrong about opening up a coffin and he did have some kind of official letter permitting him to do so. He would be in a foreign country and could only be deported back to England if he was caught in the act.

'Very well, Mr Silver, I'll take the job. But might I ask you a question?'

'Be my guest.'

'Who was Julie Kent?'

'Julie was my granddaughter, Stuart. She's been dead for quite some time.'

Cassidy stared at Silver's smiling face, the vintage brandy suddenly tasting bitter in his mouth.

'And now, Stuart, I think it is time we returned you to your home. My chauffeur will drive you back to London. I hope you don't mind wearing the blindfold again for the first half of the journey. Tarrou will tell you when you can take it off.'

Cassidy finished his drink and stood up, allowing Silver to put a hand on his shoulder and walk him to the door. 'I have every confidence in you, Mr Cassidy. I'm sure you'll be a great asset to my organisation. Here is my telephone number to take with you to Venice.'

Cassidy glanced at the piece of paper he'd been handed then placed it in his wallet.

'Whatever you find when you open up the coffin, Stuart, you must ring me as soon as possible. Is that understood?'

Silver opened the door. Cassidy wasn't at all surprised to find Tarrou standing there waiting for him on the other side.

'Tarrou will see you to the car now. Oh, and before I forget. You don't happen to know anything about those Camorra shootings in London, do you?'

Cassidy shook his head. 'No I don't, Mr Silver.'

'Thought not. Anyway, no matter. Goodbye Stuart, and have a pleasant journey.'

Four

She never wore a watch. Never much had the need for one. Time had long since ceased to have any meaning in her mind. All that mattered now was the fact she was in South London and travelling down a tree-lined boulevard on a powerful motorcycle towards her next appointment.

She reckoned it was around three o'clock in the morning. The city was dark and still. There was hardly anything moving on the road apart from the odd truck or two and a solitary urban fox that had crossed her path a while back. London could be like that in the wee small hours. It was her favourite time of the day.

It seemed like ages ago since she'd left the pub in Soho and roared off on her bike into the night. She'd stopped off at her old place to check on a few things and to make an urgent phone call to a friend. Then she'd waited until the city went to sleep. It was the way she liked to work.

So this was the London Borough of Camberwell, she thought. Leafy in parts, with some parks and gardens. A fashionable area now. Not like back in her day. Back then it had been a dump, with a few art colleges and some shabby students slumming it around in combat trousers and paint-spattered overalls. There had been a few punks too. All a long time ago.

Peckham Road. She was close. Not far now. Gearing down the bike, she cruised the last fifty metres or so then turned left down a side street and stopped at the kerb.

Turning off the engine, she looked around. The street was empty and silent. Good. That would make her job a whole lot easier.

Climbing off her bike, she began walking down the street until she came to a lamppost. Reading by its light, she thumbed through a street map until she came to the right page. Yes, this was the correct road. The map confirmed it. But where was number forty-three?

She looked at the nearest gatepost. Eighty-six—damn! She'd overshot and was on the wrong side of the street. Crossing the road, she doubled back a little until she found the right number. It was a small terraced house with a short path leading up to the front door. The amber glow from a fanlight window suggested someone was still up and about. Glancing round, she rang the doorbell.

Nothing.

She pressed the bell again.

There was a short interval of silence then the sound of someone coming down the hallway. She heard the sound of a door chain rattling and then the door opened.

'Yes… Who is it?'

He wasn't a tall man. About five-seven, with short, grey hair and a neatly trimmed moustache. Italian.

'Signor Bordoni?' she said. 'Signor Giuseppe Bordoni?'

The man let out a yell. He'd made the mistake of opening his door to a stranger. In a panic he tried to close it but the woman wedged it open with her boot. He tried to run but it was too late. Two bullets from a silenced weapon slammed into his back dropping him instantly. A third shot to his head finished him off. It was all over very quickly.

Looking down, the woman regarded her handiwork with satisfaction. Reaching into her inside pocket she removed a single black rose and placed it next to the dead man's body. 'That's for Naples,' she whispered softly in his ear. 'Have a nice time in hell.'

***

The two black youths clambered down from the open window then dropped the last couple of feet to the warehouse floor below. Dale felt a nudge to his shoulder. 'Come on bruv. Looks like there's no one about. Let's do this place over.'

'I dunno,' replied Dale. 'I've got a bad feeling about this job.'

As their eyes adjusted to the darkness, it became apparent they were standing in the ground floor well of an old loading bay. A shallow mezzanine level surrounded them on three sides which in turn gave access to the main staircase of the building.

'We go up here,' said Lee, pointing his torch at the stairs.

Silently, they climbed all the way up to the third floor landing trying every door on the way. All of them were locked, except for the last one which was set into the wall beneath an archway of red London brick. Evidently this was the oldest part of the building.

Together they passed through the door and found themselves in a long dark passageway. Fumbling for a switch, Lee made several clicks until a solitary fluorescent strip-light came on.

'It's fucking dead in here,' said Dale. 'Let's get back to Lambeth.'

'There's a door at the end of the corridor,' his friend replied. 'Maybe it's a storage area.'

Reaching the door, Lee tried the handle. It opened easily. 'Come on, he said, let's take a look inside.'

They went through the door and found themselves in a spacious chamber with a high ceiling. Lee flashed his torch around and gasped in astonishment. The room was almost entirely furnished with quality, high-end antique furniture set on an expensive Afghan carpet that covered most of the floor. Above their heads, suspended from the ceiling rafters hung a magnificent chandelier which still had a few lightbulbs remaining in it. Dale went over to the wall and switched them on. The light was dim but sufficient to make out some of the other objects in the room. A high-backed antique chair of ebonised wood together with a nineteenth-century *chaise longue* set in front of a folding screen decorated with faded press-cuttings and photographs of pop stars from a bygone era. A tapestry hung down the wall behind the screen.

'What is this place?' said Dale peering into the gloom.

'Must be storage for the antique trade,' replied Lee. 'Sotheby's or something.'

'I dunno, bruv. Looks like someone lives here,' Dale went on, going over to a small octagonal table beside the chair. There was an ashtray on the table filled with discarded cigarette butts. Lee shone his torch. 'Looks like this someone does coke as well,' he said running the palm of his hand across the surface of the table. Then he licked his fingers with the tip of his tongue. 'Good stuff an' all.'

Dale bent over the table to take a look. Then he heard the sound of an engine revving in the street outside.

'Someone's coming!'

'Relax man. It's probably just a bit of traffic in the road. Anyway, what's that over there?'

Lee was pointing to a large, square object in the shadows at the far end of the chamber. Curious to know what it was, they both went over to investigate.

The object was set on top of a wooden pallet and covered in black plastic sheeting. Lee gave his torch to Dale and lifted the sheeting. What he saw almost made his heart stop. There, stacked beneath the plastic sheeting was a large quantity of clear polythene bags filled with white powder. Lee looked at Dale.

'You thinkin' what I'm thinkin', bruv?'

Dale nodded and shone the torch directly at the bags while Lee went in search of something sharp. It wasn't long before he returned with an antique dagger in his hand that he'd found in the drawer of an old writing desk. Piercing one of the bags with its blade, he watched as a thin stream of white powder trickled out onto the floor. Then he bent down, picking up some of the powder and holding it to his tongue. 'Fucking A-grade Charlie!' he declared. 'Must be three hundred kilos of the stuff here, Dale!'

'You joking—'

'No. I'm speaking up! This stuff's got to be worth a fortune on the street. And there's something else on top of the stack. Looks like bags of crack.'

Carefully, he slit open one of the top bags and tested a sample on his tongue: 'It's pure, un-cut fentanyl. About fifty kilos—and there's some compressed cannabis resin as well.'

Another sound. This time it was the noise of an electric shutter-door opening up somewhere deep inside the building. Then there came the sound of a revving engine.

'It's a motorcycle,' said Dale. 'It's coming from the loading bay downstairs.'

Lee froze and listened, clutching the dagger in his hand. The sound stopped abruptly, like someone had switched off the engine. They waited for an interval... Nothing.

'Everything's cool,' whispered Lee. 'We've got to figure out a way of lifting some of these bags. We can't take the lot. Maybe ten kilos each. Just the coke mind you. We don't want to get caught with the fentanyl.'

A quick search produced a holdall large enough to take about twenty bags which they quickly transferred from the pallet. Then they rearranged the plastic sheeting back over the stack to make it look as though nothing had been disturbed.

'What do we do now?' said Dale.

'We hide. Whoever's downstairs might come up here. If they're on their own we can probably deal with them.'

He was about to add words to the effect that they might even bargain some sort of a deal with the owner of the drugs when he felt the hairs on the back of his neck suddenly begin tingling. Someone was watching them.

Slowly he turned, still clutching the dagger in his hand only much more tightly this time. Dale followed, mirroring his movements. What they saw next chilled them both to the bone.

Standing in the half-light beside the folding screen was the figure of a young woman, her feet planted slightly apart on the Afghan carpet. She was clad in a black leather biker jacket and wearing reflector sunglasses. From the moment he clapped eyes on her, Lee realised he was in the presence of a hardened killer.

'We were looking for a place to sleep for the night,' he said nervously. 'We're homeless.'

The woman looked unmoved.

'It's a big problem in London,' Dale put in. 'Especially for young people.'

Again the woman made no reply but turned her head slowly in the direction of the holdall then back once more to Lee.

'How did you get in?' he said, mystified at how the woman just seemed to have materialised inside the room.

'I came up the backstairs,' she answered. 'There's a hidden doorway behind the tapestry. I use it occasionally.'

'So, you're the owner of the bike then?'

'It's not mine. I'm looking after it for a friend.'

Lee glanced at the holdall. 'Look, I'm sorry about your drugs—'

'They're not mine either.'

'Fuck this,' he hissed, going for the dagger.

A single bullet struck him square in the torso and he dropped to the floor, the blade following him with a thump. Dale made to run but the woman fired again – three shots fired in quick succession, then it was over.

Certain they were dead, the woman walked over to where Lee had fallen and picked up the dagger, caressing it lovingly in her hands before putting back in the desk drawer where it belonged. Glancing down at the bodies on the floor, she frowned. She hadn't bargained on there being intruders in the building. They would have to go.

A few minutes later, two bodies slid down a metal service chute and out into the cold river Thames below. Satisfied the bodies had exited the building and hadn't got jammed in the chute, the woman walked upstairs to the roof and looked out across the water. Then she took the gun she was holding and threw it out as far as she could into the middle of the river where it sank with a splash. The bodies would probably wash up on the Isle of Dogs in the morning and no one would be any the wiser. Another job for the coroner and nothing more.

***

Dawn was a grey smudge on the horizon by the time Cassidy arrived back in London. Walking up the road in the muddy half-light, he could just about make out the familiar shape of the old gas tower silhouetted above the other buildings in the area. Not far now.

The ride back from Silver's place had taken ages. Much longer than the journey down. They must have taken a different route, he thought as he turned the corner leading down to the canal towpath. Up ahead he saw his home.

Home for Stuart Cassidy was a houseboat called the *Dog Star*, moored to a permanent berth on the Grand Union Canal. It wasn't much, but the rent was cheap and the overheads practically non-existent. Glad to be back, he wandered up the path and was just about to board the vessel when something caught his eye. It was an old, abandoned hotel about forty metres up the road from where his houseboat was tethered. The place had been closed for almost as long as Cassidy had lived in the area, but he had noticed quite a lot of activity in recent months with people coming and going at all hours of the day and night in cars, vans and big, swanky muscle bikes. Rumour had it that the place was being used as a meth-lab by the Hells Angels but Cassidy had never had the nerve to check it out. Now it seemed he never would. There was a line of police-tape stretched across the road and a squad car parked outside the building. Evidently, the place had been raided while he'd been away.

For a few moments, Cassidy looked on to see if anything was happening. Then, satisfying himself that most of the action was over, he opened the door of his houseboat and went inside, thankful for his warm bed and a nice hot cup of tea. It had been quite a night and one he would probably remember for the rest of this life.

Five

Two piercing eyes framed in heavy kohl and black mascara peered out above the horizon line of a strategically placed newspaper. The eyes watched intently as crowds of early morning commuters disembarked from their trains at St Pancras Station and filtered down the long Victorian platforms toward the exit signs and the sprawling metropolis that was the City of London.

But there was nothing particularly Victorian about St Pancras Station these days, following its recent makeover into an international rail terminal, courtesy of its link with the rest of Europe via the Channel Tunnel. Even the grand old station clock that hung on the wall facing down the length of the platforms looked strangely out of place when compared to the ranks of computerised information boards and twenty-first century paraphernalia which greeted the eyes of all weary travellers when they first set foot on British soil. Nothing was real anymore, thought Linda as she sat crouched behind her newspaper quietly observing the multitude of folk as they passed through the station concourse directly in front of her table. Had any of them had an inkling of why exactly they were being watched so purposefully they would have all shaken their heads in disbelief. But then they weren't to know, were they.

Linda sighed and recalled a different time... *her time.* A time when London still possessed enough of its own character to render it unique among all the other capital cities of the world. A certain discreet charm that was neither overtly bombastic nor as yet so unsure of itself as to necessitate a ghastly makeover to please its cosmopolitan elite and the rest of the corporate world.

Linda Bailey had been a fashion model once – queen of the catwalk in fact – with the whole world at her feet and a six-figure salary to match. But all that had been well over three decades ago in a different century, before the thud of a redundancy notice on her doormat had changed her life forever and turned her into the creature she was today. And yet strangely, she hadn't aged much since that time – at least not that anyone would have noticed. Not a single wrinkle or frown-line marked her delicate features, which remained as fresh and as youthful as they had been back in… god, when was it? – 1981 or 1982 when the event happened? She'd forgotten. Perhaps time heals all wounds eventually.

She could scarcely remember any of her friends and acquaintances from that bygone era. They would all be middle aged by now, all gone and grown up without her, whereas she'd just stayed the same – a picture postcard punk from yesteryear, living out a nightmare existence in a city she just didn't recognise anymore. Sometimes she wondered how some of the older ones of her kind managed to cope with it all – her boss for one. Now he'd certainly been around for a long time.

What if her life had been different? What if she'd taken that secretarial course back in 1978 like her parents had wanted her to instead of running off to London and joining that mad carnival of youthful rebellion known to history as the age of Punk and New Wave. That period seemed so distant now it might just as well have been the eighteenth century for all that it mattered. So much had happened since then. She'd met so many people – so many faces – most of them now no more, deceased and vanished into the collective memory of the city – Steve Tulloch, Belladonna, Claude Dubois and a good many others – all of them now dead. Then she remembered the woman called, Sterling and suppressed a shudder of fear, as if the very recollection of the name could bring her old enemy back to life.

She was glad Sterling was dead. Sterling had been one of her worst nightmares made flesh. And why was this? It was because Sterling had been very much like Linda in many ways, only ten times more brutal and cunning. Yes, she was glad Sterling was gone, and even more delighted that she'd had a hand in putting Sterling down herself. Let's hope she stayed dead and didn't come back from the grave to haunt the city which Linda had made her own personal fiefdom for the better part of thirteen years. With Sterling out of the way, Linda's own career had begun to blossom, for now she could truly set her sights on becoming the queen of London's underworld without any serious competition to worry about. Well, at least not until lately.

Trouble had been brewing in the city over the last few months, and rumours were rife among the old London firms of how more powerful foreign crime gangs were moving in from Central Europe, Russia and the Balkans – whole ethnic groups with their own way of doing things, unlike the traditional English gangs who preferred to contract their business in isolated units of two or three individuals, only calling in the muscle when absolutely necessary. That's where guys like Jimmy Silver came in handy.

'Big Issue, luv?'

The voice came from a hooded streetvendor as he suddenly thrust a magazine under Linda's nose.

'Fuck off!' replied Linda. 'Can't you see I've got my own newspaper to read! Go away and pester someone else, why don't you.'

'It's your funeral,' snorted the man as he pulled up an aluminium chair and sat down at the table without removing his hood. 'How's business, Linda?'

A glimmer of recognition crossed Linda's face as she realised who the man was.

'Oh, it's you, Barry. You shouldn't creep up on folk like that – especially folk like me. It might prove bad for your health.'

'Sorry about that. I just happened to be passing by on my rounds, so to speak, and I saw you sitting there all on your lonesome.'

The man kept glancing around nervously as he spoke, only occasionally making eye contact with Linda. It was the body language of someone who was used to having to watch his back at all times. A deeply entrenched scar running down the right side of his face provided ample explanation of why this was so.

Barry Flanagan was as hardcore as they came. The type of man you only went to see if you needed a gun in a hurry, but who never actually carried one themselves. Linda smiled and continued to watch the crowd intently, all the while making polite conversation as she did so, so that by now both figures seated at the aluminium table came to resemble a pair of paranoid meercats forever on the alert for threats to their territory.

'Since when did you start selling the Big Issue, Barry? I'd never have thought charity work was that close to your heart?'

'It ain't. This little job is my cover for the week. I'm doing a bit of spotting for Tulloch's old firm and happened to wander into the station to keep warm. Anyway, what brings you here, Linda?'

'Much the same as you, Barry, only I work for different masters these days and don't happen to feel the cold as much as you on account of this new fur coat I'm wearing. It's real leopard skin. Like it?'

'Wow! Where'd you get a thing like that, Linda? Nicked it from Bond Street or what?'

Linda took a sip of coffee and purred with satisfaction: 'I bought it, Barry – with all the money I earn these days.'

'Oh... I see. So you're still working for the toffs then?'

'If you mean, Jimmy Silver, then yes I am. Heard anything I should know about?'

'Such as?'

'Oh, you know; Trade Union trouble. Terrorist cells. Left-wing unrest – the usual.'

'Not so much as a whisper, Linda. Go tell your political masters they can sleep easy in their beds tonight without any fear of getting their throats cut.'

'And how's your end of the crime scene, Barry?' replied Linda, quickly changing the subject.

'Well, word on the street is that some Albanian firm are moving into the city. At first we thought they were just here to purchase a bit of property in the West End and put their feet up for a while, but then we got news they were taxing some of the clubs and poker-dens as a sideline so now it's all on top. They can screw the property market all they like, but they're not moving in on Steve Tulloch's old manor as a matter of principle. His brother, Shaun won't allow it as mark of respect to Steve. That's why I've been sent to keep watch down here on the Euston Road, and Danny Drake's been sent to cover Heathrow Airport—'

'What? All of it?'

'Nah. Only Terminal 2. Danny reckons the Hells Angels are spotting the rest and they've got orders to deal hard with the situation.'

'The Angels and Tulloch's crew working in tandem, Barry? I never thought I'd live to see the day when Tulloch's firm and the Angels would be working together as a team.'

'Yeah, well the game's changed, ain't it kid.'

'Nothing the chaps can't handle I hope?' replied Linda.

'It'll all blow over soon I reckon. If it don't, the coppers will have to muck in and then Tulloch will have to square his contacts in the Met with a few grand to turn a blind eye.'

'Is that likely, Barry?'

'As ever. The coppers were cool about letting the Jamaicans muscle in on Sterling's old fiefdom down in Southwark, and as far as I'm concerned they're welcome to it. That old warehouse of hers just sucks in the bad vibes like it's the gateway to hell or something. Danny reckons she put a curse on the place before she fucked off to America with Skinner and what was left of the Southwark crew after the coppers flushed them out of their little nest. Still, that's all ancient history now. Our main concern for the moment is in keeping everyone sweet until the North London firms can mobilise enough support to take on them gangs from Russia and Romania.'

'Russia and Romania? I thought you said you were on the look-out for Albanians?'

'Romanians, Albanians—what does it matter? They're all bleedin' competition at the end of the day. Things have changed, Linda. It's not like it was back in your time—'

'Back in my time, Barry! And what's that supposed to mean exactly?'

'Oh, nothing. Just a turn of phrase, that's all.'

'Well keep it that way, okay.'

'Yeah, sure. It's just that... well, it's just like you've always sort of been around you know. Like, you were on the go when Sterling's crew were running their tickles south of the river back in the 1980s and Steve Tulloch's firm were taxing most of the nightclubs in the West End. I've heard tell they practically had the whole city sewn up between the two of them until they fell out. Skinner was telling a mate of mine about it only the other week.'

'Skinner? You mean, Jerry Skinner?'

'Yes, old Jerry Skinner. You remember him don't you? He's been out of the country for a while on account of his having had some problems with the feds, but my mate reckons they've let him back in again because they can't pin anything on him.'

'And did your friend say exactly why Skinner had left the country in the first place? He was never a full member of Sterling's crew from what I remember – merely an acquaintance of hers.'

'Nope. All he said was that Skinner had done a runner and fucked off out of the UK for a while until things cooled down. That was back in 2003. He's only just got back apparently.'

'That's very interesting, Barry. Thanks for the information.'

'It's a pleasure, Linda. Anyway, what are you doing sitting here all on your own?'

Linda shrugged. 'Like I said before, I work for Jimmy Silver, looking after some of his European interests. At the moment I'm helping a few Italian geezers settle down in London. Silver has contacts with a number of continental firms – the Camorra for one. Part of the deal is to bring some of their used hitmen into Britain so they can lie low for a while. We do it for the Sicilians as well. That's why I'm sitting here this morning. I'm expecting someone arriving by train.'

Barry thought for a moment. 'Sounds interesting. Here, Linda, there's something I've always been meaning to ask you.'

'Mmm, and what's that, Barry?'

'Is it true you were caught up in that big police raid in Harringay back in 1984 when Danny Drake went down for a seven and that bloke got half his throat torn out?'

'That's all history now, Barry. Old news. I don't want to talk about it!'

'So it is true then. How did you manage to make your escape? I heard the place was crawling with coppers.'

'Through a skylight if you must know. Now, like I said, it all happened a long time ago and I don't want to discuss the matter, okay,' replied Linda, staring hard into Barry's face like she meant it.

Realising he'd overstayed his welcome, Barry apologised and made his excuse to leave.

'Sorry, kid. I was just curious, that's all. Anyway, I must be going. I can't sit around here all day when there's work to be done. Bye for now.'

Linda said nothing as she watched Flanagan get up out of his seat and walk out of the station. He did not turn to wave as he disappeared into the crowd on his way to the city streets outside. From all that he had said, it looked as if things were once more hotting up in the underworld and battle was about to commence as the older, more established London firms locked horns with the newcomers from abroad. It would be a savage fight with a good many casualties on all sides, but it was only the endgame that counted as far as Linda was concerned. Could she keep her nerve long enough to stand any chance of coming out of it on top she wondered? Well, only time would tell, and time was certainly something she'd seen plenty of over the years.

Twenty minutes later and the crowds were beginning to thin out, enabling her to relax a little and read her newspaper. The broadsheet contained all the usual chaff – trouble with the banks; more carnage in the Middle East; celebrity coke-heads caught with their noses in the trough; international white-trash out on the lash in elitist West End nightclubs, as well as the usual bevy of celebrity cannon-fodder photographed doing the wrong thing with the wrong person in the wrong place at the wrong time. Nothing new there she thought, casually turning the pages and scanning the column inches for something just that little bit more stimulating to read. Even the chess problem on page thirty-seven was trifling and mundane – an aesthetic construct offered up for public consumption by some unpronounceable wanker from Finland. She solved it in ten seconds flat and was just about to order another coffee when her mobile rang. Rummaging around in her shoulder bag, she eventually located her phone and pulled it out from beneath a pile of feminine clutter. The phone revealed a familiar number and the even more familiar voice of Jimmy Silver when she finally answered it.

'Ah, Linda. I'm glad we've made contact. Where are you now exactly?'

'St Pancras Station – on surveillance duty. What's up boss?'

'I've got some bad news.'

'How bad?'

'About as bad as it could be, Linda.'

'What's happened, Jimmy? Tell me—'

'I'm afraid there have been some unforeseen developments.'

'Such as what?'

There was a pause on the other end of the line. Then:

'You are no doubt aware of the death of two of our Italian clients. Both were shot dead recently.'

'Yes... What of it? Given their line of business it was only a matter of time before someone caught up with them and stamped their card—'

'Linda! A third man has been shot. It was Bordoni. He was found dead early this morning up in Camberwell.'

Now it was Linda's turn to sweat. Giuseppe Bordoni had been in a different league to the other two men. She'd only met Bordoni a couple of weeks ago when she'd taken him to an introduction agency in Oxford Street so he could familiarise himself with London society. She'd even got him the flat in Camberwell where he'd been found dead. *How had his killer known where he lived?*

'Who do you think it was, boss? You reckon the Sicilians did for him?'

'No, Linda. I don't think it was the Sicilians. A single black rose was found next to his body. I think the killer may have been a tad more esoteric than the Mafia, even though they're prone to leaving the odd message or two themselves with a body when it suits them.'

'You think it might have been *one of us?*' said Linda, her voice filling with anxiety.

'Perhaps,' replied Silver. 'I've heard reports of the Bathory and Teluescu clans moving in on our territory, but somehow I don't think it was them.'

'Then who?'

There was another pause before Silver answered her question.

'I'm sending someone to Venice, Linda. He's gone to have a little chat with Lady Westvale. Hopefully, she may be able to shed a bit of light on the situation.'

'Venice? But what's that got to do with—'

A sharp intake of breath told Silver that he'd made his point. When Linda spoke again, her voice was urgent.

'Christ all fucking mighty! What the hell am I going to do? I'm a sitting duck!'

'Just watch your back,' said Silver. 'That's all you can do for the moment.'

'It's all very well for you to say that, Jimmy but I'm stuck right out here in the open. She'll pick up my scent for certain.'

'We'll cross that bridge when we come to it, Linda. I've given the man I'm sending to Venice your phone number by the way. His name is Stuart Cassidy. He will contact you as soon as he has some news.'

'You've done what?'

'Don't worry. Mr Cassidy is very discreet, Linda. Look, I'm dreadfully sorry but I'm going to have to close for now. I have some urgent business to attend to. Speak to you soon. Bye.'

'But—'

Too late. Silver had rung off, leaving Linda in nothing short of a blind panic. A few minutes ago she'd been her usual self, taking the piss out of Barry Flanagan something shocking. Now she was reduced to a quivering wreck, her hand shaking as she reached deep inside her bag for a cigarette. She was just about to light one up when a female platform attendant came over to remind her that smoking in the station was strictly forbidden and would she please go outside if she wanted to smoke. Linda just glanced up at the woman and looked directly into her eyes with an almost hypnotic stare before replying quietly, *'Go fuck yourself, bitch!'*

The woman blinked two or three times, swayed slightly on her feet and then wandered off down the platform in a daze.

Linda got to smoke her cigarette.

Six

Stuart Cassidy stood at the junction of Charing Cross Road waiting for his ride. Presently, a black London taxi pulled up at the kerb and he climbed in.

'Where to matey?' said the driver of the cab.

'Islington. Take me to Islington,' replied Cassidy, still in a state of mild shock following the events of the previous day. More to the point, he'd just been to the bank to check his account. Sure enough, two thousand pounds had been deposited in it from a remote source in the Channel Islands. His visit to Jimmy Silver hadn't been a dream after all. He really was in the big league now.

'That where you live then—Islington?' the driver responded, setting his meter for the journey.

'No, I'm visiting a friend,' replied Cassidy, counting out the notes in his wallet. He'd just taken the better part of five hundred quid out of his account and changed the rest into euros in preparation for his trip to Venice. With a couple of days to kill before his flight, he thought he'd go and visit an old mate of his who had recently arrived back in the country.

Fifteen minutes later and the cab pulled up outside a coffee shop. Cassidy paid the driver in cash then glanced at the name on the café signboard. Yes, this was the place. He wandered inside and looked around. There was no sign of his friend yet, so he ordered an Americano and took a seat by the window.

Half an hour passed and Cassidy lost count of the number of times he'd skimmed through the generous supply of newspapers and magazines in the rack by the door. He was just about to attack the chess problem in the *Spectator* when he felt a firm hand on his shoulder.

'White to mate in three—' came a voice with a broad east-end accent. Cassidy turned to see a thickly-set man of middling years clad in a brown bomber jacket and blue jeans standing close by. It was Jerry Skinner, the man he'd come to see.

'How's it going, Jerry?' said Cassidy rising up out of his chair and greeting his friend warmly. 'Here, take a seat. I'll get you a coffee.'

'No, Stuart. It's my manor around here. Let me do the honours. Americano, isn't it?'

Cassidy nodded and sat back down by the window. Presently, Skinner returned carrying a small plastic tray with two large Americanos in white Costa-style cups. Soon, both men began chatting.

'I've been out of the country for a while, Stuart. Just got back a few months ago. Strictly on the quiet you understand.'

'Oh, yes; I heard there was a bit of a problem. You were with that Goth woman's crew down in Southwark when everything went bad for them with the law back in… when was it… 2003 or thereabouts?'

'That's all history now. These days I'm working for Steve Tulloch's old firm as a go between with the Hells Angels.'

'But Tulloch's dead.'

'Happens as how his brother, Shaun took over the running of the firm. Got me a job minding the doors of a Bloomsbury club, didn't he. I also collect protection money from some of the smaller shops around here. Look the other way, Stuart, there's a good chap.'

Cassidy turned away as the owner of the shop came over and passed Skinner a plain brown envelope which he immediately pocketed without expression. Yes, that was Skinner all right, regular brown envelopes an' all. His hair might be greyer and the ponytail had long gone, but there was no getting away from the fact that his friend was still up to his old tricks in spite of his years. The number of gold rings on his fingers said it all.

'So, what happened after you left England, Jerry? I heard you went to America with that young woman... funny name she had...'

'Who—Bricabrac? Best shoplifter in the business, Stuart. Still is.'

'No, I meant the other one. The Goth bird—'

'There was no *other one,*' replied Jerry firmly. 'I went with Bricabrac and her pal, Domino. We lay low for a while until the heat was off. We reckoned that once the feds had busted the old warehouse in Southwark everything would cool off.'

'So, what happened to the Goth?'

Skinner made no reply. Instead, he took a sip of his coffee and glanced nervously out of the window. He seemed alert for danger and strangely distracted. Clearly there was something on his mind.

'So you've got your foot in the door with the Hells Angels now,' said Cassidy changing the subject. Skinner turned his gaze from the window but his expression didn't alter.

'I do a bit of business for them now and then,' he replied. 'Why do you ask?'

'No particular reason. I expect you've heard about all that trouble up in Harlow. The feds busted a Hells Angel clubhouse the other week. Seized some computers and stuff for evidence. The bloke inside got away though.'

'Yeah, tell me about it!' exclaimed Skinner tetchily.

'What do you mean?'

'The bloke inside was me, Stuart. I was minding the place for them when it happened. Went and left a bleedin memory stick in one of the computers, didn't I; and now we're in deep shit with the Californians.'

'Oh..!'

'Never mind, Stu,' you weren't to know. It's my problem anyway. More to the point, what are you up to these days?'

Cassidy ordered some more coffee and proceeded to tell his friend all about his latest exploits. As he did so, Skinner's eyes widened. At the mention of Jimmy Silver's name those same eyes narrowed and a frown creased his brow.

'You want to stay the fuck out of that!' Skinner exclaimed. 'You don't know what you're getting yourself into mixing with people like that.'

'What do you mean?'

'I mean, Silver isn't your regular sort of geezer. He's not like you and me, Stuart.'

'All right, I know he's a bit of a toff, but—'

'That's not what I meant, Stuart.'

Skinner glanced out of the window once again then regarded Cassidy closely. 'Jimmy Silver isn't normal and neither are some of the people he associates with. A friend of mine had a run in with him a while back. Come to think of it, she wasn't fucking normal either. None of those bastards are.'

'He pays well,' said Cassidy. 'I'm on two grand a day expenses at the moment.'

'What for?' enquired Skinner, his eyes narrowing once again.

Cassidy pulled up his chair and leaned across the table. 'Well,' he said conspiratorially, 'it's all very strange and I'm not supposed to tell anyone, but...'

'Go on,' said Skinner, 'I'm listening.'

'...Silver wants me to go to Venice for him.'

'Why?'

Cassidy lowered his voice to a near whisper. 'He wants me to visit this posh bird who goes by the name of Lady Caroline Westvale. You don't happen to have heard of her, have you?'

'No, I haven't Stuart. She's a new one on me. Carry on...'

'Well, happens as how I've got to give this woman a letter of introduction from Silver and she has to give me a key, right—'

'Yeah. She gives you a key. And what happens then?'

'It's the key to someone's tomb. I've got to check if there's still a body inside the coffin what's interred there.'

Skinner sank back in his seat, his face suddenly growing pale.

'Stay the fuck out of that, Stuart! You don't know Silver like I do. There could be anything inside that coffin.'

'His granddaughter more than likely. That's who he told me was inside.'

'Bollocks! Silver hasn't got a granddaughter. At least none that I'm aware of.'

'Swears as how he has. Her name was... was... Oh, I forget, but that's what he said anyway.'

Sensing he'd struck a raw nerve, Cassidy changed the subject. 'So, what about this memory stick then, Jerry? You reckon you've got any chance of getting it back for the Angels?'

'Not in a million years, Stuart. The coppers have probably got it stored in a secure safe in Scotland Yard by now. There's no way I can get my hands on it.'

Just then, Skinner's mobile rang. Pulling the phone out of his pocket, he answered it. The call barely lasted a minute, during which time, Skinner said very little, occasionally muttering a few words in the affirmative. When he had finished talking and the person on the other end of the line had rung off, Skinner regarded Cassidy gravely.

'I've just had an urgent call, Stu. I've got to go now. Watch yourself with Silver, that's all I'm saying. Here's my card. It's got my address and telephone number on it. Call me if you need any help. *Ciao!'*

With that, Skinner got up and left the café, leaving Cassidy on his own to ponder all that he had said. What exactly had Skinner meant when he described Silver as not being *"normal"?* It just didn't make any sense. He would certainly be on his guard over the next few days, but he would carry out his strange task regardless. He was in too deep now and he needed the money anyway. What other option did he have?

Seven

Venice

Moored gondolas bobbing on the waves like tethered seahorses. Streets filled with water instead of clay and tarmac. A city of petty thieves but very little serious crime, where everyone knows your business and you are forever being watched. Cassidy was relieved when he discovered that most people spoke English and was even more surprised when he found out that some of them actually spoke it a whole lot better than he did. But he could never get used to the ever-present feeling of being watched.

He was about to take a water taxi to his destination when another glance at his map told him he could probably walk the distance in half the time if he took a series of narrow alleyways and small bridges that linked his hotel to the address that Silver's man, Tarrou had given him.

Twenty minutes later and Cassidy found himself standing outside the stuccoed façade of a five-storied stone palazzo that had undoubtedly seen better days. The house was situated at the end of a long winding lane, and unlike many of the other grander houses of Venice, its front entrance did not open out onto a canal but instead graced the shadow side of a quieter square inhabited solely by a couple of stray cats and a public well. Cassidy walked up to the plain wooden door and rang the bell. It wasn't long before he heard an electronic crackle and the distinct sound of someone's inbreath.

'Yes. Who is it?' came a dark Tuscan voice over the intercom. The voice seemed to belong to a woman but he couldn't say for certain.

'My name is Stuart Cassidy,' he replied. 'I have an appointment to see Lady Westvale.'

'Just a moment,' came the voice once more. Yes, it was a woman's voice all right, only coarse and dry like cheap whisky.

There was a silent interval lasting for a few seconds. Then: 'Lady Westvale will see you now. Take the stairs to the first-floor landing and knock.'

An electronic click told Cassidy that the door lock opened automatically. He pushed the door gently with the palm of his hand and ventured inside. The entrance hall was quite spacious with an eerie baroque staircase that ascended in successive flights of stone up the central spine of the building. Cassidy's footsteps echoed in the stairwell as he climbed.

Reaching the first-floor landing, he paused. Though tidy and well-kept, the place had an air of melancholy about it like so many of the older Venetian palazzos. Set into a classical portico of solid marble was a double door with two brass doorknobs in the shape of lion's heads. Cassidy knocked three times and waited.

'Come in,' came a feminine voice that sounded surprisingly English.

Cassidy entered and was astonished by what he saw. The room was exquisitely furnished and decorated in contrast to the plain stairwell outside. Paintings in antique frames hung on the wall; neo-classical landscapes, views of Venice and several eighteenth-century female portraits, most of them bearing a remarkable resemblance to the woman he now glimpsed sitting on a sofa next to the fireplace. Some remote ancestors perhaps?

The woman got up from the sofa and walked towards Cassidy. Of an indeterminate age, she wore her auburn hair high off her forehead and tied in a chignon at the back of her neck just like some of the women in the portraits on the wall. A grey knee-length skirt and a white cotton blouse brought her firmly into the twenty-first century, however, even though Cassidy somehow got the impression that she didn't really belong there at all. A pair of dark glasses completed the picture, which she removed as they met.

'Ah, you must be, Stuart,' she said brightly. 'I am Caroline Westvale – Lady Caroline Westvale – though some people call me the *countess*. Silver told me you were coming.'

'I have a letter of introduction,' said Cassidy, rummaging in the inside pocket of his coat.

'No need,' replied Lady Westvale. 'I know who you are and why you are here. Please remove your coat and be seated, Mr Cassidy. I will have my maid fetch us both a drink. What would you like?'

'A coffee would be fine for me thanks.'

Cassidy watched as the woman walked over to the fireplace and gently pulled on a length of red tasselled rope. A servant's bell rang somewhere deep inside the house, followed by the sound of approaching footsteps. Presently a smaller, much younger looking woman entered the room. With her black geometric hairstyle and dark Italian eyes, she couldn't have been much more than twenty years of age and spoke in the same rich, dry tones that Cassidy had heard over the intercom.

'Yes, Lady Westvale?' she enquired, barely able to suppress a giggle. From the expression on her face, Cassidy surmised that her relationship with her mistress more likely approached the lesbian end of the spectrum with a smattering of bondage thrown in for good measure.

'A coffee for our guest, Nicoletta,' said the older woman. 'And make it French. It's still morning.'

'Very good, your ladyship. And will you be having one too?'

'Yes. The same. Black. No sugar—'

As the maid went off to prepare the coffee, Cassidy and Lady Westvale exchanged small talk.

'And how is your hotel, Mr Cassidy? I hope Sir James has booked you a good one.'

'It's the *Principe,* Lady Westvale. Just off the Grand Canal.'

'Ah yes, the *Principe.* A first-class establishment. It's not often Jimmy puts someone in there. You must rank very highly in his esteem.'

A picture of structured elegance in her patrician hairstyle and bright red lipstick, Caroline Westvale resumed her seat on the sofa. Yes, she did bear a strange resemblance to the women in the portraits, thought Cassidy. Her family must have been resident in Venice for quite some time. Long enough for her to have been accepted as a native, even though he'd heard her referred to as *"the English lady"* when he'd asked directions of passers-by in the street earlier on in the day. Just how long did you have to live in Venice before you finally got accepted by the locals he wondered.

The coffee arrived just as Lady Westvale was about to put another handful of wood pellets on the fire. 'I don't feel the cold that much myself, but these old houses have a tendency to get a bit damp in winter. Isn't that right, Nicoletta?'

'Yes, m'lady,' the maid replied with a mischievous grin before putting her tray down on the low coffee table that separated her mistress from the new guest. 'Will that be all?'

Westvale nodded and watched as her companion left the room. The two women were obviously having a private joke between themselves that was lost on Cassidy. He waited until Nicoletta had disappeared through an adjoining door before continuing with his conversation.

'How long have you lived in Venice, Lady Westvale?'

He did not think it too personal a question but was surprised by his hostess's response.

'Why do you ask?' she enquired coldly. Her gaze was as steady as a candle flame and it made him feel uncomfortable.

'No particular reason,' he responded quickly, 'only I noticed that some of the portraits in this room seem to bear a close relationship to yourself and I was wondering if they might be some of your ancestors.'

There was a pause as Lady Westvale allowed her gaze to wander slowly around the walls. Her cold expression was gone, replaced by an almost wistful look as she studied each portrait in turn. It was almost as if she were reminiscing, thought Cassidy as he picked up the porcelain cup he'd been offered and took a sip. God, but it was good. He'd never tasted coffee quite like it before.

'Yes,' she said, 'they are my ancestors. These portraits were painted well over two hundred years ago. That one above the fireplace is by the artist George Romney.'

The countess faltered abruptly then recovered her composure only to change the subject.

'The coffee is organic, of course. It's an old French blend I have Nicoletta prepare with bottled spring water from the Swiss Alps. Would you like some more?'

Cassidy couldn't bring himself to refuse and held out his cup for Lady Westvale to fill from a generous cafetiere. Ordinarily, he would have felt secure with such warm displays of hospitality, but for some reason he didn't.

She's hiding something, he thought. *There's something not quite right. Am I being set up here...?*

The countess smiled and offered him a biscuit. 'How long have you worked for Jimmy Silver, Stuart?'

Cassidy had been about to ask her much the same thing and got the impression that she had somehow anticipated the question and turned it back on himself. *She's being evasive. Why...?*

'About two or three years, your ladyship,' he replied. 'It's the first time he's asked me to do anything like this though.'

Again, Lady Westvale smiled. 'I'm sure Jimmy has a good reason for your visit here. Do you plan staying long on the island?'

'What island?' said Cassidy, almost choking on his biscuit.

'Oh, didn't he tell you?' replied Westvale raising her eyebrows in mock surprise. 'How thoughtless of him. He usually briefs all his agents as a rule.'

'He didn't mention any island, Lady Westvale. At least, none that I can recall.'

'Never mind,' said the countess putting down her cup. 'The tomb he wants you to investigate is on Poveglia.'

'Poveglia? Where's that?'

'It's small island out in the Venetian lagoon. The locals call it the Island of the Dead.'

'Island of the Dead!' Cassidy responded, his mouth opening slowly, allowing a few biscuit crumbs to tumble down the front of his shirt.

'But of course, silly. Where else would you expect to find a tomb – in a kindergarten?'

Suitably admonished, Cassidy brushed away the biscuit crumbs from his shirt. 'Is it far?' he asked querulously, not wanting to travel any further than he already had.

'No, it isn't very far, but I doubt if you will find many boatmen who would be willing to take you there without charging a hefty price.'

'Why? What's the problem?'

'Poveglia has a bad reputation, Stuart. It's not called the Island of the Dead for nothing.'

'How do you mean?' said Cassidy growing increasingly apprehensive.

The countess paused for a moment and took a sip of coffee. Then, when she was satisfied that she had Cassidy's full attention, she proceeded with her explanation.

'Poveglia is reputed to be the most haunted and evil location in the world, Mr Cassidy. The first mention of it is in an ancient Roman chronicle when the place was being used as a burial ground for plague victims. The island served the same purpose centuries later during the Black Death when the dead were dumped into large pits in the ground in a state of panic. It has been estimated that upwards of 160.000 bodies lie buried or incinerated there, so much so that even the soil of the island is still black and sticky with their remains.'

'That's all very interesting,' observed Cassidy, 'but why should the island have such a bad reputation. I mean, it's only an abandoned graveyard after all.'

Now the countess regarded him strangely. Her gaze became steady, almost hypnotic, and he experienced a distant floating sensation almost as if he were being lifted out of his body. The sensation barely lasted for a few seconds before the sound of Lady Westvale's voice brought him back down to earth again.

'...Ever since Silver abandoned me here in Venice, I have made it my business to study certain of the more obscure branches of esoteric knowledge that contemporary science has chosen to ignore. What you have just experienced, Mr Cassidy is but a fraction of that knowledge. On Poveglia you may well experience a good deal more.'

What is she driving at? thought Cassidy, still unnerved by the event. *Is she trying to intimidate me?* He continued listening as the countess went on with her narrative:

'Everyone who has visited the island says that a heavy, dark and evil atmosphere haunts the place. Psychics who have investigated it have left Poveglia in a hurry, scared to death and unable to return. A fitting place for Silver to bury his granddaughter, wouldn't you say, Stuart?'

Now she was playing with his mind. It was almost as if she were using him for her own amusement rather than treating him as a fellow colleague. Cassidy became irritated.

'I don't know what all this has to do with the matter in hand, your ladyship. All I have to do is search for a tomb with a body in it and report back to London. It's not exactly rocket science, is it?'

'No Stuart, it is not,' said the countess softly. 'It is most definitely not that. But come! I have kept you dangling long enough. I shall get the key you requested to open up the tomb and you can be on your way. Just a moment—'

With that, Lady Westvale got up and walked out of the room leaving Cassidy on his own. Wondering what to do, he allowed his gaze to wander. Yes, it was true. Most of the female portraits on the wall did indeed bear a strong resemblance to Caroline Westvale. Clearly, her family must once have been very powerful at one time back in eighteenth century England. Indeed, only one of the portraits actually depicted a former Westvale as being resident in Venice, and in this particular one, the woman portrayed standing in front of a long colonnaded terrace seemed to lack all the gaiety and confidence of the others, instead exhibiting a rather bleak and wistful expression reminiscent of someone who has suffered sadness and great loss. He was wondering just who this rather sad and lonely woman might have been when his hostess returned brandishing a large iron key.

'The key, Stuart!' she announced sharply. 'Take it and guard it well. When you have completed your task, leave it with the manager of your hotel. I will send Nicoletta round to collect it when you have gone. Now, are there any further questions you would like to ask me before your trip to the island?'

Cassidy could think of several he would have liked to have asked the countess, but in the end he settled for only one, 'What exactly is Poveglia used for now, Lady Westvale?' he enquired, eager to know what perils might lie ahead of him.

'Now, Stuart? Why, nothing at all. A lunatic asylum was built there early in the twentieth century but it had to be abandoned shortly after it opened. No one could stand the place for any length of time – not even the inmates.'

'That bad, huh?'

'Indeed. I have recently heard news that the place has been bought by an Italian businessman from the mainland. Rumour has it that he plans to carry out some building work on the island. Personally, I don't fancy his chances. Nothing has ever flourished there and I doubt if it ever will. Anyway, don't just take my word for it. You'll be able to see for yourself soon enough. The best of luck with your task, Stuart, and don't forget your coat. The lagoon can get quite chilly this time of the year. Nicoletta will see you out. Goodbye.'

***

Lady Westvale had been right. The lagoon was a chilly, lonely sort of place and not at all as he had imagined it. Grey, translucent and silent, the island of Poveglia came into view out of a thin mist, blurred and encircled with illusory reflections like an aqueous mirage – wavering trees, a deserted bell tower and the long silhouette of an abandoned building. The perfect setting for a low-budget horror movie.

After a good deal of haggling, Cassidy had managed to persuade an elderly Venetian boatman to take him out to the island for what seemed like a reasonable fee. Even so, the man had insisted that they should stay there only for a few hours and leave before nightfall. There was no way he said that he would stay on the island for any length of time after dark and if Cassidy had not returned to the boat by late afternoon then he would leave without him. This, Cassidy agreed to and so without any further debate they set out for Poveglia around midday hoping to arrive there before one o' clock.

The trip out was largely uneventful, but as the island of Poveglia appeared out of the mist, Cassidy's sense of foreboding steadily grew. He couldn't say why exactly. There was nothing about the place that seemed remotely out of the ordinary. It was just like any other island in the lagoon – silent and wave-lapped by shallow water with a dense canopy of trees covering most of it. But as he drew closer, this pervasive sense of imminence seemed to grow stronger until he felt as if it would penetrate his very soul.

The boatman wasn't happy either, he could tell. The guy, whose name was Matteo, had hardly uttered a single word throughout the entire journey even though his English was reasonably good. Now, as they approached the island, he remained stoically silent, guiding his small craft up the narrow channel toward the quayside until they drew level with another boat that was moored to the landing stage with a length of nylon rope. The other boat turned out to be a police launch manned by two uniformed officers who were preparing to cast off and leave. One of the men recognised Matteo and waved. Cutting the engine, Matteo waved back and pretty soon both of them were engaged in an animated conversation.

Unable to understand anything of what they were saying, Cassidy bided his time until the exchange was over and the police launch pulled away allowing Matteo to dock. As they both climbed the steps of the landing stage, Cassidy enquired of the elderly Venetian what the conversation had been about.

'The policeman is my nephew,' Matteo replied in a thick local accent. 'We were mostly talking family, that's all. Everyone knows everyone else's business here in Venice. It's that sort of a place. He also told me that he and the other officer were investigating an incident that took place here a few days back.'

'Oh...' said Cassidy, his curiosity aroused, '...and what was that if I may ask?'

'Seems like there was a gang of construction workers on the island doing some renovation work to the old asylum building. According to my nephew, Paolo, they came across something weird and left the place in a panic.'

'"Something weird...,"' Cassidy heard himself echo in reply. 'Did they say what it was they found?'

'A tomb,' Matteo replied in a matter of fact sort of way.

Cassidy was guarded with his response. He couldn't very well say he'd come to the island himself looking for a tomb because it was now a police matter. Instead, he questioned the boatman further.

'And what happened?'

'Well, from what my nephew told me, one of the workmen came across a coffin when he was demolishing an old brick outhouse behind the asylum building. He accidentally put the front shovel of his bulldozer through an adjoining wall and found a casket had been interred behind it. Turned out, the place had been used as a tomb. There are plenty of burials on the island but this one was fairly recent. The coffin was of a modern design made out of ebonised wood with solid gold handles. Must have cost a fortune.'

Silver's granddaughter, thought Cassidy. *He's not going to be very pleased.*

'What did the man do then?' he asked, hoping no further damage had been done to the tomb.

'Then?' said the boatman. 'Why, then he went to tell his mates, that's what he did. They spent the night in their cabin debating what best to do. At some point in the early hours of the morning they heard what sounded like wood being splintered, then shortly after that came the sound of a motor launch engine being started up. They went out to investigate and noticed that one of their boats was missing. Whoever had taken it must have been very strong or else very desperate—'

'Oh, and why do you say that?'

'Because the rope used to secure the vessel had been torn in half.'

'Torn in half...?' Cassidy went on, his curiosity overcoming any feelings of apprehension he may otherwise have had. 'Go on, tell me more.'

'That's all really. The men left the island at dawn and never returned. According to my nephew, all work on the island has been halted until the construction company in charge can recruit some new workers. So far, no volunteers have come forward in spite of the offer of higher than average wages. Looks like the builders will have to go as far south as Calabria to get anybody. News travels fast in the north.'

65

Cassidy glanced toward the old asylum building. No more than three storeys high, its lengthy façade was obscured by a forest of scaffolding pipes recently put there by the builders. There was no evidence of any work currently in progress.

'I'm going to look for the tomb,' he said. 'You want to join me?'

'I stop here,' Matteo replied. 'You do what you have to do. I'm not going any further. Understood?'

Cassidy nodded. 'I'll go round the back of the asylum. That's where the men said they found the coffin. I won't be long.'

After what seemed like an hour, but which couldn't have been more than twenty minutes, Cassidy eventually managed to find his way through the dense undergrowth of bushes and ferns to where the workmen's cabin stood. The door of the cabin was open as if it had been abandoned in a hurry. Wasting no time, he looked around hoping to see a bulldozer. There was none. Instead, he saw the imprint of its tracks in the soft black earth and followed them until he came to a small clearing in the woods. In the centre of the clearing he spied a low brick building, and, neatly embedded in one side of it, was the bulldozer, its front shovel having punched a large gaping hole clean through the brickwork just as Matteo had said.

Curious, he walked towards the building and took a closer look. Yes, this must be the place. There was a solid iron door on the front side of it, and although he no longer needed to use the door to enter on account of the damage done by the bulldozer, he nevertheless took out the key Lady Westvale had given him and tried it in the door. It fitted perfectly. Turning the key in the lock, he pushed open the door which let out a creaking sound as it opened. It only moved a few inches, however, before it stopped. Something was jamming it. Putting his shoulder to the door, Cassidy managed to force it open a few more inches and squeezed through the gap, snagging most of the buttons on his coat as he did so. There was no turning back now.

Inside, the light was dim, but as his eyes adjusted to the gloom he saw what it was that had blocked the door. Lying flat on the dusty floor was the long, black lid of a coffin. The top half of the lid had been shattered beyond recognition, while its interior lining of crimson velvet was torn and ripped to shreds, clear evidence perhaps that someone had entered the tomb after the accident with the bulldozer and desecrated the grave. How was he going to explain that to Jimmy Silver? The thought of it appalled him, but even this idea shrank into insignificance when he went over to examine the coffin.

The solid black casket lay open on top of a long stainless steel trolley which stood at about waist height from the floor. In an instant, Cassidy realised what the building must once have been used for. It was the old asylum mortuary. Silver had interred his granddaughter in an abandoned hospital morgue. But if that wasn't bad enough, nothing prepared him for what he witnessed next.

The coffin was empty!

Yes. There was the unmistakable imprint of a human head on the red velvet pillow inside the casket, but of a body there was no sign.

In vain, Cassidy searched about the room looking for a corpse. He found nothing. Instead, what he saw chilled him to the bone. Four black candles had been placed on the floor around the trolley on which the coffin lay. One at the head. One at the foot, and one on either side. Beyond this, and encircling the trolley all around, someone had laid a circle of salt. One section of the circle had been broken where the bulldozer had caused part of the wall to collapse into the room. Apart from this, the circle was complete.

Black Magic!

It was the first thing that came into Cassidy's mind. Someone had entered the tomb and removed the body of Silver's granddaughter for the purposes of some unspeakable ritual or other. That would at least explain the damage to the coffin lid.

Now his thoughts were racing. The door to the tomb had been locked when he'd tried the key, so that would mean that whoever had entered the tomb could only have done so after the bulldozer had hit the wall. Teenagers perhaps? They were always dabbling with the occult, weren't they? Innocent enough fun when you regarded the matter in a juvenile context, but not when a body went missing. That was desecration and a criminal offence. More to the point, what the fuck was he going to say to his boss? *"I'm sorry Jimmy, but your granddaughter's body has just been nicked by a gang of Italian teenagers out on a jolly?"* No. That wouldn't do. He would have to think of something else and think fast.

Reaching into his pocket, he fished out his mobile and dialled the number Silver had given him. When he couldn't get a signal, he went outside and tried again. Still nothing. Maybe all the ghosts and spirits of the island were conspiring to block his call. Oh well, it was time to go anyway. He'd have another try when he got back to his hotel. There was no point staying around here anymore.

***

The balcony of his hotel room overlooked the Grand Canal. It was evening by now and from where he was standing, Cassidy could hear the sound of laughter rising up from a group of revellers being ferried up the famous waterway in a gondola. The atmosphere was jolly but Cassidy wasn't in a party mood.

At half past eight, he went downstairs to the hotel bar. He had yet to phone Silver and needed some alcohol to calm his nerves. Sitting at a small table in the lobby, he sipped his drink – vodka and tonic – not his usual tipple but he needed it.

Nothing made any sense.

Why was he here? Why had he been sent all the way to Venice to check on a coffin, and why had Jimmy Silver interred his granddaughter in a tomb on a lonely island out in the Venetian lagoon? Things just didn't add up. But that wasn't all. The body was missing. The body of... oh, what was her name? He couldn't remember... Julie something... Yes, that was it!—Julie Kent! The body of Julie Kent had been stolen by grave robbers; that was what had happened, and with a bit of black magic thrown in for good measure. Maybe that was what the two police officers were investigating when he and Matteo had arrived at the island. That much at least did not appear in any way out of the ordinary. It was just a pity that nothing else did.

He went to the bar and ordered another drink. This time it was neat vodka – a double, and without any tonic. Perhaps the vodka blast would stimulate his grey cells sufficiently well enough for him to start fitting it all together. He certainly hoped so.

Sitting down once more, he began to think hard, retracing his steps until he was back again with Lady Westvale in her spooky old palazzo – one, two, three… the coffin, the key, the portraits on the wall, then his mind went blank again. It was almost as if someone had flicked a switch in his brain. For a moment, he could have sworn he heard the sound of feminine laughter and glanced round, half expecting to see the countess standing there beside his table in the hotel vestibule. She wasn't. It was just the lobby porter yawning by the reception desk as he gazed vacantly into space waiting for his next call.

Cassidy finished his vodka in a single gulp and banged the glass down on the table. Was he going crazy or what? There was nothing else for it. He would go back to his room immediately and ring Jimmy Silver from the landline beside his bed. That way he could be sure of getting through.

For some reason he ignored the hotel elevator, preferring instead to climb the main staircase up to the fourth floor. As he climbed, he couldn't help thinking again. It was an offhand remark that Lady Westvale had made during their meeting. Unless he was very much mistaken, he could have sworn the countess had said that she'd been *"abandoned"* by Silver in Venice. What exactly had she meant by that remark he wondered? More to the point, exactly *when* had Silver abandoned her and why had she never returned to England herself? Was she in some sort of trouble with the law, preferring to remain in

Europe rather than risk being arrested back home? The thought intrigued him.

Walking down the corridor, he reached his room and swiped his key card in the lock. The door opened with a click and he went in. Without hesitation, he walked over to his bed and sat down by the bedside telephone, searching in his pocket for Silver's number. Then he looked at the phone. Reaching out with his hand, he was almost about to pick up the receiver when he stopped. *No, not yet,* he thought. *I need another drink first.*

Getting up, he walked across the room and took a miniature bottle of vodka out of the minibar. Pouring it into one of the small plastic tumblers provided, he downed it in one gulp then went back to the phone, picked up the receiver and dialled the number. There was a short pause followed by a ring tone. A woman's voice answered his call.

'Hello. Who is it?'

'My name is Stuart Cassidy,' he replied. 'I'm calling from Venice.'

'What about?' the woman enquired, her voice now sounding alert.

'I've got a message for Jimmy Silver – who are you?'

'My name is Linda – Linda Bailey. Jimmy said you might call. What's the problem?'

'It's complicated. I need to talk with the boss in private.'

'He doesn't take direct calls. You can tell me and I'll pass it on.'

'It's about his granddaughter's tomb—'

'What about it?' Linda replied, her voice now edged with concern.

Cassidy sensed Linda's growing anxiety and was guarded in his response. 'It would appear that the body of Julie Kent has gone missing.'

There was a long silence on the other end of the line that ended in a single word:

'*SHIT!*'

The phone went dead in Cassidy's hand. Whoever this Linda Bailey person was, she'd obviously taken the news very badly and had rung off. He dialled the number again but it was engaged. Evidently, she was contacting someone else with the news. Oh well, he'd done his job. Perhaps he could get a good night's sleep now and—

The phone rang. Someone had returned his call.

'Hello, Stuart,' came an all too familiar voice on the line. It was Jimmy Silver.

'Boss?'

'Yes, it's me. Where are you now, Stuart?'

'I'm in my hotel room, boss. In Venice.'

'Ah yes, the *Principe*. I do hope it is to your liking. It used to be a palace back in my day. I remember staying there with Lady Westvale when she and I were younger.'

'You knew the countess well then?'

'Indeed I did. We used to be partners once you know. Ever such a long time ago it was. How is the countess by the way?'

'She's fine, boss. Look, I've got some news about your granddaughter and you're not going to like it.'

'I've heard, Stuart. Linda's just told me. She's got herself worked up into a terrible state and isn't making very much sense so I was hoping you might be able to fill in some of the details for me. What happened on the island?'

Silver listened intently as Cassidy outlined the events of the day in chronological order, only occasionally asking questions as the narrative progressed.

'And you say that the circle of salt was definitely broken?'

'Yes, boss. The collapsed wall did it.'

'What about the coffin lid?'

'It was vandalised, boss. Must have been the grave robbers.'

There was a pause on the line. Cassidy waited for Silver to speak first.

'How exactly had the lid been vandalised, Stuart?'

'It was smashed, boss.'

'In what way?'

'You know, like, *smashed!*'

'That's not what I mean. Had the lid of the coffin been smashed inwards from the outside or outwards from within?'

Now it was Cassidy's turn to pause. Thinking back, he tried to visualise the coffin lid as it had lain on the floor of the outhouse.

'Hard to say, Mr Silver. The top half of the lid was badly broken. The inner velvet lining of the lid had been torn to shreds as if it had been done by someone in a frenzy.'

'Hmm. "*Someone in a frenzy*," you say. That's very interesting, Stuart. And when exactly did the workmen on the island hear the engine of their spare motorboat being started?'

'In the early hours of the morning, boss. They also heard the sound of splintering wood a short while before that.'

'And they hadn't seen anyone else on the island during the whole time they'd been there?'

'No, boss. Nobody.'

Cassidy could almost hear Silver thinking on the other end of the line. When his boss spoke again, his message was short and polite; 'Thank you, Mr Cassidy. You have just confirmed all of my worst suspicions.' Then the line went dead. Silver had hung up.

In vain, Cassidy tried to reconnect, repeatedly jabbing in the numbers until he could almost do it without thinking, but it was no use. His boss had rung off and left him dangling.

'Well, you can fuck off!' he shouted, banging down the receiver and falling backwards onto the bed. Now he knew he would never get the twenty-grand bonus Silver had promised him. He'd been played for a fool and taken for a ride. Jimmy had long firmed him royally.

Staring up at the ceiling, Cassidy considered his options. He was in unfamiliar surroundings dealing with a situation he couldn't even begin to understand. All of the subterfuge – what had it all been about? And what had Silver meant when he said that Cassidy had confirmed all his worst suspicions? Was Silver scared of something? Linda certainly had been – whoever Linda was. What the hell was going on?

He tried to get up, but his head was spinning with vodka. He hadn't drunk very much but he wasn't used to it. Slowly and inexorably, he succumbed to the effects of the alcohol, eventually drifting off into a deep sleep.

He was dreaming now. He was still in his hotel room in Venice but somehow it didn't look the same. The room was much larger and furnished in the style of an earlier age. There were also several people in the room. Most of them were wearing Venetian carnival masks and all were clad in the clothes of the late eighteenth century. One of them was Lady Westvale, and it was she who appeared to be the hostess of the party.

Up until this part of the dream, Cassidy had only been an observer, but he soon became aware that it was now he himself who was being observed. Out of the corner of his eye he spotted someone sitting on a chair gazing at him intently. It was the same woman he had encountered in the bar in Soho – the mysterious biker-chick with the black hair and mirrored sunglasses. He was just about to walk across the room and talk to her when a man entered the salon and began speaking with Lady Westvale. An argument quickly developed between the pair causing the man to utter an oath and make for the door. As he did so, Cassidy got the shock of his life, for the man was none other than Jimmy Silver, only not the same Jimmy Silver he was familiar with. This particular version of Silver wore an eighteenth-century frock coat and a three-cornered hat, complete with rouged cheeks and a powdered wig – the very epitome of the English aristocrat abroad. In vain did Lady Westvale implore him not to leave, but he thrust her aside causing her to fall sobbing to the floor. If anyone else in the room had noticed the argument they didn't say anything, for at this point the overall mood of the dream changed and everyone was at the window looking out across the lagoon. By now, the normally bright blue sky had visibly darkened and someone let out a cry: "Napoleon!" at which point there came the sound of distant cannon fire and the whole of the lagoon was engulfed in flames. War had come to Venice.

Suddenly, the dream changed. Now, Cassidy was at another party. This time he was in London in the 1970s. The party was a posh kind of affair with people standing around dressed in the clothes of that era – flared trousers, silk shirts and wide ties. Some music by the Rolling Stones was playing in the background. A man who Cassidy did not recognise stood talking to a woman wearing a yellow kaftan and smoking a large joint. Just then, a punk girl entered the room sporting an alarming hairstyle with swirling tattoos on her arms and shoulders. She was followed by a far more timid, but equally outrageous younger woman with ginger hair who was dressed in a ripped school blazer festooned with safety pins and zips. The girl with the alarming hairstyle pointed to a tall patrician lady who was standing talking with a group of people near a huge fireplace. At this point, Cassidy's attention was caught by another young woman with black hair sitting on a chair by the wall. She was staring fixedly at him from behind a pair of mirrored sunglasses and shaking her head sorrowfully.

For some reason, Cassidy became aware that he was witnessing the beginnings of a terrible tragedy but didn't know quite what it was that was about to take place. That it had something to do with the girl with the ginger hair and the woman standing by the fireplace he was fairly certain, but apart from that there were no other clues. Then the dreamscape changed again and he found himself standing alone on a desolate shingle beach somewhere on the south coast. It was dawn and there was a fine mist blowing in from the English Channel. As he looked around he saw another figure standing about forty metres away. He waved and the figure began walking towards him. It was the girl with the ginger hair and ripped blazer and she was dripping wet as though she'd only recently been immersed in the sea.

As she drew closer, Cassidy became aware that her footsteps made no sound as she walked. Silently, she approached with her head bowed low, gliding over the shingle beach like a ghost. Then, when she was about two or three metres away from where Cassidy stood, she halted abruptly and looked up. The girl had no eyes. Just two empty sockets where her eyes once had been. Cassidy's heart skipped a beat. He knew he was looking at a dead person but for some reason he didn't panic. Instead, he asked the girl a question.

'Who are you?'

'My name is Julie,' the girl replied, '– Julie Kent. This is the place where they drowned me.'

'Who drowned you?'

The girl – she couldn't have been more than twenty years of age – seemed to shimmer and fade with the dawn's early light and Cassidy realised he didn't have much more time.

'Who drowned you?' he repeated urgently, but it was no good. The girl with the ripped blazer and ginger hair disappeared right before his eyes leaving him alone with his thoughts.

The sky was getting lighter as Cassidy walked along the shore, stopping occasionally to pick up pebbles from the beach. It wasn't long before he came to a patch of wet sand with a stream of fresh water running through it. Looking down, he saw the body of a dead fox. It must have drowned in a storm and got washed downriver overnight. Just like the ghost girl, the fox had no eyes, but its big bushy tail was bright red just like the girl's ginger hair and he marvelled at the similarity. Then everything went dark and his dream location changed once more.

Now he was standing in an alleyway in London. It was night. There were two people in the alleyway apart from himself. A man and a woman. The woman wore a long dark coat that reached down to her ankles. Her black hair was cropped short on top with a long plaited strand of it handing down one side of her face and a small black tattoo of a star high up on her right cheek. More like a Hollywood B-movie vampire than any living human being, her skin was chalk-white beneath the moonlight and she carried a black ebonised walking stick with a silver handle by her side. She didn't look normal.

The other person in the alleyway was a young man who Cassidy guessed must have been the woman's drug dealer. Evidently, some kind of transaction was taking place. There was a short argument and some angry words were exchanged. Then a series of shots rang out. The young man had pulled out an automatic weapon and emptied the entire magazine into the woman's torso in a panic. As the man turned to run, Cassidy caught sight of his face. It was someone he recognised as Claude Dubois, a former acquaintance of his. Then the dream faded and Cassidy woke up in a sweat. He was back in his hotel room in Venice staring up at the ceiling in an alcohol-induced coma. It took several minutes for him to pull round, but when he did he sat up on the bed and shook his head. *That's the last time I touch vodka,* he thought, running his fingers through his hair and reaching for a cigarette. Then he remembered that he'd been trying to give them up for the better part of six months and let out a curse. A good old-fashioned cigarette would have been just the thing to take the edge off things and clear his mind. Maybe he could try one of those electronic vapes when he got back to England and see what they did. Then he would go and seek out his boss. The guy owed him the better part of twenty grand. He wasn't going to let him get away with that.

Eight

The weather was grey and overcast by the time Cassidy arrived back in England. He didn't linger at the airport, instead taking the tube as close to home as he could before walking the rest of the way in the rain, finally arriving at his houseboat at around four o'clock in the afternoon.

Once he got inside, he filled the kettle to make himself a pot of tea then removed a small package from his travelling bag. The package contained his new vape and there were some instructions to go with it. Instinctively, he reached for his cigarette lighter then realised he didn't need one.

Damn! But lighting up was half the pleasure, wasn't it? You light the tobacco then you take your first draw. Magic! But not with a fucking vape. A vape was different. All you had to do with a vape was suck on the mouthpiece and inhale the steam. Oh well, he'd give it a try and see how he got on.

Just then, the kettle clicked and went off the boil. Earl Grey tea, that's what he needed. Cassidy had always thought of himself as a connoisseur of tea. His galley cupboard was full of the stuff. Green tea, black tea, Indian tea and Chinese tea; you name it, he had some. He even ordered exotic blends on the internet when he couldn't source any locally. His favourite was a South African blend which he usually drank first thing in the morning. Most afternoons, however, he preferred the Earl Grey. It calmed and soothed his nerves which was exactly what he needed right now.

So, what do you actually smoke in a vape? he wondered as he waited for his Earl Grey to brew in its pot. There was a bottle of flavoured liquid in the starter pack he'd purchased at the airport. It had a funny sounding name.

'Lime Breeze?' Cassidy exclaimed in disgust. 'How the fuck do you smoke a Lime Breeze? Then he looked at the actual vape and scratched his head. 'Forty quid this lot cost me! I could have bought a whole load of duty-free for less than that and sold it down the pub for a ton. What a con!'

Hurling the vape across the room, he went in search of his emergency supply of tobacco. At first he couldn't find it and spent the better part of ten minutes rummaging through every nook and cranny of his houseboat until the place came to resemble the aftermath of a very nasty burglary. Then he remembered the spare yellow teapot which he kept on the top shelf of his galley cupboard and went to fetch it. Lifting the lid of the pot, he looked inside. To his relief, he found the small packet of hand-rolling tobacco and cigarette papers exactly where he'd left them. He also found his old cigarette lighter and pretty soon he was seated in his favourite armchair sipping his tea and enjoying the first decent cigarette he'd had in weeks. It wasn't long before his thoughts began wandering over the events of the previous few days.

How was he going to get his hands on the twenty grand that Jimmy Silver still owed him? He still didn't know where Silver lived. Of course, he could just put it all down to experience and let the matter drop, but Stuart Cassidy wasn't that kind of a bloke. A deal was a deal when all's said and done, and the twenty grand would have set him up for the better part of nine months. He couldn't let it go as easily as that, but where was Silver's actual place of residence? All he knew was that the guy lived somewhere near the sea, but the precise location of his boss's whereabouts still remained a mystery to him. It could be anywhere on the south coast, thought Cassidy – Folkestone, Hastings, Eastbourne or a myriad of other places – there was simply no way of knowing, and, as far as he could tell, no way of finding out either. Silver was more than likely living under an assumed name at an obscure address and that was that. Guaranteed anonymity for the rest of eternity.

The situation seemed hopeless, but then he remembered his old mate, Jerry Skinner, and their meeting in the café in Islington a few days before. He seemed to know something about Silver and could probably point him in the right direction. That was always assuming his friend wanted to get involved of course. From all that Skinner had said, he appeared to have his hands full dealing with the fallout from the police raid on the Angels' clubhouse in Harlow. What on earth Skinner was doing getting himself involved with a bunch of has beens like the Hells Angels, Cassidy couldn't begin to imagine. Didn't the guy realise that things had moved on since the 1990s? Nobody did business like that anymore. The future was in fraud and cyber-crime. The days of the HA were long gone, just like that meth-lab the cops had busted up the road from where Cassidy lived. According to local gossip, the place had been a Hells Angel concern until some little wanker had dobbed it in to the drug squad. Imagine anyone running a crystal-meth factory in this day and age. Stupid bastards. He hoped his friend hadn't been implicated. Probably not, but you could never tell with men like Jerry Skinner. He usually kept things so close to his chest that you'd hardly think he was involved in anything as serious as organised crime. *But he was.*

Sinking deeper into his thoughts, Cassidy considered his position. There was still quite a lot that he didn't know about Jimmy Silver and his associates. Just how much power and influence did his former boss actually have in the underworld and how far did his influence extend? Evidently far enough for him to have an agent running things on his behalf in Italy by all accounts. The existence of the mysterious Lady Westvale was ample proof of that.

Westvale... He ran the name through his head several times. Where could he find out about a toff called Lady Westvale he wondered? Perhaps if he did a bit of digging around on the internet he might come up with something. Yes, he would give it a try. After all, what did he have to lose? He might even discover some clues as to Silver's whereabouts and the precise nature of his business interests in Italy while he was at it. Now where had he put his laptop?

Cassidy was no academic. Half an hour's searching still hadn't yielded him any results. There was simply no mention of the name Westvale to be found in association with an aristocratic title anywhere on the web. Either the name "Westvale" had never belonged to the nobility or he was looking in the wrong place. Further searching and another pot of tea revealed an additional list of websites for him to investigate. Most of them required some form of monthly or annual subscription which he wasn't prepared to fork out for, but after a while one of them caught his eye. It was a free-view website specialising in aristocratic names dating from the year 1700 to the present day. Without hesitating, Cassidy lit up another smoke and clicked on the text line. Again, there were no modern-day Westvales to be found, but to his surprise something did crop up for the year 1807. It was a reference to a Lord Bartholemew Westvale and there were some biographical details to go with it.

Apparently, Bartholemew Westvale had been born in the year 1739 and had married a certain Mary Anne Montague of the county of Dorset in 1763. They produced two children – a boy and a girl. The male child was christened Percival Augustus Westvale and the girl was named Caroline Elizabeth Westvale. Young Percival joined the British navy as a junior officer when he was sixteen while his more wayward sister eloped with a country gentleman by the name of Sir James Blackthorne and went to live in Europe. Percival Westvale was later killed in action during the Napoleonic War and when Lord Bartholemew Westvale finally died a widower in 1807 the family line of the Westvales became extinct.

'So what happened to the daughter?' muttered Cassidy scrolling further down the page. There wasn't very much apart from a brief footnote stating that Caroline Westvale had so scandalised society by her elopement with Sir James Blackthorne that she was disowned by her family and never heard of again. It was later believed by some that she may have become involved in espionage when she was in Europe, but other than that the historical record appeared to fall silent after 1797 and there was no further mention of her name.

Cassidy's thoughts were racing: *If there aren't any Westvales anymore then who was the woman I saw in Venice?*

Either she's a highly accomplished con artist or an extremely gifted eccentric. More likely the former if Silver's got anything to do with it. Damn! Looks like I've been set up by a regular pair of grifters. But who the hell was Julie Kent? The creepy island. The desecrated tomb. The empty coffin. What the fuck was all that about and why did Silver want to know? No, there's a lot more going on here than meets the eye...

Now he found himself searching furiously for Julie Kent. He looked in all the UK obituary websites he could source but found nothing. Then he looked in all the Venetian civic death records and drew a blank – he couldn't gain access. He even tried all the social websites in the hope that Julie had profiled herself before she died, but all he came up with were two middle-aged women from Scotland and a teenager who lived in Florida. None of these were likely candidates so he paused for a few seconds and then for some reason typed in the words "missing persons" on the top bar and waited until something appeared. The FBI website he discounted immediately on account of Julie not having been an American citizen. Then he discovered a site called "UK MISSING PERSONS" and clicked on the text line. For some reason the screen froze and he had to wait for a whole minute before it began working again.

'What the fuck do they want – blood? murmured Cassidy as he answered the battery of questions needed to confirm his identity. It took another minute before he gained access to the website, but when he did, what he saw proved to be quite a revelation.

Cassidy had never realised there were so many missing persons in the British Isles. The majority were teenagers and young adults, the quality of their photographic images and hairstyles more or less determining the decade in which they had vanished. The earliest dated back to the 1940s. There weren't too many of them, but as he scrolled down the page, more and more pathetic little faces appeared until the entire screen was filled to capacity. *So many people,* he thought. *There must be hundreds of them. How do people just go missing like that and which one of them is Julie Kent?*

It wasn't long before he found out.

Selecting from the menu of search criteria, Cassidy began typing in what little he knew about Silver's granddaughter. Her name; her gender; her ethnicity and her nationality; all of these proved easy enough questions for him to answer, but he found himself at a loss as to the precise age she'd been when she went missing and the place where she was last seen, so he just clicked on the search box and hoped for the best. It wasn't long before the pale, faded image of a young white female appeared on the screen. In an instant, Cassidy realised who this person was and his blood ran cold. It was the same young woman he'd seen in his dream. The one who'd called herself Julie Kent. There was also a short piece of text beneath the photograph which Cassidy began reading out loud to himself: "Julie Kent, daughter of Albert and Molly Kent. Born in 1957. Studied music at London University between 1975 and 1977. Pale complexion. Blue eyes. Ginger hair. Last seen at the Roxy Nightclub, London, 21 July 1977."

The entry was dated November 1977 which was most likely when the police team investigating her disappearance had drawn a blank and placed her name on the missing person's file. That clinched it. The woman he was looking at in the photo was Julie, which would mean that her mother, Molly, must have been Silver's daughter who had married a bloke called Albert Kent. Well the logic seemed to fit, but unfortunately the maths didn't.

Creasing his brow, Cassidy rolled another cigarette and counted down the years. If Julie Kent was born in 1957 then she would have been twenty years of age when she went missing. Jimmy Silver, her grandfather, was now aged somewhere in his late fifties which would have put him at around twenty years of age himself when Julie disappeared.

'Impossible,' he muttered. 'A grandfather and a granddaughter of the same age? The woman in the photograph must be someone else…?'

Sensing he was getting nowhere, Cassidy closed down his laptop. The whole thing was simply a no-brainer. Whoever it was that had been in the coffin, it certainly wasn't Julie Kent. So, who could it have been?

Cassidy knew nothing of Silver's activities in Italy. Maybe his former boss had gone in for a bit of murder on the side and had interred the corpse of one of his female victims on the island for reasons best known to himself. But why go to all that trouble when there were a myriad more effective ways of disposing of a body? No, there was something definitely out of the ordinary about whatever he thought he'd witnessed out there on the Venetian lagoon. Something far more sinister and arcane. The black candles; the expensive coffin; the circle of salt? Yes, maybe he was better off out of it, safe and sound back here in his cosy little houseboat on the Grand Union Canal. Perhaps he'd just forget about everything and open up a four-pack of cider.

There was a movie coming up on the horror channel in about half an hour's time. It was probably a complete load of shite, but anything was better than just sitting here slowly going out of his mind thinking about Jimmy Silver and Julie Kent. Well it was worth a try.

***

Joe Rackham was sitting in the living room of his council house when his phone rang.

'I'll get it,' said Sheila going into the kitchen where the Rackhams kept their landline.

'Right,' muttered Joe, only half-interested in what was going on. He was watching an episode of *Crimewatch* on TV that was broadcasting some footage of the police raid on the Hells Angels' clubhouse in Harlow. So far, the police body-cameras had only shown the faint, ghostly image of Jerry Skinner as he legged it off down the road before the police SWAT team could catch up with him.

'Thank fuck for that,' whispered Joe under his breath. 'You can't tell who the cunt is at that distance. Looks like he's cleared that fence an' all. Not bad for an old bloke.'

'It's for you Joe,' said his wife popping her head round the door.

'Oh… Who is it?'

'A woman. Someone called Sterling. Do you know her?'

'Uh… yeah,' replied Joe, getting up from his seat with a grunt. As he did so, the TV remote slid off his knee and fell to the floor. Stooping down to pick it up, he turned down the volume on the telly and went into the kitchen, plucking the phone receiver out of his wife's hand. She looked concerned.

'It's okay, Sheila. Everything's cool. Don't worry.'

Sheila wasn't convinced. She recognised the name of Sterling from way back and she wasn't happy. If this was the same person she was thinking of then things could possible turn out very badly for Joe and his crew. The woman was bad news.

'Be careful,' said Sheila as Joe took the phone.

Joe smiled and nodded. Then he ushered his wife out of the room with a wave of his hand and began speaking into the phone in a low voice so he wouldn't be overheard.

'Sterling, is everything all right? Nothing's happened to the consignment, has it?'

'Your drugs are safe and sound, Joe,' the woman replied. 'I caught two black guys snooping around the warehouse a couple of days ago but they're gone now.'

'What do you mean *they're gone?*'

'Like I said, they're gone. You know what I'm saying…?'

Joe should have known what she meant the first time round. The woman he was talking to had such a fearsome reputation among London's criminal elite that anyone who had ever crossed swords with her and lived to tell the tale still spoke her name in hushed tones even years after the event. It was how she worked.

'So, why are you calling?' continued Rackham, swapping the phone over to his good ear. He'd worked in a noisy factory in his younger days and now suffered from partial deafness. His obsession with heavy metal music hadn't helped much either.

'I'm calling about the bomb, Joe. The one that blew up the pub.'

'What about it?'

'Silver's men definitely planted it. I've just had it confirmed.'

'Thought as much. So, it wasn't a rival chapter then?'

'No it wasn't. And I've got some other news as well.'

'What's that?'

'The feds have busted your meth lab. The one by the canal.'

'Fuck! Anyone get collared?'

'I don't think so. At least, not that I've heard.'

'Have you told Skinner? He needs to be warned.'

'Not yet. I'll be up in his neck of the woods tomorrow so I'll tell him then. Don't worry.'

'But I am worried, Sterling. I've got enough on my plate without all this happening. The Californians are threatening to disband the whole chapter if I don't get the memory stick back from Scotland Yard within a fortnight—'

'Could be less time than that if I have anything to do with it, Joe.'

'How do you mean?'

'Never you mind. Just leave it to me, okay. In any case, I've got something else I need to tell you.'

'Like what?' enquired Rackham, almost reluctant to hear the rest of her news.

'I've shot Bordoni.'

The revelation dropped like a stone in a pond and rippled out into Joe's mind. He paused and took a short breath. You've done what—?'

'Giuseppe Bordoni. I've shot him. Did it a couple of days back. Is that a problem?'

'It might be. What if Silver thinks the Hells Angels have done it?'

'He won't. He knows it was me. I can sense it.'

'What do you mean you can sense it? You psychic or something?'

'In a manner of speaking, yes I am. It kind of comes with the package when you're a thing like me.'

'I don't follow. What are you saying?'

'Don't worry, Joe. Just ask Skinner the next time you see him. Anyway, I've got to go now. There's some business I need to attend to. Bye for now.'

And with that, she rang off, leaving Joe with a hollow feeling in the pit of his stomach. Jimmy Silver ran a cushy little racket settling Italian hitmen in England long enough for the heat to die down in their own country. It was quite a lucrative sideline by all accounts and now Sterling had gone and rubbed out one of his best payers. He wasn't going to be well pleased to say the least.

But why had she done it, thought Joe? It wasn't as if she'd ever had any bad blood between herself and the Italian mobs – at least, none that he was aware of. Well, no matter. What was done was done and there could be no turning back. He needed to call a meeting of all the southern Hells Angel gangs right away. It looked as if there was going to be trouble.

Nine

'You don't have to answer that question, Mr Cassidy.'

It was the duty solicitor who spoke, sitting next to Stuart in the interview room. Cassidy had been held in police custody for the better part of twelve hours now on account of him having been found in possession of two kilograms of crystal meth which the drug squad had discovered under his bed when they'd raided his houseboat in the early hours of the morning. Naturally, the presence of the drugs hidden beneath his bed was a complete mystery to Cassidy who had never dealt in illegal narcotics in his life, preferring instead to leave that kind of activity to the younger end of the criminal food chain while he busied himself with other things.

The interview room was quiet compared to the rest of the police station. Even the sounds of the London traffic outside were dull and vague in here, so that Cassidy had to continually force his mind to concentrate on everything the interviewing office was saying.

'Very well then, I shall put the question to you in a different way, Mr Cassidy. Can you please tell me for the benefit of this interview exactly what it was that you were doing on your trip to Venice?'

'Like I said before, I was just visiting the place. It's not a crime, is it?'

'No it isn't, but we are trying to establish as precise a picture as possible of your movements in the days leading up to your arrest so it would be advisable if you could be a bit more co-operative. What exactly was the purpose of your visit to Venice?'

'I was sightseeing.'

'Sightseeing?'

'Yeah. I was sightseeing. There, does that answer your question?'

'I see,' replied the interviewing officer glancing momentarily at his colleague. 'And do you usually take your holidays in Venice during the winter months?'

'Yes I do. It's cheaper this time of the year and you get to see some lovely mists. Look! Like I said to you before, I've no idea how those drugs got to be under my bed. I was away for a few days and when I got back I had a few drinks and fell asleep in front of the telly. Next thing I know, your boys are turning my houseboat over searching for the crystal meth. It's a complete mystery to me how it got there.'

The officer glanced at his colleague once again then regarded Stuart quizzically.

'And you claim that during your stay in Venice you made the acquaintance of a certain Lady Caroline Westvale, is that correct?'

'It is.'

'And what is your relationship with this woman, Mr Cassidy?'

Stuart looked at his solicitor. The man nodded, indicating it was all right to answer the question.

'She's a friend,' Cassidy replied. 'Just a friend.'

'That's very interesting, Stuart,' continued the interviewer, 'only we haven't been able to trace anyone called Lady Caroline Westvale against that name and title anywhere in Europe. She's not on any database we know of and the Venetian authorities have no trace of her either. According to our records she doesn't exist.'

Cassidy thought, *they've drawn a blank. Now why doesn't that surprise me?*

'Look officer, it's all been a mistake. Someone is trying to set me up.'

'Trying to set you up? And why would anyone want to do that?'

Suddenly he was at a loss. How could he tell them the real reason for his visit to Italy? That he'd gone on an errand on behalf of a criminal mastermind to see if there was an unregistered body still interred in a tomb on an island in the middle of nowhere? No, that would only make things worse for him, so he turned to his solicitor for guidance.

'Do I have to answer that?'

'Only if the matter is directly relevant to what you are being accused of, Stuart.'

Cassidy understood. 'No comment,' he replied, half expecting his interrogator to lay off him for a while, but he didn't. Instead, the officer just changed tack and continued on with a different line of questioning.

'Our investigations show that you made no calls from your mobile phone all the time you were abroad, Mr Cassidy. Is there any particular reason why you maintained phone silence during your stay in Venice?'

'The reception was bad,' Stuart replied. 'I couldn't get a signal.'

He's hiding something, thought the interviewing officer. *It's got something to do with his trip to Venice. Maybe if I push him a little bit further I can find out what it was.*

But he didn't, for at that moment the mind of DC Collins suddenly went blank and he threw a massive fit, falling to the floor of the interview room where his body continued to lie, trembling violently for about thirty seconds until his colleague put him in the recovery position and called for an ambulance.

It was a full fifteen minutes before the paramedics arrived. Cassidy looked on as they carried DC Collins out of the room. He was about to offer his assistance when he felt a firm hand pressing down on his shoulder. 'No you don't!' came a voice from behind.

Turning round, Cassidy found himself standing face-to-face with a uniformed senior officer who was glaring at him through a pair of steel-rimmed spectacles.

'What have you done to him, you little bastard?' the officer seethed, almost spitting out his words as he spoke.

'Me? I haven't done anything,' Cassidy replied innocently enough, but his gauche manner only seemed to infuriate the police officer even more. 'Don't lie to me, you little scrote. I know what you fucking well are!'

'What do you mean? I don't understand.'

The officer glanced round the room before looking Cassidy directly in the eye.

'Did *she-e-e* send you?' he enquired lowering his voice menacingly.

'Who?' said Cassidy, looking to his solicitor for support.

'You know who I mean. The woman who calls herself, Sterling. No one could have done what you've just done without her help.'

'Done what?'

'DC Collins, that's what! He's in a right old state. You've gone and scrambled his brains for him, haven't you!'

This was a new one for Cassidy. He'd been interviewed by the police many times before in his career but he'd never come up against anything like this. Was it some new interview technique they were trying out to get him so disorientated that he would confess to practically anything? Again, he looked to his solicitor for support but the man just shrugged his shoulders. He didn't know what was happening either.

At that moment, a female officer entered the room and walked over to where Cassidy was standing. She appeared to outrank everyone else and began speaking to the man who'd just given Cassidy the third degree: 'I don't think this is appropriate, Inspector Lefarge. He's just a drug dealer, that's all.'

'Sod the drugs, Louise! I've been in the police force a long time and I've seen this sort of thing before. What we've got ourselves here is a right fucking goblin!'

The woman took Lefarge gently aside. 'I think a spot of annual leave would be a good idea George, don't you? What about a couple of weeks in Devon? I've heard you're thinking of retiring to that part of the world soon.'

Ten minutes later, Cassidy was standing in front of the police station reception desk. 'What happens now?' he asked the duty solicitor as the station sergeant handed him back his property and personal effects.

'For the moment you're free to go,' replied the man. 'Lefarge screwed up the interview so there would have been complications if your case had gone to court.'

'So I can just walk out of here scot-free then?'

'Not entirely. The matter will most likely be sent to the Crown Prosecution Service to establish what, if anything, you can be charged with. It's possible you might get done for possession, but I doubt if they'll do you for intent to supply.'

'What about Inspector Lefarge? All that weird stuff he was coming out with. What was all that about?'

'To be perfectly honest with you, Mr Cassidy, I haven't got a clue. Stress of the job I suppose, though I haven't seen one go off like that before. Given what happened in the interview room I doubt very much if the police will follow things up. You know how it works.'

***

It was getting late when Cassidy left the bar. He hadn't meant to stay for so long but his ordeal at the police station and the strange turn of events in the interview room had so unsettled him that he needed a few drinks to calm his nerves.

The street outside was dark and quiet compared to the place he'd just left, and the odour of stale beer soon evaporated on the breeze as Cassidy walked the few dozen yards or so toward the turning that would take him closer to the taxi stop he needed. As he walked, he spotted a young woman in a leopard-skin coat and heels on the opposite side of the road. Seeing him, the woman crossed over and asked him for a light. 'I must have left my lighter in my other bag,' she said coyly. 'I'm always doing it. Silly me.'

Cassidy obliged and they soon began exchanging small talk.

'What's your name?' said Cassidy casually. 'It's not important,' she replied. 'What's yours?'

'It's Stuart,' he replied, thinking the woman must be a local prostitute. She was certainly dressed that way, though the faint reddish glow that hazed around her head and shoulders was something he'd never seen before. Presumably, she was wearing some new kind of cosmetic that was currently in vogue among the *demi monde* of society.

'I'm not soliciting,' she said smiling, almost as if she could read his thoughts. 'I just wanted a light, that's all. Bye—'

And with that, the young woman crossed back over the road and disappeared into the night. Thinking nothing of it, Cassidy shrugged his shoulders and continued on down the street before turning left into a narrow lane. It was then that he realised he was being followed.

Trying not to show any fear, Cassidy quickened his pace but it was no good. The two men came up behind him, flanking Cassidy on either side as he walked. Unable to do very much else, he turned and stood his ground. Big mistake. One of the men – the taller of the pair – grabbed Cassidy from behind pinning both his arms behind his back while the other man stared at him hard.

'This is to make sure you keep your mouth shut,' said the shorter man. 'The boss doesn't like people knowing too much about his business.'

Before he could reply, Cassidy felt all the air in his lungs escape in one agonising gasp as the man's fist slammed into his stomach. Then the man drew back his hand to deliver a second punch, but as he did so, Cassidy wrenched his arms free and lashed out at his attacker, catching him square on the chin with a clenched fist.

His assailant staggered backwards, blinking at Cassidy in disbelief. In response to this, the man behind produced a claw hammer from the waistband of his trousers. 'Linda didn't say anything about him being handy,' he said, preparing to deliver a blow to the back of Cassidy's skull.

'Leave it out,' said the shorter man, nursing his bruised jaw with the palm of his hand. 'I think he's got the message.'

The man holding the hammer wasn't convinced. 'What difference does it make if he's dead? Best finish him off now and get the fuck out of here. We don't want to stick around for too long, especially with that biker bitch around.'

Panic seized Cassidy's mind. He knew he was going to die and tried to make a run for it, but his legs were trembling so much he doubted if he could manage more than a few metres before his assailants caught up with him and worked him over a bit more before killing him. Despairing of the situation, he surrendered himself to the inevitable and waited for the hammer blow that he knew would shortly come. When it didn't, he wondered what was up and why the man had hesitated. Pretty soon he had his answer.

She was standing beneath the acid glow of a security light which had switched itself on to register her presence. Clad in jeans, a leather jacket and motorcycle boots, she stared directly at Cassidy's two attackers as if she were sizing them both up.

'It's her,' said the shorter man urgently. 'What are we going to do?'

Cassidy watched as the pale slender figure moved out of the glare of the security light and walked several paces forward. As the light clicked off, he could see that her body was surrounded by a glowing crimson aura just like the woman he'd seen earlier wearing the leopard-skin coat, only much stronger and deeper in hue. If the two men could see it as well, they made no comment, only drawing back a little as the lone figure in the biker jacket continued staring at them malevolently from behind her dark mirrored sunglasses.

'Screw this,' hissed the taller man brandishing his hammer in his right hand. 'I'm gonna settle this fucker's hash for good!'

To Cassidy's surprise, the woman made no attempt to move out of the way, preferring instead to stand her ground as her assailant approached. Then, just as the man was about to raise his weapon for a lethal downstroke, she neatly sidestepped him and grasped his head with both her hands, twisting it sideways in one swift action causing his neck to break with a sickening crunch.

This was enough for the other man. No sooner had he watched his comrade's lifeless body drop to the ground than he turned on his heels and fled in the opposite direction with the crazy biker woman chasing after him in hot pursuit. As she brushed past Cassidy in the narrow lane, the edge of her hand accidentally touched his for a split second and he felt an ice-cold chill run up his arm. Then there was a sound like a clap of thunder going off inside his skull which caused him to jerk his head back in shock. A series of images now flooded into his mind as if all the events of his life had suddenly flashed before his eyes in an instant, except that these particular images didn't belong to his own life. They belonged to somebody else's.

He saw a swish 1970's house party in full swing in an upmarket London apartment ... flared trousers, psychedelic shirts and lots of people standing around smoking marijuana. Then he saw a deserted beach and the woman with the skeletal eyes and ginger hair who called herself Julie Kent. Next, came the image of a young man lying face down in a pool of blood with his nose severed. His name was Claude Dubois. All of these images and a good many more now ran speeding through Cassidy's mind like an express train until the final sequence of events when things seemed to slow down a bit. In these last scenes, a woman wearing a long dark coat with cropped black hair was crossing a public square somewhere in Italy when a motor scooter suddenly pulled up behind her and its pillion rider stepped off brandishing an automatic pistol. Then, a series of shots rang out and the woman lay dead on the ground as the crowds scattered around her. Shortly after this, everything went blank and Cassidy came to his senses once again.

It was then that he noticed the woman in the leather jacket. She had paused in her pursuit of the man she was chasing and was looking at Cassidy in a strange way. Then she jerked her head back with a snarl and ran, disappearing off into the darkness before Cassidy had time to speak. He felt dizzy, as if he had just stepped off a roller-coaster ride at a fairground. All he wanted to do was get back home to the safety of his houseboat and sleep, but something told him that the images he'd just witnessed were somehow connected with the woman in the leather jacket. Then he realised where he'd seen her before. It had been while he'd been waiting for his ride to see Jimmy Silver. She'd been the woman sitting in the Soho bar staring at the clock on the wall.

He started back to his home. It was almost midnight and the streets beyond the lane were jammed with revellers determined to savour the last few minutes of enjoyment from what remained of their night out. The noise and excitement they generated almost made him forget the events of the previous twenty-four hours.

At first, he thought it was the breeze that whispered in his ear. Then the breeze spoke his name.

Cassidy turned to see the pale, smiling face of a young man in his early twenties, dressed in an expensive loose-fitting suit. The stranger lifted a cigarette to his lips, his eyes shadowed by the glare of the nearby streetlight. It was then that Cassidy noticed that the young man was missing his nose. Realising who it was, he took a step backwards and his heart began to pound.

'You're dead!' he exclaimed with an almost accusatory tone.

'It's not a fucking crime, is it?' replied Claude Dubois taking another draw on his ghostly cigarette. 'I've been trying to catch your attention for the better part of the night, you stupid bastard!'

Cassidy noticed that significant parts of Claude's body were semi-transparent and that his feet and the lower half of his legs were practically non-existent.

'I don't have much time, Stuart, so listen up. Us dead men aren't supposed to communicate with the living, but I've never been one for following the rules. Take my advice mate. Just get the fuck out of this town while you still can. Forget you ever laid eyes on her.'

'Who—?'

'Who the fuck do you think I mean? Why, Sterling of course! The girl in the leather jacket. She's death, mate! Death on two legs!'

'What do you mean?'

'Look, Stuart. I'm telling you in no uncertain terms to get as far away as you can and don't come back. The way she just zero'd in on you back then means she's got your scent. Things like her can pick up on your psychic vibes like nobody's business.'

'I don't understand.'

Claude shook his phantom head.

'Being dead has given me a different perspective on things. It ain't the best way to be but it's better than how things were when I was alive. Maybe she was doing me a favour when she topped me, but you're different see.'

Cassidy suddenly realised what the ghost was saying. 'Are you telling me that she—'

'Killed me? Yeah, that's what I'm saying. And she cut my nose off too. It's them what found my body that I feel sorry for. I must have looked a right mess.'

'Why did she do it?'

'Because I once tried to kill her, that's why. Shot her with a machine pistol not too far from here back in 2003.'

'Then what have you come to warn me for? What did I have to do with it?'

Cassidy's fear of the ghost had diminished by now and he was beginning to feel irritated.

'Let's just say that we're kindred spirits, you an' me, if you'll pardon the pun.'

'I don't follow…?'

Claude let out the spiritual equivalent of a sigh and looked Cassidy straight in the face.

'You used to work for Jimmy Silver, didn't you?'

Cassidy nodded. 'Yes I did. So what?'

'So did I. They use people like you an'me, Stuart. People they can manipulate to do their dirty work. Silver and one of his associates compromised me into shooting the bitch. Well, I was young and easily led, wasn't I. They said I could do the job easily with an uzi. I couldn't miss they said. But killing something like her ain't that simple.'

'You messed up?'

'Yeah. Big time. I capped her square in the tits with a full magazine and that put her down for a while.'

'Then what happened?'

'The bitch woke up in the morgue, that's what happened! Then she comes after me to finish the job and the rest in history.'

Cassidy replied, 'What exactly did you mean when you said that they use people like us? I don't understand.'

'Look, Stuart, it's all very simple. Men like Silver and that creature you saw back there in the alleyway are one in the same kind. They pick up on folk like us because we're useful to them. So far you've only had a taste of what they're capable of, but if you stick around much longer you'll get the full deal. Take my advice and leave town now. It's your only way out.'

'How do you mean?'

'Sorry mate,' replied Claude, his body becoming more transparent. 'My time's run out here and I've got to go. I've told you all I can. The rest is up to you.'

'No. Wait! Why are you telling me this?'

The ghost laughed. 'You'd best ask that biker bitch next time you see her. Maybe she can fill you in on the details...'

Claude's body appeared to shimmer like vapour rising up from a rain-soaked summer road. Then he vanished into thin air almost as suddenly as he had appeared – a visitor from another world with a salutary warning to impart.

Everything was silent. The late-night revellers and party-goers had vanished too. Cassidy glanced at his watch. To his dismay, he found that it was 2:30 in the morning. He'd been talking with the ghost of Claude Dubois for well over two hours and hadn't noticed the time go by. As he climbed into his taxi, a feeling of bone-deep weariness came over him and he realised that he needed to rest. Maybe after a good night's sleep, things would become clearer in the morning. He certainly hoped so.

Ten

Cassidy could tell from the thin sliver of light seeping through the gap in his bedroom curtains that it was almost dawn and the start of a new day.

He hadn't slept well. At around 4:30 in the morning he'd been woken by the sound of footsteps crunching up the gravel towpath outside his home. Then he'd fallen back to sleep again, too weary to investigate whoever it might be.

He couldn't remember when it was that he'd first taken to sleeping in his clothes. He'd been doing it for so long that it had become a habit with him. People in his line of business usually slept in their clothes if they had any sense. You never knew when you might have to make a run for it, and getting yourself dressed all of a sudden just took up too much valuable time.

Getting out of bed, he wandered into the bathroom for a few minutes before going into his kitchen to fix breakfast. Breakfast was his favourite meal of the day. Three rashers of bacon, two pork sausages and a fried egg, all washed down with a steaming hot mug of coffee. Lovely.

When he'd finished eating, Cassidy sat back in his chair, cupping the mug of coffee to his lips in silent meditation. He usually drank tea, but not first thing in the morning.

Mulling over the events of the previous day, Cassidy considered everything that had happened. He hadn't really seen a ghost, had he? Claude Dubois had been found dead in a gay bar in Soho back in 2003. That was well over thirteen years ago. Impossible.

He hadn't known Dubois that well when he'd been alive. All he could remember was that Claude had been a rent boy in his younger days before graduating up the ladder of crime and vice to carrying out major underworld hits in support of his heroin addiction. Life could be cheap in the capital.

Then there had been the altercation with the two men in the alleyway. Now that had definitely been real. Real enough to make him consider taking the ghost's advice to leave town and never come back. But then, Claude didn't exist anymore, did he? And what about the crystal meth? It could take months before the Crown Prosecution Service decided what they were going to charge him with. If he scarpered now, they would take it as a sign of his guilt and come looking for him. He was in a no win situation whichever way he looked. Damn!

Feeling the need to smoke, Cassidy got up and went in search of his tobacco and rolling papers. Then he rolled himself a cigarette and lit it with trembling hands.

'Cassidy?'

He spun round so fast he almost dropped his lighter.

She was standing in his kitchen dressed in a pair of faded blue jeans, a brown t-shirt, black leather jacket, scuffed biker boots and sunglasses. It was the girl from the alleyway, and even though he could not see her eyes, Cassidy was aware of being watched.

'You are Silver's agent?' she said in a menacing voice.

He tensed. 'I was… but not anymore.'

Her lips twisted into a thin smile. 'That's what they all say.'

'Who?'

'Men like you, Stuart. Those lucky enough to be alive, that is.'

'What are you saying?' said Cassidy, preparing to defend himself.

'Those two men you met in the alleyway last night,' said the woman, 'it was Silver who sent them to rough you up. It's his way of telling you to keep your mouth shut.'

'How do you know Jimmy Silver?'

'Jimmy is my grandfather – *in a manner of speaking.*'

Cassidy's scalp began to tighten and a cold chill ran up his spine.

'You're Julie Kent?'

Again the woman's lips twisted into a smile. 'No, my name is Sterling. Julie is dead.'

Cassidy paused, unable to follow the logic. For some reason, he allowed his gaze to wander and noticed that the woman wore a long ginger fox tail hanging from a leather strap attached to the belt of her jeans. 'How did you get into my houseboat?' he said without taking his eyes from the strange ginger talisman.

'You left the front door open, Stuart. Careless of you in the circumstances.'

'Then how did you know where I live?' replied Cassidy raising his gaze.

'Jerry Skinner told me. He's a friend of yours I believe.'

'You know Skinner?'

'Yes. We go back a long way, Skinner and me.'

Relaxing his guard, Cassidy relit his cigarette and sat down. 'You killed that man in the alleyway last night. The one who was going to top me with the hammer…'

'Yes, I did. And I slotted the other fucker too once I caught up with him.'

'Thanks, I'm grateful.'

'So you bloody well should be! It's not every day a small-timer like you has someone watching their back.'

'But why did you do it? What's so important about me?'

'Because I need you alive, Mr Cassidy. That's why.'

Again, Stuart paused and took a long draw from his cigarette. 'What's going on?' he demanded firmly.

'Going on?' replied the woman extending her pale narrow hand toward him. 'I'll show you what's going on.' As their fingers touched, Cassidy experienced what he could only describe as a strong electric shock going off somewhere deep inside his skull. The room disappeared and he found himself standing in the middle of a large city plaza somewhere in central Italy. It was Christmas 2003…

The body of a young woman lay on the ground riddled with bullets. Someone had just emptied the magazine of an automatic weapon into her chest at close range. Cassidy looked down and saw to his surprise that the woman's face was the same as that of the woman he'd seen in the alleyway and with whom he'd recently been talking. Only her hairstyle was different. As Cassidy looked on, a young couple – a man and a woman – walked towards the body. The woman he didn't recognise – she was American. But the man he recognised immediately. It was Jerry Skinner and he looked concerned…

Sterling retracted her hand. That's enough for now, she thought. He's got psychic ability but he can't take much more.

'What did you do just then?' said Cassidy coming to his senses.

'I can't explain just yet,' replied Sterling. 'Whatever the case, you can't stay around here for much longer. It's too dangerous, and Silver probably knows where you live. Meet me at Skinner's flat tonight at nine o'clock and all will be revealed. There's a lot more going on here than meets the eye.'

Reaching into the pocket of her jacket, she produced a small calibre handgun. 'It's loaded,' she said, checking the weapon. 'Here. Take it. You may well need it before the day's through.'

'I can't,' replied Cassidy, shaking his head. 'I don't want nothing to do with guns.'

'Take it!' yelled Sterling thrusting the gun into his hand. Then she turned and left, leaving Cassidy alone in the houseboat. It wasn't long before he heard the sound of a motorcycle engine starting up outside. As the sound receded, he glanced down and saw his cigarette lying on the floor. Picking it up, he examined it carefully and noticed that it had burned all the way down to the filter. That would mean he'd been out for almost fifteen minutes while all those scenes were playing around inside his head. Just what exactly had he got himself involved in this time, he wondered?

It was mid-morning before Cassidy had calmed down sufficiently enough to focus his thoughts. From all the woman in the biker jacket had said, it looked as though he was a marked man. So far he'd been lucky, but sooner or later, Silver's agents would catch up with him and then things wouldn't be so cosy. He had to think of a plan.

It was no good him hiding away in his houseboat. Better to stay on the move he thought and keep his enemies guessing. Putting on his coat, he grabbed his house keys and tobacco then made for the door.

The morning air was fresh as he stepped out onto the jetty and began walking down the canal towpath towards the narrow pedestrian footbridge where he wanted to be. The towpath was almost deserted apart from an elderly couple out walking their dog and an over-enthusiastic cyclist who pedalled like fury, almost knocking Cassidy into the canal.

'Wanker!' he shouted after the man on the bike, then he kept on walking until he reached the middle of the footbridge. Here he paused and took his bearings. From where he was standing, he could see most of central London spread out across the horizon together with several of its more familiar landmarks protruding above the skyline like pins in a wall chart. Silver's men could be lurking anywhere out there in that vast metropolis. It was only a question of time before they caught up with him.

Reaching into the pocket of his coat, his fingers came into contact with the handle of the gun that Sterling had given him. He wasn't the sort of criminal who usually carried a gun. It was a mug's game. Get yourself caught in possession of one of those things and you went down for certain.

What to do?

Making sure he wasn't being observed, Cassidy took the gun out of his pocket and examined it carefully. Then, leaning over the parapet of the bridge, he allowed the weapon to slip from his grasp into the dark waters of the canal below where it sank with a plop; an interesting find for some future archaeologist but no longer a problem for him now.

Satisfied that he'd made the right decision, he pulled up the collar of his coat and continued walking across the bridge as if nothing had happened. For some reason, getting rid of the gun made him feel more secure. It shouldn't have he knew, but the knowledge that he could be arrested by the police at any time and without any warning made parting company with the weapon seem like a good idea. Another good idea would be to go and get himself a haircut. He hadn't been to see his barber in weeks and by now he was beginning to feel untidy. It was time to pay Mick a visit and catch up on some local gossip.

Mick's Place was one of the least expensive barber shops in the district, which was the main reason why Cassidy went there. The other reason was that he could usually rely on Mick giving him the haircut he'd actually asked for rather than some trendy new style that just so happened to be in vogue for the season.

'How are we having it this time?' said Mick as he draped the blue barber shawl across Cassidy's shoulders.

'Just tidy it up a bit,' replied Cassidy as he examined his reflection in the mirror. Somehow his face looked different. Evidently, the events of the past few days had left their mark.

As Mick set to work with his scissors, the conversation turned to matters of a less technical nature. The government, the cost of living, and of course, the inevitable subject of holidays.

'Going abroad this year?' said Mick, over the sound of a radio playing away in the background.

'I've been,' Cassidy replied with more than a trace of irony in his voice.

'Anywhere interesting?'

'Venice. Just for a few days.'

'Oh, and how was it?'

'Lively.'

Well he couldn't tell his barber the full story, could he? About the haunted island complete with its own personal loony bin and desecrated tomb? No one would have believed him anyway.

'Off the ears is it?' said Mick, glancing momentarily at Cassidy's reflection.

'Yes, and I need it tapering at the back too.'

'What happened to the square cut then?'

'Makes me look old,' said Cassidy, still surprised by the face he saw staring back at him from the mirror.

Mick made no comment and carried on snipping away with his scissors until more and more of Cassidy's hair began to accumulate on the floor around his feet. Then, just as he was about to finish the job, his telephone rang from the back office.

'Won't be a moment,' said Mick putting down his scissors. Seconds later, he returned trailing the telephone cord and clutching the receiver in his hand. 'It's for you, Stuart—'

'Who is it?' Cassidy exclaimed in surprise.

'Don't know. They didn't say.'

Mystified, Cassidy removed his barber shawl and took the receiver from Mick.

'Hello… Who is it?' he said inquisitively.

'It's Jimmy,' came the reply.

Cassidy swallowed hard. 'How did you know I was here?'

'That's not important, Stuart. All that is important for now is that you co-operate with me, is that understood?'

'I don't get it. What do you mean *co-operate?*'

There was a moment of silence before Silver spoke again.

'I hear you met my granddaughter last night... in an alleyway.'

Now it was Cassidy's turn to pause. Silver seemed to know everything about his movements over the last twenty-four hours. He was being watched.

'She's wasted two of my best men,' Silver continued. 'I'm not well pleased about that.'

'So what! Those two blokes tried to kill me,' Cassidy protested. 'She saved my life—'

'And you'll wish she hadn't if you don't provide me with the information I require.'

'What information?'

'The precise details of her whereabouts, Mr Cassidy. I have assumed that she may be hiding out in one of her old haunts but I was wondering if you might have heard otherwise. I want to know where she is.'

'Can't help you with that one, Silver. I don't know where she is myself and even if I did I wouldn't tell you.'

'Don't be silly, Stuart. I can pick you up whenever I want to. Remember that other woman you met before your unfortunate encounter in the alleyway – the one wearing the leopard-skin coat?'

'What about her?'

'Her name is Linda. She's one of my agents too, in case you were wondering. I've got the city well covered, Stuart. There's nowhere you can hide.'

Now Cassidy was angry. Silver's mocking voice was more than he could stand. Holding the mouthpiece closer to his lips, he replied, 'Yes, Mr Silver. I'm meeting your granddaughter tonight at nine.'

'Oh, you are, are you? And where might that be?'

'You mean you don't know?'

'No, I don't,' Silver responded calmly.

'Well you can fuck off then!' Cassidy snarled, banging the receiver down on the handset which had been conveniently placed on the worktop in front of him.

'Anything the matter?' asked Mick, wide-eyed with concern.

'Just some bleedin muppet thinks he can fuck me over,' replied Cassidy reaching for his wallet. 'How much do I owe you?'

'I haven't finished yet. I still need to run the shears over the back of your neck.'

'Don't worry. I'll do it myself with a razor when I get home. So how much was it?'

'Seven quid, and mind you don't get razor burns. Thanks…'

***

It's a good job this place has got some bogs, thought Cassidy as he downed his fourth coffee of the afternoon.

Visiting art galleries wasn't his usual leisure time activity. The world of fine art had been a closed book to him ever since he'd left school at the age of fourteen. Still, the National Gallery in Trafalgar Square was a different matter. He'd never realised the place had so many famous paintings on display – and it had toilets as well.

Feeling hungry, he purchased a small snack-pack of biscuits at the cafeteria then settled back down at his table with a newspaper from the communal racks. His evening rendezvous at Skinner's flat was still a long time away. Until then, he would have to keep a low profile and hope that no more of Silver's goons caught up with him.

There wasn't much of interest in the newspaper. Only the horoscopes in the middle section attracted his attention. Capricorn was his sun sign and the reading was a mixed one at best. It told him to keep a low profile and avoid arguments if possible. Apparently, accidents were a distinct possibility.

Dammit! Even the heavens were against him. Could it be karmic payback time for his life of crime, Cassidy wondered? It wasn't as though he'd been a particularly bad sort as far as criminals went. He'd never worked someone over so badly that even their mothers wouldn't have recognised them and he'd never stolen from old ladies either. All right, there was some small-time fraud and the rent collecting he'd done for Silver but it was nothing compared to what others had done. Maybe karma was somehow cumulative in nature and you got the bill all at once instead of in regular instalments. It certainly felt that way.

He needed the lavatory urgently now, but public toilets could be lethal places if you were trying to dodge a hitman. It only took a moment's lapse of concentration and you could end up lying dead in front of the urinals for the next punter to find and report to the janitor. It didn't bear thinking about really.

Ten more minutes went by. It was no good. He had to go. If there were any of Silver's agents lurking in the vicinity, he would use the opportunity to give them the slip. All he needed was a pair of spectacles and a spare coat to provide him with a suitable disguise.

The spectacles were easy. He had a pair in his pocket which he seldom wore on account of him being only marginally astigmatic in one eye. The coat was a different matter, however. Where could he get another coat from? He would have to improvise.

Reaching the gent's toilet, he went inside. Once he'd completed the purpose of his visit, he turned his own coat inside out and put on his glasses. *There,* he thought, regarding himself in the mirror. *No one would mistake me for Stuart Cassidy now. I look completely different.*

Satisfied with his disguise, Cassidy walked out of the toilets making his way along a series of corridors and stairways until he eventually reached the front of the building. Here he stopped for a moment and gazed out across Trafalgar Square. Apart from a few pigeons, the square was almost empty and devoid of people. It was four o' clock in the afternoon which meant he still had five hours to kill before his meeting at Skinner's place. What on earth could he do till then?

His best strategy would be to stay on the move. It was the only method of avoiding Silver's agents that he knew might work. With this in mind, he descended the steps of the National

Gallery and turned left up Charing Cross Road, walking in the direction of Leicester Square tube station. There, he could use London's underground rail network to his advantage in giving Silver's men the slip.

Purchasing a ticket from the nearest booth, Cassidy went through the turnstiles and down onto the platform below. It wasn't long before a tube train snaked its way out of a tunnel and came to a halt alongside where Cassidy was standing. Glancing around to make sure he wasn't being followed, he waited for the carriage doors to slide open before stepping on board the train and sitting himself down in an almost empty compartment. Then the doors slid shut and the train moved off, slowly picking up speed as it went. If he could endure the monotony of travelling to-and-fro across the city for the next five hours, then he stood some chance of reaching Skinner's flat alive. If his plan didn't work, then at least he would die secure in the knowledge that he'd tried his best and given his pursuers a hard job of hunting him down What did he have to lose?

Eleven

Sterling watched as Cassidy boarded the train. Satisfying herself that all was well, she turned and made her way back up to street level. It was getting dark by now, but that didn't bother her. She had excellent night vision. One of the few advantages of being one of her kind.

Halting at a street corner, she sniffed the air. There was a slight breeze and it carried the scent of the metropolis on its wings. Somewhere out there in that big old city, Silver was waiting. Waiting for her to make a mistake. Linda was out there too. Linda Bailey, the cute little fashion icon of yesteryear with a taste for human blood and high-end criminal activity. Just like herself in many ways, only not as cunning.

Sterling frowned and pulled the envelope from her pocket. It had arrived mysteriously that afternoon; a small parchment envelope shoved unceremoniously under her door at the old warehouse beside the Thames. Turning it over in her hands she sensed who it had come from.

Silver…

Was it over thirteen years ago since they'd last clashed? Like most vampires, her sense of time had become distorted. Days could seem like weeks. Weeks seemed like months, and months could seem like years. That was how things were for the Undead.

Running her fingers over the wax seal, her mood darkened as she recalled Silver's treachery on the streets of Naples. It had all been a long time ago, but the moment was still burned fresh in her mind as if it had happened only yesterday.

The seal broke easily, falling into pieces at her feet. The message inside was written on expensive pale blue stationery and scented with perfume. Its calligraphy was exquisite. No doubt, Silver favoured the fountain pen over the biro.

My Dear Sterling

Please forgive the formal nature of this communication. I have made several attempts to contact you since your arrival back in England but all to no avail. I do not hold your recent disposal of my two menials against you. Nor do I chafe at your treatment of Bordoni and the other two Camorra shooters. Indeed, I find your talent for carnage almost reminiscent of my own when I was your age. But one thing I will not tolerate is a threat to my business interests here in the capital. So, with this in mind, might I suggest we stage a meeting to discuss these matters further and attempt to find a satisfactory solution of mutual benefit to ourselves. You can contact me through Linda. I feel sure you will both have a lot of catching up to do.

Yours truly
Silver

Sterling crumpled the letter up in her fist and threw it in the gutter. Her hands were trembling. He wants a meeting, she thought. That's good. Now I can pay him back for what he did. Setting that joker, Claude, on my case. The Camorra shooting in Italy. All those years of interment in that tomb – the fucker's got it coming in spades, and that bitch Linda too if she gets in my way. But I won't just walk straight into his hands. I'll take him by surprise on his own turf where he least expects it. That's what I need Cassidy for—

A sudden flash of mental static broke her train of thought. Curious, she sniffed the air and caught the scent of something not altogether human lurking somewhere in the immediate vicinity. Then her body tensed as she saw a huge troglodyte of a creature shuffle across the road moving in the direction of the underground station.

Ogre!

It was the first word that came into her mind but the only one that made any sense. Silver was using an ogre to track Cassidy, she thought. That's bad…

Instinctively, she backed into the shadow of a nearby doorway just as the creature glanced round. Hesitating at the entrance to the tube station, the beast lost Cassidy's scent, mingled as it was with that of all the other people using the underground. Emitting a low growl, the ogre shook its head and moved off up the road in the direction of Oxford Street, causing a young couple to step quickly out of its way. The thing looked human from a distance, but seen up close you couldn't be sure.

Relieved, Sterling made her way down the road to where she'd parked her motorcycle. Ogres were creatures straight out of folklore and mythology. They weren't supposed to exist, but they did, along with a myriad of other beings that science had thought convenient to dump in the rubbish bin of history. The one tracking Cassidy even had an aura a bit like her own – dark crimson tinged with black around the edges – not quite as pronounced as a vampire's but close enough. She'd clashed with an ogre once before and had barely survived to tell the tale. This son of a bitch was even bigger than its predecessor so there was no telling what damage it could do. Best keep out of its way, she thought, stamping down hard on the kickstart of her bike and driving away. There was no point tangling with a thing like that unless it was absolutely necessary.

***

'So, there I was at the barber's,' said Cassidy sitting on the sofa in Skinner's flat. 'The phone rings in the back shop and Mick says it's for me, so I take the receiver out of his hand and guess who it was on the other end of the line...'

'Who?' said Skinner, taking a sip of whisky from a glass.

'Silver, of course.'

'Oh... and what did he want?'

'He wanted to know where Sterling was.'

'Uh-huh. And what did you say?'

'I told him to fuck off.'

'You did what?'

'I told him to fuck off and then put the phone down on him.'

Skinner looked at Cassidy hard across the table. 'Please tell me you didn't say that,' he said imploringly.

'I did, and what's more I meant it too. The cunt's got a bleedin nerve calling me up when he owes me the better part of twenty grand—'

Skinner banged his whisky glass down on the table and stood up from his armchair. 'You know what you are, Stuart? You're an accident waiting to happen, that's what!'

'Don't worry,' Cassidy replied taking his third shot of Jack Daniels, 'I can handle Silver any day—'

'No you frigging can't!' Skinner snarled, rounding on Cassidy and grabbing him by both lapels of his coat. 'You don't know what Silver is!'

'Oh, and what is he then?'

Skinner relaxed his grip. It was no good. Cassidy just didn't appreciate the full extent of the danger he was in. How could he? It had taken Skinner the better part of his entire adult life to come to terms with it himself. 'Best wait until Sterling gets here,' he said pushing Cassidy gently back down onto the sofa. 'She'll fill you in on the details much better than I can.'

'What do you mean?'

'You'll find out soon enough. Here she comes now.'

Cassidy listened. Someone was coming up the communal stairway. There was a coded knock on the door and Skinner went to open it. Two figures stood in the doorway. One of them – the one wearing sunglasses, Cassidy recognised immediately as Sterling and she was carrying a plastic shopping bag at her side. The other woman he'd never seen before.

'What's she doing here?' said Skinner as the pair walked into the room.

'I took the liberty of calling in some of the old team,' replied Sterling, regarding Cassidy as he sat on the sofa. 'Stuart, allow me to introduce you to Debbie Stephenson, alias "Bricabrac". She's the best little shoplifter in London, aren't you, Bricabrac?'

'If you say so, Sterling,' replied the young woman with the ska hairstyle. Bleached blond and cropped short on the top of her head and back of her neck with longer strands of it hanging down in front of the ears. Her forearms were heavily tattooed and she wore a new pair of Levi 501s which looked as if they'd recently been stolen from a chic West End store. A pair of Doc Marten boots and a denim jacket completed the picture.

'Why bring Debbie into this?' said Skinner accusingly.

'Yeah,' echoed the young woman. 'Last time I got involved in one of your schemes, Sterling I ended up stranded in Colorado with that American bint of yours. Tell me it's not going to be a repeat of that?'

'Don't worry, Bricabrac. We're not leaving the country for this job. At least, not that I'm aware of.'

Debbie sat herself down on a vacant chair. 'So what's this *job* if you don't mind me asking?'

'We're going after Jimmy Silver, that's what.'

'Silver? No way!' replied the petite blond shoplifter throwing back her head. 'You've got the wrong woman, Sterling. Go and pick some psychotic dyke fresh out of prison, why don't you. It's not me you want.'

'Relax,' said Sterling, placing a reassuring hand on her friend's shoulder. 'Make yourself comfortable and have a drink, Bricabrac. I've got loads of booze in this bag here. Yours was always vodka I seem to recall.'

The blond woman nodded. 'Yeah. Make it neat. And stop calling me Bricabrac! It's Debbie or Debbs now, okay?'

Cassidy listened as the mood in the room lightened and became more convivial with the consumption of alcohol, tobacco and dope. It didn't take long for him to realise that he was witnessing the reunion of three former companions as well as a meeting to decide the fate of his former boss. Much of the talk he didn't understand, and it soon became evident that a great deal of what Sterling, Skinner and Debbie were discussing had more in keeping with the plot of a late night horror movie than anything resembling the antics of the London underworld.

'So what happened in Italy, Sterling?' said Debbie, lighting up an enormous joint and sucking in the smoke. 'You were with Skinner and that American woman... what was her name...?'

'She was called Samantha Russell.'

'Yeah... Her... So what happened?'

'It's complicated,' interrupted Skinner, casting a fleeting glance in Cassidy's direction. Obviously, whatever had taken place in Italy wasn't for the ears of the uninitiated.

'It's okay,' said Sterling, regarding Skinner from behind her sunglasses. 'It's all history now, and in any case, Stuart wouldn't understand.'

'What wouldn't I understand?' Cassidy put in as more of Skinner's eye movements followed, this time ending up fixated on the ceiling in mute resignation.

Sterling looked at Cassidy: 'I was on a mission to return a precious object to the underworld if you must know.'

'The underworld? You mean the Italian mafia?'

'No, Stuart. I mean THE underworld. There's an entrance to hell a few miles north of the city of Naples. It was the winter of 2003 and the goddess Hecate was demanding the return of an ancient magical amulet to its rightful place in Hades. Lucifer was also demanding its return so I couldn't very well refuse, could I?'

'Urm... no you couldn't,' replied Cassidy, suddenly feeling way out of his depth. He glanced at Skinner for some reassurance that Sterling was having a joke at his expense but the reassurance didn't come. Instead, Skinner leaned forward in his chair and spoke calmly but firmly. 'She's speaking the truth, Stuart so you'd better listen. Go on, Sterling; tell him what happened next.'

'Thanks, Jerry. Anyway, like I said, I delivered the amulet back to its owners and then I returned to Naples...'

'And what happened then?' said Cassidy, feigning interest. He didn't believe a word of what he was hearing but could see that Skinner did, so in deference to his old friend he pretended to listen as Sterling continued with her story.

'I arrived back at the railway station in Naples where I'd planned to meet up with Skinner and Samantha Russell who were waiting for me in the Piazza Garibaldi...'

'And...?'

Sterling paused to light a cigarette. 'Well, the next bit gets confusing. I was crossing the square in front of the station when two men pulled up behind me on a motor scooter. The pillion rider gets off the bike and opens up on me with a machine pistol. Next thing I know, I'm lying on the ground staring up at the sky with Skinner and Samantha kneeling beside me. I don't remember anything after that until I woke up in my coffin on that island in Venice when the bulldozer went through the wall—'

'It was Silver who ordered the shooting,' said Skinner, eager to embellish the story. 'He got a guy called Bordoni to organise it. You see, Stuart, Jimmy Silver thought Sterling still had the amulet on her when she returned to Naples and he wanted it so badly that he was prepared to have her shot so he could get his hands on it. He even had special bullets made for the job as well—'

'That's enough, Jerry!' interrupted Sterling. 'Cassidy doesn't need to know all the details.'

'Sorry, Sterling, I got a bit carried away there. In any case, Silver doesn't know you're here, does he?'

Sterling looked askance. 'I'm afraid he does, Jerry.'

'What do you mean?' replied Skinner, putting his drink down on the table.

She faced him and he saw himself reflected in her mirrored sunglasses.

'Jerry, there's something important you should know.'

'Go on... Tell me.'

'I've shot Bordoni.'

'Fuck! That was you?'

'Yes, I'm afraid it was, Jerry. And I left my calling card as well... a single black rose... you know what I'm saying?'

'Your way of telling Silver that you're back in town?'

'Yeah,' Sterling grinned, showing an unusually long pair of upper canine teeth. 'And it worked too!'

'How do you know?'

'I know because Silver sent that poor cunt sitting opposite you all the way to Venice to see if I was still in my box!' exclaimed Sterling, jabbing her index finger in Cassidy's direction. 'You see, Jerry, it was like this. About three days before Silver got Cassidy to go to Venice, I killed two other Camorra hitmen – Lorenzo Molinari and Francesco Bianchi – and left a single black rose with each of their bodies. Silver guessed it was me, but he had to be sure, so he sent Cassidy to find out. It's all quite simple when you think about it.'

Up until this point, everything that Cassidy had heard had seemed to belong to the realms of science fiction , but with the revelation about Molinari and Bianchi, events had begun taking on a far more sinister complexion than he was comfortable with.

'Well, I think it's high time I was on my way now,' he said. 'I've got to get back home and feed the cat.'

'No you frigging don't!' growled Sterling. 'You're in this up to your bollocks as it is. In any case, you don't have a cat and you can't go home because Silver's men are probably lying in wait to stamp your card just as soon as you put your frigging head round the door. And I'll tell you something else for free. The thing that's been stalking you could probably rip your frigging head off without even breaking into a sweat.'

'What?'

'You were being tailed by an ogre, Stuart and it's got your scent. I saw it lurking outside the underground station shortly after you boarded your train.'

'So, you've been following me too,' Cassidy exclaimed in surprise.

'Only to save your fucking neck,' Sterling replied. 'I need you alive.'

'Why? What possible use can I be in all of this?'

'You worked for Silver, didn't you?'

'Ye-e-e-s... so?'

'Then you know where he lives... where he keeps his lair.'

'Not exactly,' Cassidy replied. 'I've only ever been to his place once before and I had to wear a blindfold for most of the journey.'

Sterling looked down at her hand. The hand Cassidy had accidentally touched in the alleyway. *Damn! I hadn't counted on that,* she thought. *Silver's not taking any chances, but maybe Cassidy could still be of use to me.*

'Think, Stuart,' she said, looking directly at him. 'Was there anything that you noticed on your journey to meet with Jimmy Silver? Anything at all…'

'Not a lot,' Cassidy replied. 'The journey was a long one and I think he might be living somewhere near the coast because I could smell the sea when we arrived.'

'Anything else?' said Sterling with growing interest.

'No, not really. But judging from your description of that creature you mentioned—'

'The ogre?'

'Yes. I think he's called Fetch. He's one of Silver's minders.'

'Hmm. That would make sense. You really don't know what you're dealing with, do you Stuart?'

'Not entirely,' Cassidy replied, 'but I'm not afraid of no ogre. I've got this—'

Fumbling in his coat pocket, Cassidy searched for the weapon Sterling had given him earlier in the day.

'You've got what?' enquired Skinner glancing apprehensively at Debbie across the table. The young shoplifter was so full of dope that she'd almost passed out.

'I've got a gun,' continued Cassidy still searching for the pistol.

'So, where is it?' said Sterling sharply.

'Dunno. I'm certain I had it a moment ago. I…'

It was then that Cassidy realised what he'd done with the weapon and suddenly went pale. 'I... I seem to have lost it...'

Sterling leaned closer, her lips drawing into a thin line. 'Stuart, what did you do with the gun I gave you?'

'I threw it into the canal, Sterling. I don't usually have anything to do with guns. Sorry.'

Sterling stared at Cassidy hard. For a second he caught his reflection mirrored in her sunglasses and was struck by how small and insignificant he looked. 'I hope the gun didn't cost you too much,' he added in an attempt to placate her rising anger.

'It's not the frigging gun I'm concerned about so much, Stuart as the bullets that were inside it. They were special.'

'Special? How do you mean?'

Ignoring Cassidy for a moment, Sterling reached inside the zip pocket of her jacket and drew out a small plastic bag. Laying out a huge line of coke on Skinner's coffee table, she rolled up a ten pound note and snorted the lot straight up her nose before continuing:

'Those bullets were the only thing that would have saved your life if Silver had decided to come looking for you himself—'

'Whoa! Calm down, kid,' exclaimed Skinner. 'Cassidy is right. This thing is starting to get out of hand. Guns bother me as well. I mean, nobody wants to get themselves caught in possession of a firearm.'

'Oh, really? And what makes you so damn certain, Silver won't come looking for you as well?'

'Eh—?'

Sterling took another line of coke and regarded Skinner with a smile. 'Jerry, there's something you should know about Jimmy Silver. It's something I've suspected for a long time.'

'What's that?'

'Silver is a police informer, Jerry. It was Silver who tipped off the coppers about the existence of the Hells Angels' clubhouse in Harlow.'

'Who told you that, Sterling?'

'Joe Rackham, if you must know. And there's more...'

'Tell me.'

Sterling sat back in her chair, her brain soothed by the effects of the enormous amount of cocaine she'd just taken. 'Jerry, the meth lab got busted by the police a few nights ago. The one by the canal—'

'Jesus fucking Christ... Have you told Joe?'

'Yes, he knows about it. But what's more to the point, is that it was Silver who told the cops about its existence in the first place. Then he took some of the crystal meth and had it planted on Cassidy here to stitch him up with the law.'

'He doesn't mess about then, does he?'

'No, he doesn't, Jerry. He's still the same old Silver we knew, only now he's got a lot more influence with the authorities.'

'That would account for his knighthood then. He's called *Sir James* now, apparently.'

'That doesn't surprise me, Jerry, knowing the way this shithole of a country works. No change there, huh?'

'Damn right,' replied Skinner, taking another swig of whisky before handing the bottle over to Cassidy who accepted his refill only too gladly.

'So you see the danger we're all in, Jerry. Which is why I gave this little twat here the gun he so cleverly decided to get rid of. He'll need it all the more now that Silver's put an ogre on his case. The beast has got Cassidy's scent now, which of course will lead it to us. You savvy?'

Skinner eyed Cassidy with disdain. 'On second thoughts, Stuart, maybe getting rid of that gun wasn't such a bright idea after all. Ogres aren't too fussy about who they kill. They also eat children as well, in case you wanted to know.'

'He's just a big bloke,' replied Cassidy. 'I don't understand what all the fuss is about. There's three of us against one of him and...'

'Four! There's four of us!' exclaimed Debbie who had just recovered from her cannabis trance. 'I need another vodka. Make it a double.'

Sterling poured out the vodka, thinking hard. Then she looked at Skinner. 'Whatever the case, we're going to need another gun... and some bullets.'

'Who are you going to use, Sterl? Most of our old contacts are either dead or in the nick.'

'Hmm. You've got a point there, Jerry. I'll give Maz a call and see what he's got in stock. He usually has what I need.'

'What are you going to use for money? Guns don't come cheap.'

'Not a problem. I can trade some of Joe Rackham's coke that I've got stored in the warehouse. I'm sure he won't mind donating a couple of kilos. It's all in a good cause and seeing as how Silver fucked him over with the Harlow bust, he'll want to get even anyway.'

'Yeah, tell me about it! I've got to get the memory stick back from the cops pronto or my life ain't going to be worth living.'

'We can cross that bridge when we come to it, Jerry. In the meantime, we've got to get to Silver before he gets to us.'

'And how do you intend dealing with Silver?' said Cassidy. 'You don't even know where he lives.'

'That's where you come in, Stuart. Give me your hand.'

Before he could argue, Sterling had reached across the table and grabbed him by the wrist.

'Don't worry,' said Skinner, 'she does stuff like this from time to time. Just think of it as a game.'

Placing the palm of her left hand against Cassidy's right, Sterling closed her eyes. Cassidy flinched as she made contact. Her flesh was ice-cold to the touch. The last time he'd touched flesh as cold as that was when he'd had to visit a hospital mortuary to identify the body of a dead relative.

'Concentrate, Stuart,' she said. 'Think of your journey to visit Silver. 'What direction were you travelling in when you left London?'

'South, I think. Difficult to say really. It always feels like I'm going downhill whenever I'm traveling south and I think that's what it felt like.'

Good, thought Sterling. *He's thinking like a Sensitive. Let's see how far I can push him…*

'Think of a name, Stuart. Anything that comes into your mind.'

'Okay… I'm thinking.'

Cassidy's mind went blank. He felt the palm of his hand begin tingling. Whether it was the coldness of Sterling's skin or a surge of energy passing into him, he couldn't say. Presently a name popped into his head.

'Blackthorne,' he said. 'Sir James Blackthorne… and he's been dead a long time.'

'Keep going, Stuart. Is there anything else?'

Cassidy thought hard. A series of faces came into his mind. They were people from a long time ago. First there was the man called Blackthorne who looked uncannily like Jimmy Silver, except that he wore his hair in the style of an eighteenth century gentleman and had rouged his cheeks. Next came, Caroline Westvale, the same woman he'd met in Venice, only now she looked more like the faces depicted in some of the portraits that had hung in her room. Then he saw the image of Claude Dubois followed by another face he didn't recognise, but received the impression that it was a woman called Virginia Cavendish.

'That's very good, Cassidy,' commented Sterling, pressing her hand ever closer to his. 'I need the name of the place now. Where did Silver's men take you to?'

'It was somewhere on the south coast… maybe it was Dungeness? No, not there. It was somewhere else, but near there…'

For an instant, Cassidy's dream image returned. It was the one of the ginger-haired girl with the empty eye sockets and there was a date to go with it. Recoiling in horror, he broke contact with Sterling who sat back in her chair with a look of concern.

'What did you see just then, Stuart? Tell me.'

'A woman with ginger hair,' answered Cassidy. 'She was standing on a shingle beach. It was the year 1977... She was called Julie Kent and she'd been murdered.'

Cassidy came out of his trance and looked at Sterling. There was a sad, empty expression on her face that he'd never seen before.

'It was me,' she said solemnly. 'The girl on the beach was me. It was where Silver dumped my body back in 1977... on Dungeness beach... So, now you know.'

But that was the whole point. Cassidy didn't know. Nothing seemed to fit, including the chronology. All he had was a sequence of names and faces spanning a period from the late eighteenth century all the way through to the present day. Whatever it was that he was involved with, certainly liked to spread itself out across the centuries.

He was about to ask a question when Sterling got up from her chair and spoke to Skinner.

'I need to make a phone call, Jerry. Can I use your landline?'

'Sure, be my guest,' replied Skinner pointing to his phone which was over by the window.

'What's she up to now?' said Cassidy nervously.

Skinner jerked a thumb in Sterling's direction. 'She's probably giving Maz a ring. Maz – or should I say, Malcolm Green – is one of the Jamaicans we used to deal with when Sterling was running her old crew down by Tower Bridge. I think she's getting us some artillery by the sound of it.'

Cassidy listened. Sterling was speaking into the phone almost out of earshot of the others, but he managed to catch the gist of what she was saying:

'I want a Glock 17 and some ammunition to go with it. Not the usual kind, if you know what I mean.'

There was a pause, followed by Sterling's reply to what the person on the other end of the line had said:

'Okay, Maz, it's a deal. Two kilos of cocaine it is and don't fuck me about, I haven't got much time. Oh, and there's something else I need to know. Where does Linda Bailey hang out these days? I need to have a little chat with her about Jimmy Silver.'

A few more words were exchanged then Sterling banged the phone down hard and looked at Cassidy.

'That cost me a lot, Stuart. Have you any idea how many wraps you can trade on the street these days from two kilos of Charlie?'

Cassidy shook his head. He honestly didn't know.

'More than the fucking gun was worth, that's what! So, don't you go chucking it away this time, is that understood?!'

Suitably admonished, Cassidy nodded and watched as Sterling resumed her seat and began giving orders. Clearly, she held a lot of respect in the underworld and it went back a long way.

'Jerry,' she said, 'I want you to arrange a meeting with Joe Rackham and the Angels. Tell him that it's urgent.'

'What about the memory stick, Sterl? I'm not exactly on the best of terms with the Angels at the moment.'

'Tell Joe the matter is being dealt with and mention my name. If I can't arrange something with my old contacts in the Met, then we'll have to send in some of Debbie's mates to burgle Scotland Yard.'

'What?' shrilled Debbie, now well and truly lifted out of her cannabis trance.

'Don't worry, Debbs. It probably won't come to that,' said Sterling reassuringly. 'Just tell Orlando to remain on standby. He might be needed, okay?'

The young shoplifter nodded reluctantly and rolled herself another joint. Her hands were trembling.

'Are you sure we can get the Angels' support?' said Jerry. 'I mean, it's been a long time since you were last on the scene. Things have changed a lot since then.'

'We've no option,' Sterling replied. 'In any case, I'm minding their stash of drugs for them, so they owe me a few favours. They also owe me for the tip-off about the bomb in the pub. Silver planted it, so now they need to pay him back quickly before he does them over for good. Now, does anyone else have any questions?'

'Yes, I do,' said Debbie. 'Where's the toilet? I think I'm going to be sick.'

'Down the hallway, first on the right,' said Skinner, 'and remember to flush it when you're done.'

Debbie got up and left the room. It wasn't long before the sound of violent retching and someone being monumentally sick drifted down the corridor.

'She's always like this before a job,' confided Skinner in Cassidy's ear.

'No change there then,' put in Sterling with a laugh. 'She was like that when we went to the States, remember?'

'How could I forget,' Skinner answered. 'She was never out of them bogs on the plane going over, and it wasn't as if we were asking her to do very much either.'

'She's all right once the job starts,' Sterling replied, 'and that's all that matters. Anyway, like I said before, has anyone got any questions?'

Cassidy nodded. He'd got a lot of questions to ask and hardly knew where to start.

'There's a lot I don't understand about this situation,' he said coolly. 'I mean, I've been doing quite a bit of research lately but nothing seems to fit together.'

'Uh-huh... go on, I'm listening,' Sterling replied, laying out her third line of coke. 'What is it you don't understand?'

Cassidy took a swallow of his drink, glancing over the rim of his glass at Sterling. He was still uncertain as to whether he trusted the strange woman in the reflector sunglasses, but couldn't see that he had any other option.

'Is Jimmy Silver really your grandfather?'

Sterling shrugged. 'Some would say so. But if you mean is he my *human grandfather*, then no, he is not.'

'I didn't think so. You see, I found out something when I was searching on the internet. It was about the woman's body Silver sent me to Venice to check on.'

'Julie Kent?'

'Yes, Julie Kent. According to the UK Missing Persons Files, Julie Kent went missing in July 1977 and her body was never found.'

'Go on, Cassidy; I'm listening,' replied Sterling, her lips pursing with barely suppressed mirth. Clearly someone was having a huge joke at his expense.

'Well, according to the records, Julie was born in 1957 and was the daughter of Albert and Molly Kent. She studied music at London University between 1975 and 1977 when she mysteriously disappeared. She was last seen at the Roxy nightclub on the 21 July 1977 and there was no sign of her after that. She had ginger hair and blue eyes, and...'

'What's your point, Cassidy?'

'My point is that Silver certainly couldn't be your biological grandfather. He's not nearly old enough to have a granddaughter your age.'

'Jimmy Silver is at least four hundred years old, Mr Cassidy.'

She wasn't pursing her lips together this time and looked in deadly earnest. Even so, Cassidy guessed she was just playing with his mind and carried on talking.

'...And you look way too young to be Julie Kent, if Julie was born in 1957.'

'But I'm not Julie Kent. At least, not any more...'

Puzzled, Cassidy took another drink and continued looking at Sterling. 'What about the woman called Westvale?' he said. 'The one Silver sent me to see. Who is she?'

'Who was she would be a better phrase to use, Stuart. In fact, you could use that expression to describe all of us – me, Silver, Caroline Westvale and Linda Bailey included.'

At this point, Skinner interrupted. 'I don't think Stuart needs to know, Sterling.'

'I'll be the best judge of that, Jerry. In any case, he'll have to be told sooner or later.'

'Told what?' said Cassidy putting down his glass.

'That I used to be Julie Kent,' she replied.

'But you couldn't be. You're the wrong age and Julie had ginger hair and blue eyes. Oh, you might have dyed your hair and had plastic surgery to disguise your age, but the eyes… Julie had blue eyes… Let me see your eyes. Take off your sunglasses.'

'Oh, fucking hell,' muttered Skinner looking away. *'I don't want to see this…'*

'What's wrong?' said Cassidy. 'I only want to see her eyes, that's all.'

'No you fucking don't,' Skinner replied. 'You definitely don't want to do that.'

Sterling waved Skinner into silence, never taking her gaze off Cassidy as he sat on the sofa. 'Keep quiet!' she said. 'It's better he finds out the hard way.'

Satisfied she had Cassidy's full attention, Sterling leaned forward in her chair with both hands resting on her knees.

'Do you believe in vampires, Mr Cassidy?'

'I don't disbelieve… I mean, my mother was a Catholic and—'

'Do you believe in vampires?' Sterling repeated slowly, gazing directly into his eyes.

Cassidy blinked, taken aback by the sudden change in subject matter. 'If you mean, do I believe in the sort of vampires you see on the TV horror channel, then no, I don't. Why do you ask?'

Sterling took off her sunglasses and looked at him, channelling her gaze directly into his mind. He remembered seeing two piercing orbs of crimson light where there should have been eyes, then fear took hold of him and he began trembling violently in his seat.

At first he thought he was having an epileptic fit. There was a flash like an electric shock surging through his brain. Then the room disappeared and Cassidy found himself in a very strange place.

The smell of sweat and fear was strong. He knew he was witnessing everything Sterling had ever seen and done over a lifetime. He saw scenes of violence that would have shocked even the most hardened forensic pathologist, so intense were the images that now paraded before his mind's eye. In some, the hapless victims were seen trying to make a run for it before Sterling closed in for the kill. The screaming was the worst part, but it usually didn't last long before each individual was quickly despatched and drained of their blood with fiendish mechanical precision. Others weren't quite so lucky however, including Claude Dubois and the particularly grotesque manner in which he had died at her hands. Clearly, the killing had been an act of calculated revenge on Sterling's part and it wasn't the only one. More examples of her handiwork followed in rapid succession, each more cunning and brutal than the last. Exactly what manner of creature he was dealing with, Cassidy did not know, but all these acts of carnage he was now witnessing certainly weren't the work of a 1970's music student called Julie Kent. No, the person who had carried out these attacks was clearly something else; a homicidal maniac, an escaped lunatic, or someone who was demonically possessed, he couldn't say. All he wanted to do now was tear himself away from Sterling's gaze and run. But he couldn't...

'Not yet, Cassidy!' came a voice out of the darkness. 'There's more...'

The scene now shifted to the interior of a fashionable London apartment where a party was in full swing. It was 1977 and a young woman with ginger hair dressed in the style of that period had just entered the room. Cassidy guessed the girl was Julie Kent and that this would be the last time she would ever be seen alive. The next series of images saw Julie as the victim of a frenzied vampire attack by a well-to-do patrician lady called Virginia Cavendish, followed by an interval of time that concluded with Julie's body being washed up on a beach after Jimmy Silver had arranged to have it dumped somewhere out at sea. Several months passed by in an instant, during which time Julie's face underwent its final metamorphosis into the creature that Cassidy now saw staring at him from across the table in Skinner's front room. The change was subtle at first, but when it was complete there was no sign in those long pale features and jet-black hair of Sterling's that Julie Kent had ever existed.

As the days passed into years, Julie assumed the name of Sterling and developed an alarming drug habit. Now it was the 1980s and her desire for human blood and random acts of violence had increased to such an extent that she could no longer control it without taking enormous quantities of cocaine. A short while after this and her reputation as an underworld enforcer had been established in one sickening act of carnage that would have made the Kray twins green with envy. The cat was now well and truly out of the bag, and she became known to the authorities simply as "Sterling"; one of the most notorious villains on the streets of London, with the exception of those who wanted her dead. And the strangest thing was that she didn't seem to have aged very much either. By the late 1990s when by rights she should have been well into her forties, instead she had the fresh and unblemished appearance of someone in their early twenties. She was now running a crime gang who used an old Victorian warehouse near Tower Bridge for their base of operations. Everything was going smoothly until she decided to seek revenge against the woman called Virginia for what she had done to her. In one single night, Sterling and her associates descended on a mansion house in a remote part of rural Buckinghamshire and slaughtered everyone inside, including Virginia Cavendish who back then was a well-known figure in the British Establishment. This was too much for those who held power in the land, and Sterling was forced to flee the country and seek refuge in America before travelling to Naples where she was gunned down in the street by two Camorra hitmen operating under the instructions of Jimmy Silver...

'They used special bullets, Stuart. You know what I'm saying?'

'They did what?' murmured Cassidy coming out of his trance.

'They used special bullets,' repeated Sterling, putting her sunglasses back on. 'The bullets were made of silver. Does that mean anything to you?'

'No… should it?'

Sterling looked at Skinner. 'What more do I have to do to him?' she said imploringly.

Skinner shrugged. 'It's up to you, kiddo. You're the boss.'

Just then, Cassidy coughed and cleared his throat. 'Werewolves!' he declared. 'You need silver bullets to kill werewolves! I've seen it on the telly.'

'Good,' said Sterling. 'You're getting warmer. Anything else…?'

Cassidy was silent for a moment as he considered the matter. Running a series of B-movie titles through his head, he utterly failed to make the necessary connection, at which point Sterling decided to intervene:

'Do you remember me telling you that Jimmy Silver was over four hundred years old?'

'Yes I do. I presumed you were having a joke.'

'Well I wasn't. Why do you think I was born in 1957 as Julie Kent but only look twenty years of age?'

'You've had plastic surgery.'

Sterling shook her head.

'Good genes?'

'Quite the opposite, Mr Cassidy. There's nothing good about my genes now, or Jimmy Silver's for that matter.'

'I'm still not following you.'

'Okay, let me put it another way. What is it that myself, Jimmy Silver and Caroline Westvale most have in common?'

'You all look a whole lot younger than you should be.'

'Correct. And why do you think that is?'

'I don't rightly know. Are you all related or something?'

'Yes, in a manner of speaking we are.'

'But how? You told me that Silver wasn't your human grandfather.'

'Indeed I did.'

'Then how are you related? I don't get it.'

Sterling lowered her head in despair. Then she raised her gaze once more and answered him:

'Because we're all vampires, Stuart. Every last one of us – Linda Bailey included.'

Twelve

'So, Mr Cassidy, do you really want to know what it means to be a vampire?' continued Sterling, staring hard at him from behind her mirrored shades.

'I suppose so,' Cassidy replied. 'Will it take long?'

'Not really. You can have the short version if you like.'

'Okay, I'm listening. Tell me…'

'I do not remember being Julie Kent.

'All I know is that Julie ceased to exist on the night of 21 July, 1977 after visiting the Roxy nightclub in London and was never heard of again. Everything I have since learned about my predecessor, I have had to piece together from newspaper cuttings of that era. Other than that, I know practically nothing about her at all, other than she had been heavily into the punk scene, could play the piano reasonably well and had a strong preference for members of her own sex.

'I adopted the name of Sterling because it must have been Julie's old punk name. Leastways, it was the only name I could remember when I woke up on the beach at Dungeness the following day after I had been attacked by Virginia at the party.

'I guess I must have been human once. At least that's what the newspapers say, so I suppose it must be true. Of course, there was a time when creatures like me were almost hunted to extinction. That was when people still believed we actually existed, along with all the other ghosts, ghouls and goblins that haunted the forests and graveyards of medieval Europe. And I am not the oldest of my demonic brothers and sisters. No, I am a fairly recent creation if the history of our race is anything to go by. There are older vampires than Jimmy Silver and Virginia Cavendish if you can believe it, though I have never yet encountered one myself and hope I never do.

'My first victim must have been the truck driver. It happened shortly after I regained consciousness on the beach. I was walking along the road in a daze when a man driving a white truck stopped to give me a lift.

'On the surface, the driver of the truck seemed to be a decent sort of a chap, but after a while I began having my doubts. Mind reading was the first skill that I had evolved since becoming one of the Undead, and from the few images I picked up from his memory, I could tell that he'd given lifts to young women before and I knew what the consequence might be.

'It wasn't long before the man turned off down a side road and stopped his truck. Then he leaned over and tried to kiss me. When I refused to give the man what he wanted, he grabbed my breasts through my shirt and began mauling me. It was then that my mind went blank.

'I came to in what was left of the cabin of the truck. Every muscle of my body ached and it felt like I'd broken several ribs and all the fingers of my right hand. It was then that I saw all the blood. There was blood everywhere I looked and the interior of the driver's cab showed evidence of an immense struggle. The driver was dead. His arms and legs were all broken and twisted into funny shapes and there were two huge puncture marks on the side of his neck. My life as a vampire had begun.

'After the incident with the truck, I hitched a lift to Folkestone and crossed the English Channel, finally entering France at Boulogne where I spent several weeks surviving on my wits. I couldn't very well live on Social Welfare because I was an illegal, but through a contact I knew, I managed to find employment at a seedy strip-joint situated on the outskirts of Paris where I was to remain for the better part of three years.

'There weren't many changes in my appearance over this time, and for the most part, I still looked like Julie Kent, complete with her ginger hair and bright blue eyes. But then one night while I was examining my face in the dressing room mirror I was shocked by what I saw. For a fleeting moment I could have sworn I had no reflection. There was nothing there except for the image of the wall tiles visible behind me. Then, when my reflection finally returned, I noticed to my surprise that my normally ginger hair had turned completely black.

'But that wasn't all.

'Regarding myself a little closer, I could see that my upper lip had taken on a pout reminiscent of someone who had recently undergone cosmetic lip surgery. Then, hardly daring to breathe, I lifted my upper lip with the tip of my finger and saw what the problem was...'

'And what was it?' said Cassidy who had been listening intently for the better part of fifteen minutes.

'Canine teeth, Stuart! Two enormous canine teeth in my upper jaw. That was when I first realised exactly what it was that I was turning into.'

'Urm... I think I'd better leave now,' replied Cassidy, uncertain as to where the story was leading.

'You'll stay right where you are, Stuart! There's quite a bit to go yet...

'Shortly after my metamorphosis, I decided to leave France of my own accord, eventually arriving back in England in the November of 1979. It was now almost three years since Julie Kent had gone missing and the world had moved on. Julie Kent was old news now; just a name and a photograph in a Missing Persons file but nothing more. Her case was eventually closed in 79 and never reopened.

'Compared to France, England in those days was a drab and dismal place with unemployment at its highest rate since anyone could remember. By the early 1980s, I was making a living solely out of prostitution. My taste for cocaine was developing too, and since the price of coke was still very high, I often thieved a lot more than I could use and sold the surplus on for a profit out on the streets. It was also around this time that I met, Sharon Stapleton.

'Sharon was my best friend and lover. We shared a flat together in London and earned a living working as prostitutes until we managed to land ourselves with a job at a nightclub called the Jabberwock up in the Kilburn district. The place was managed by a man called Jack Malone and was the number one alternative venue of its time for that part of the capital. Sharon worked at the club as an exotic dancer, while I functioned as a female bouncer, hired to deal with some of the rowdier women customers who sometimes visited the place.

'It was also around this time that I met a young West German student called Rosa Korsch. Rosa was twenty-three years old. Her father was a wealthy German financier who had family connections with the British aristocracy. She was living in a flat in Chelsea and studying art history at London University with the aim of working in a fashionable West End gallery as a picture dealer.

'One day, Rosa invited Sharon and myself to a party that a group of her more wealthy and influential friends were attending in Curzon Street. She thought it would be a bit of a laugh if I came along and tried to read the minds of some of the more important guests she knew would be attending the party that evening.

"This is Professor Alexei Stanislavsky," she announced proudly. "He's a world famous art historian. He taught me during my first year at university. Alexei, these are my friends Sterling and Sharon. They're both in the entertainment industry."

'As we made polite conversation with the professor, Rosa left our little group for a few minutes. When she returned, her expression resembled that of someone who had just won first prize in the national lottery.

"Sterling," she said, "You'll never guess who is in the drawing room. It's none other than Baron Ulrich von Geisenheim, the German art collector. Apparently, he's visiting London for a few days attending an auction at Sotheby's. Isn't that simply fabulous?"

'Sharon and I made our apologies to Professor Stanislavsky and followed Rosa into the drawing room. Although I didn't realise it at the time, this was going to be my first real meeting with one of my own kind and I wasn't going to like it.

'The baron was a paunchy, red-faced gentleman who had made himself comfortable on an antique sofa. He was wearing a collarless grey suit and was flanked on his left by a pretty young sex-worker called Zhora, and on his right by a handsome brown-haired rent boy who I was later informed went by the name of Claude Dubois. Beside them stood their patron, a rather fleshy looking woman in her late twenties who had frizzy blond hair and who was wearing an evening gown made entirely out of fine grey leather. This person I immediately recognised as a former prostitute called Belladonna who was now operating an escort agency catering for the wealthier and more privileged elite of society. I could tell she didn't like me from the outset, but just then, Rosa introduced me and Sharon to the baron:

"Herr Baron, I would like you to meet my friends, Sterling and Sharon…"

'The baron rose smartly to his feet and politely kissed each of our hands in turn, visibly delighted to have been introduced to two unattached young women who both looked as if they had the experience to revive even the most jaded of sexual appetites. The look from Belladonna's eyes could have stalled a tank.

'It was while we were talking to the baron, that Sharon was taken suddenly ill. She swayed slightly on her feet and gave me the impression that she was going to faint.

"I think it must be the heat, Herr Baron," said Rosa, quickly making up any explanation that seemed plausible. In actual fact, she had no idea what was wrong with Sharon and didn't want to be embarrassed in front of the baron.

'The baron helped Rosa and me take Sharon over to the French windows and out onto the terrace to get some air. Alexei Stanislavsky met us at the window, took hold of Sharon's arm and went outside with Rosa, while the baron and I stood by a small table near the curtains attempting to make polite conversation.

"Does your friend, Sharon, have some sort of a medical problem, Fraulein Sterling?" he inquired politely.

"It's very stuffy in this drawing room," I replied. "She must have been overcome by the heat, I expect."

"I don't think so, Fraulein. I think that maybe it could have had something to do with me perhaps, hmm?"

'Von Geisenheim stepped closer to me so that our faces were almost touching. As he did so, I caught a whiff of his breath. It smelled foul and it was hard for me to keep my gaze steady without screwing up my eyelids at the sickly sweet stench of decay that was coming out of his mouth. I didn't have to wear sunglasses back then, but when I looked at the baron again, his face had changed. A grinning skull, complete with a few tattered remnants of flesh protruded from the collar of his shirt and stared back at me with empty eye sockets. A few strands of hair still clung to the dead thing's scalp, but otherwise all semblance of life had long since vanished from the cadaver, leaving only the mummified husk of what had once been a living human being.

"Just as I thought," said Von Geisenheim, studying my reactions closely. "You're one of us. But the question remains, Fraulein Sterling, as to just how old you are and who was your creator? Was it Virginia or that pathetic excuse for a vampire, Jimmy Silver? I should have finished that bastard off during the war while I still had the chance. Too late now though.Pity."

"I haven't got the faintest idea what you're talking about," I replied, all the while looking desperately around to see if anyone else in the room was witnessing the deadly gambit that was developing near the French windows. They weren't, and pretty soon I found out why.

"Don't bother shouting for help, Fraulein. Nobody can hear you. We're both outside of time now, you and I. As far as the other people in this room are concerned, we both left the party several minutes ago. No one saw us leave this room and no one will see us return. It will be just as if this meeting never took place. In fact, I could kill you now with my bare hands and no one would be any the wiser. Here, let me show you how!"

'As the baron made to grab hold of my throat, I dropped my mental screen and shot out a flare of crimson red energy from my mind the equivalent of a psychic uppercut. Von Geisenheim swayed a little on his feet and blinked several times as if he couldn't believe what I'd just done. Then he lowered his gaze for a moment, appearing deep in thought. *"Ach so,"* he murmured to himself, and then, looking me straight in the eye, he addressed me as if he were speaking to one of his peers.

"You think yourself so clever, don't you, Sterling? So young and high-minded that it makes me want to retch. It won't do you any good in the long run though. Soon you'll become like all the rest of us and there won't be any turning back then! Slowly your soul will begin to deteriorate and you'll die from within, just like myself and Jimmy Silver. Then you will wander the earth like me, marvelling at the passing of the years and envying the dead their rest. Why don't you just end it all now before it's too late—"

"Ah, Herr Baron! There you are! Rosa mentioned you were looking after Sterling for a while. Sharon is quite recovered now, but desires to leave the party early. She needs to go home and rest."

'It was Alexei Stanislavsky who had interrupted Von Geisenheim. As Alexei stood there in front of the French windows with that soft gleam in his eyes, I could tell that he'd come to rescue me…'

'And what happened then?' said Cassidy, eager to know more.

'Well, reaching into his jacket pocket, Alexei brought out his wallet and handed me his card saying that if I was ever up in his neck of the woods I could drop by and pay him a visit.'

'And did you?'

'Yes I did, but when we next met it was to be under very different circumstances.'

'Which were?' Cassidy enquired, growing increasingly fascinated with Sterling's life story. Skinner noticed Cassidy's growing interest as well but said nothing. He'd heard it all before, including her run in with the London Chinese snake-heads and the unfortunate encounter she'd had with the teenage delinquent she'd killed in Highgate cemetery.

Then Cassidy noticed that Sterling had paused in her narrative. Her head was bowed slightly and she was shuddering in a series of small, suppressed sobs.

'What's wrong?' he said with a look of concern.

'The bastards killed her, didn't they,' she answered raising her head. 'The bastards went and killed my Sharon.'

'Who killed her?'

'…Sharon was killed a few days before Christmas 1984. She was knocked down by a speeding car in Kilburn shortly after leaving work to return home. The police never caught the driver of the car. It was a hit-and-run job, and forensics failed to find any traces of paint from the car's bonnet on Sharon's clothing...'

'I'm sorry,' said Cassidy, regarding Sterling sympathetically. 'What did you do then?'

'Then? Well then I just went to pieces I suppose. I wandered the world surviving as best I could until Alexei Stanislavsky took me in. He knew what I was and how best to control my affliction.'

'He knew you were a vampire?'

'Yes, and much else besides. You see, Alexei wasn't just a university professor. He was also an Adept.'

'What's an Adept?'

Sterling glanced at Skinner with a knowing smile. Skinner looked away and poured himself another drink. 'Debbie's been gone a long time,' he said making conversation. 'I hope she's all right.'

'She'll be fine,' replied Sterling, 'which is a lot more than I could say for Rosa and Belladonna.'

'Why, what happened to them?' inquired Cassidy, forgetting his last question.

'I killed them. That's what.'

'Both of them?'

'That's what I said, Stuart. Both of them. Rosa first, followed by Belladonna second.'

'But why?'

'I did for Belladonna because I later found out that it was her who had arranged to kill Sharon. The woman, Rosa, I killed because she knew about it and hadn't thought fit to tell me. I had to drag the truth out of her several years later and when I did, it was quite a surprise.'

'In what way?'

'Like I said, according to Rosa it was Belladonna who arranged the accident with the car that knocked Sharon down in the road. What I didn't know at the time was that the car had been meant for me.'

'How do you mean?'

'The driver had mistaken Sharon for me as she crossed the road. You see, I'd loaned Sharon my coat for the evening and Sharon had recently taken to dying her hair the same colour as mine. As we were both roughly the same height, it was an easy mistake for the hitman driving the car to make. Belladonna had planned to have me killed in revenge for an incident where I had punched her in the jaw one evening at the Jabberwock Club when she was getting a bit out of hand. Instead, she ended up killing Sharon by mistake…'

Sterling's voice tailed off for a moment as she stared blankly into space. Cassidy could tell she was upset so he said nothing. Skinner too, was silent, knowing the woman only too well and what she was capable of if she got pissed off. Just then, the door to the living room swung open and Debbie walked in looking slightly the worse for wear. Skinner put a finger to his lips, motioning her to keep silent. One look from Sterling was enough for Debbie to understand the situation and she went quickly over to a vacant chair and sat down. A few minutes later, Sterling came back from wherever it was that her memories had taken her. 'You okay, Debbs?' she said as if nothing had happened.

'I think so. Must have been the dope, I guess.'

'Want a drink?' said Skinner offering her the bottle.

'No. Just tea for me thanks. Three sugars.'

As Skinner wandered off into the kitchen, Cassidy looked on as Sterling made conversation with Debbie, gently stroking her friend on the shoulder as she did so. Whoever this strange woman in the leather jacket and sunglasses was – or whatever she had become – there must still have been some semblance of humanity remaining in her, judging by the way she was comforting the young shoplifter who had just thrown up so mightily in Skinner's bathroom. Maybe she wasn't so bad after all.

'What is it that you don't understand, Mr Cassidy?' said Sterling as she glanced in his direction once more.

'How did you know I was going to ask you something like that?' responded Cassidy in amazement.

Sterling laughed. 'Most creatures like myself develop some degree of telepathy if we live long enough, Stuart. Now, what is it exactly that you don't understand?'

'Quite a lot really. From what you've just told me, you've been around for quite a long time—'

'For a vampire, you mean?'

'I'm sorry. I didn't mean to give offence.'

'None taken, Stuart. Actually, I'm still relatively young compared to Jimmy Silver. He's been around since the eighteenth century.'

'What?'

'Yes, I thought that might shock you. There are some older ones of course. They call themselves the Ancients, but they're seldom very active these days. The oldest one I know of was born in the twelfth century. I don't know how they survive, but from what I've heard they seem to have access to some secret knowledge contained in an old book called the Incunabulum. It's been doing the rounds since Roman times apparently.'

'Oh… right,' exclaimed Cassidy with total indifference. His knowledge of ancient history was virtually non-existent and he had practically no fascination whatsoever with old books.

Sensing his lack of interest, Sterling changed the subject, only to be met with a barrage of questions about Jimmy Silver, at which point Skinner re-entered the room with Debbie's tea.

'So, exactly how much do you know about Silver,' Cassidy enquired, eager to learn all he could about his former boss. 'What's his stake in all of this?'

At the mention of the word "stake,", Debbie bust out laughing, almost spilling the entire contents of her tea mug over her jeans.

'I'm sorry, Sterling,' she spluttered in between fits of laughter, 'but it's that word… You know what I mean. Oh god, I think I'm going to piss myself. *Pah-ha-ha-ha-ha!*'

Sterling waited until Debbie had recovered her composure, then she looked at Cassidy in the same way that a university professor might regard a junior college student reading out their first essay of term.

'If you mean Sir James Blackthorne when you are referring to Jimmy Silver, then yes, I do know quite a lot about him, Stuart. What do you want to know?'

'James Blackthorne? I've heard that name somewhere before,' said Cassidy. 'It was when I was searching the internet for some information about the Westvale family.'

'You would! It was Jimmy Silver's name back in the eighteenth century. You see, Stuart, vampires change their names every few decades and assume a different identity so as to keep people guessing. In earlier times when people still believed we actually existed, it didn't do to keep the same name for too long while in possession of a body that never seemed to age. It made folk suspicious.'

'I see… So, Jimmy Silver is really Sir James Blackthorne then?'

'That is correct. They're one and the same, Stuart.'

'Then Caroline Westvale became a vampire too?'

'I expect so. Presumably, it happened shortly after she eloped with Jimmy and they went to live in Europe in the 1790s.'

'What was she doing in Venice?'

'They were both actively engaged in the war against Napoleon Bonaparte, helping to contract the support of a mercenary army for the Venetian state to oppose Napoleon's troops in Italy while he was away fighting the Austrians.'

'But why?'

'Because they were both aristocrats, Stuart… And because they were vampires. The French Revolution had upset the political status quo in Europe making it difficult for vampires to exist in all the usual nooks and crannies of the old class system. It was a dangerous time for us.'

'Then what happened?'

'Napoleon got lucky. He signed a treaty with Austria and then turned south to smash the revolt in Venice. Silver panicked and promptly dumped Caroline, leaving her marooned in Venice while he returned to the relative safety of England.'

'Why didn't she follow him?'

'Because she couldn't. Venice is effectively an island surrounded by water and some vampires can't cross water. Silver must have turned her into a vampire while they were both in Venice and then used his knowledge of sorcery to make his escape when the time came, leaving poor Caroline trapped in the city forever.'

'Just like you, Sterling—on that island. The one where I found your coffin. How on earth did you manage to make your escape?'

'Silver made one big mistake with me, Stuart. He didn't realise what I had become over the years. It must have had something to do with the fact of his having dumped the body of Julie Kent in the sea back in 1977. I developed an immunity to water when I made the change over into becoming a vampire. Oh, he'd taken the added precaution of surrounding my coffin with a circle of salt and all those black candles, but when the bulldozer finally crashed through the wall and the circle was broken, I became free.'

'Yeah, a regular little Houdini is our Sterling,' exclaimed Debbie, her mischievous face all but immersed in her tea cup. Cassidy ignored her snide remark and continued with his questioning.

'So, how come Caroline Westvale is still working for Silver after all that happened?'

'I don't rightly know, Stuart. Over the years they must have come to some kind of agreement whereby Caroline acted as Silver's agent in Europe while his criminal activities expanded throughout the nineteenth century.'

'A man of many parts then—just like Moriarty!'

'Yes, that's a very good comparison, Stuart—a Victorian criminal mastermind still active in the world today. I like it.'

'My turn,' interrupted Skinner, getting up from his seat, 'I need the bog.'

'Don't forget to put the seat down after you've finished,' exclaimed Sterling with a smile as Skinner made his exit from the room.

Cassidy waited for him to leave then turned back to Sterling with another question.

'So, let me get this straight—Jimmy, or James Silver, arranged to have you shot in Naples by the Camorra, am I correct?'

'Spot on, Stuart. I was in Naples with Skinner and an American woman called Samantha Russell. It was December 2003 and we were engaged on a mission to return a magical amulet back to its rightful owners in hell. Silver wanted to get his hands on it at all costs, even if it meant killing me in the process.'

'I see. So you were shot in Naples but ended up being taken to Venice and interred on an island in the lagoon. How come?'

'It's like I said. Silver knew how powerful I was and thought it might be prudent to have me interred on an island surrounded by water. That was his first mistake. He should have had me cremated instead.'

'What happened after the bulldozer hit the wall of the tomb?'

'I escaped from the fucking island, didn't I? The workmen had a spare motor launch so I used that to make my escape. Next day, I mugged some tourists for their money and caught a train to Holland, eventually ending up in Amsterdam which is where I met Joe Rackham.'

'Who?'

'Joe Rackham. He's one of Skinner's mates. He was over in the Netherlands attempting to clinch a drug deal with some Amsterdam bikers. The Hells Angels have a tendency to trade among themselves so that everything is on the level. It usually works most of the time.'

Cassidy regarded Sterling with a mixture of awe and disbelief. He was about to say something when Skinner re-entered the room.

'I put the toilet seat down like you said,' Skinner exclaimed, half-jokingly.

'So you bleeding well should,' Debbie put in. 'Sterling's just gone and freaked out Cassidy here with some of her old stories.'

'Which one?' asked Skinner, only half listening.

'All of them,' Sterling replied.

'What... *including your visit to hell?*'

'You've been to hell?' exclaimed Cassidy in surprise.

'Yes. Like I said, it was some time ago when I was visiting the Naples region.'

'What was it like?'

'Exactly what you'd expect and then some. There, does that answer your question?'

Cassidy shut up. It wasn't that he didn't believe what Sterling had just said, rather than he didn't want to hear the details.

Sterling looked at Debbie then lit up a cigarette. 'How would you fancy a trip to the seaside, Debbs?'

The little blond shoplifter frowned. 'That depends. What exactly did you have in mind?'

Sterling shrugged. 'Oh, nothing special. Just a bit of light reconnaissance, that's all.'

'You're going after Silver, aren't you?' said Debbie in a low voice.

'What if I am? You wouldn't be directly involved. I need Orlando for what I want to do.'

'No! You're not using my Orlando. If you want someone's house done over then just ask me, okay.'

'All right, Debbs—you it is then. We can keep Orlando on standby just in case we need him. What do you think?'

'I dunno, Sterl. It sounds like a pretty dangerous job to me. Won't Silver have lots of minders watching his back?'

'I dare say he will, Debbie. That's why I'm pulling in Joe and his gang of bikers from Harlow.'

'Oh... right. Quite a little task force you've got there, Sterling.'

'Yes, and we'll need it too. I don't know what it is that I'm walking into.'

'I see. So, where exactly is Silver's house then?'

'I don't know that either. That's why I'm going to be doing some asking around over the next couple of days. Stuart here, says Silver's place is located somewhere near the sea but he doesn't know the precise location, do you Stuart?'

Cassidy shook his head. 'I was blindfolded the only time I ever visited it. The place could almost be anywhere on the south coast.'

'Oh, great,' replied Debbie. 'That's just what I needed to hear.'

'We'll just have to cross that bridge when we come to it,' said Sterling, stubbing out her cigarette in Skinner's ashtray. 'All I need for the moment is for Skinner here to get in contact with Joe Rackham and the Harlow crew. I reckon about seven of Rackham's best hards should be enough for the job. If they're all tooled up, then all the better. Silver's probably got a few shooters himself I shouldn't wonder—I doubt if I got all of the Camorra hitmen he's been hiding under his wings over the past few years.'

'And what exactly is it that I have to do?' said Debbie, sitting forward in her chair.

'Just keep quiet about the whole thing, Debbs. You can brief Orlando, but no one else must know. Silver's probably got informers all over the city by now. I've been out of the country for so long that I don't know how far his influence extends these days.'

'What about me?' Cassidy asked, feeling a bit left out of the proceedings. 'What do you want me to do?'

'You're coming with me,' Sterling replied, running her tongue along the edge of her upper lip. 'We're going to my old warehouse near Tower Bridge—you'll be a whole lot safer there.'

'What do you mean, *safer?*'

'Remember that ogre I told you about?'

Cassidy nodded blankly. 'Yes; what about him?'

'Well, like I was saying before, the beast has got your scent and I don't much fancy your chances of survival if it ever catches up with you out in the open and I'm not around. In any case, I need you close by where I can keep my eye on you.'

'Why?'

'Because once you know what you're letting yourself in for, you're going to want to do a runner, and that would make me very angry. There, does that answer your question, Stuart?'

'I guess so, Sterling. I wouldn't want to do that.'

'No, Mr Cassidy. You definitely wouldn't want to do that.'

Thirteen
Revenge

Southwark, London

Early December 2016

Stuart Cassidy hadn't been on a motorcycle in a long time and he certainly hadn't experienced anything like the ride he was having now, perched on the back of Sterling's machine as it cruised through the dark London streets, growling at the traffic lights every so often whenever they were forced to stop at a junction.

It was getting on for around midnight by the time they crossed the River Thames at Tower Bridge and Sterling took a left turn down a thin, narrow sidestreet that was flanked on either side by tall warehouse buildings constructed almost entirely out of red London brick. Most of the warehouses had been converted into flats, shops and offices, but one in particular stood out from all the rest. It was a drab, old Victorian derelict that stood about five storeys high and it looked as though no one had lived there in years.

'This is it,' yelled Sterling above the roar of the bike's 750cc engine as they slowed to a stop.

'Where is this place?' said Cassidy getting off the bike. The building towered above him, its vast bulk casting a dark silhouette against the night sky.

'It's called Shad,' Sterling replied, jingling a set of keys in her pocket. 'It used to be a run-down commercial district until the property developers moved in and smartened it up—all apart from this building of course. They left this one alone for some reason.'

Must have known you were coming, thought Cassidy, suppressing a shudder.

'I heard that!' said his companion, revealing her teeth in a wide grin. 'Now, stand aside and let me open up.'

Cassidy watched as Sterling inserted one of her keys into an electronic lock at the side of some roller-shutter doors. Then she pushed a large red button which caused the doors to open, revealing a small rectangular loading bay inside.

'In you go,' said his friend, retrieving her keys and driving the motorcycle inside the building. Reluctantly, Cassidy followed her, noticing how much louder the sound of the bike's engine was within the poorly lit confines of the loading bay.

Once inside, Sterling switched off the engine and dismounted from her bike. Then she doubled back and locked the door. As the metal shutters slowly descended, Cassidy's heart sank. He was now trapped, all alone in the lair of a homicidal maniac who was no stranger to random acts of violence. Anything could happen.

'This way,' said Sterling, pointing to a rise of concrete steps that led up to the loading bay's operational floor. As Cassidy ascended the steps, he couldn't help but notice that the walls were pock-marked with a series of small craters, each one vaguely reminiscent of a bullet hole.

'Police raid back in 2003,' remarked Sterling reading his thoughts. 'That's when I had to clear out of here fast. A police SWAT team hit the building and didn't bother with the usual formalities. Those bullet holes are the result of automatic fire from a police carbine.'

'What were you doing here?' said Cassidy, running a finger over one of the holes.

'It's a long story, Stuart. Suffice to say, I was in charge of a large crime gang and we used this old warehouse as our headquarters all through the 1990s.'

'Oh...'

Cassidy counted four flights of stairs before they reached the third floor landing. Here they turned off down a corridor which opened out into a large room with a high ceiling. Going through the entrance door, Sterling clicked on the light switch.

'This is the main hall, Stuart. It's also where we used to hold our meetings and plan all our major jobs.'

Cassidy walked into the room. It wasn't at all what he'd expected to find in a warehouse. From where he was standing, he could see that the room was inhabited by several items of quality antique furniture set out on a beautifully patterned Afghan carpet that could easily have fetched a respectable price in any high-end auction house in the land. But it was not to these items alone that Cassidy's attention was drawn, so much as what it was that was resting on the floor partially hidden in the shadows at the far end of the chamber.

'What's that over there?' he exclaimed, nodding in the direction of a large wooden pallet covered in black plastic sheeting, a section of which had been pulled away and then hastily taped back into position without much thought of concealment.

'That, Stuart—?' said Sterling going over to the pallet— 'That is Joe Rackham's consignment of drugs and it's one of the main reasons why we are here tonight.'

'Fuck me, Sterling! There must be well over three hundred kilos of Charlie here. Where did it all come from?'

'This lot came in from Holland a few weeks ago. There's also some crack, fentanyl and cannabis resin to go with it too. One day soon, all of this shit will be legal, so Joe's trying to cash in on it while the price is still high. He reckons the narcotics trade is going to take a nosedive sooner or later, so he's trying to set himself up with a pension to tide him over for the next twenty years.'

'Nosedive, eh Sterling! That's a good one!'

'Yes, very funny Stuart. Now, if there's nothing else you want to see, might I suggest that you get some sleep. It's going to be a long day tomorrow.'

Sterling led Cassidy up a further flight of stairs to a small attic room. A narrow bed was placed where the slope of the roof met the wall.

'This used to be Debbie's room. It's not much, but there again, Debbie was even smaller back then than she is now. You should be safe here. I'll be downstairs keeping a look out.'

'Whatever for?' said Cassidy, growing alarmed.

'Silver's pet ogre, that's what. It's still another seven hours to go before dawn. Best not take any chances with that thing around.'

Ogre? Cassidy thought. *How do I know she's not lying to me? Why has she really brought me here?*

'What's this ogre like, Sterling? Have you ever seen one?'

'A good many in my time, Stuart; including the one that's been stalking you. They're big, powerful and dumb, and they like eating human flesh. Didn't your mother read you any fairy stories when you were a nipper?'

'Not the kind you're thinking of, Sterling.'

'Ah yes, I was forgetting. I was born before they started sanitising folklore. I expect you were brought up on the *Gruffalo* and *Fungus the Bogeyman*.'

'I was as a matter of fact. What's so bad about that?'

'Nothing, Stuart. It's just that if Silver's creature had caught up with you, you'd have been inside its stomach by now. Goodnight and sweet dreams. I'll see you in the morning.'

With that, Sterling closed the door of the tiny room and made her way downstairs. As the sound of her footsteps died away, Cassidy tried the door.

'Locked! She's locked the door on me, the bitch! She knew I was going to do a runner... Damn!'

Despairing of his situation, Cassidy stared at the narrow window set in the peak of the roof. Walking over to it, he pushed the window open and inhaled the cold night air. It was a long way down to the wharf below and the dark waters of the River Thames beyond. He was trapped. There was nothing else for it but to get some sleep and see what the morning would bring.

Always assuming the ogre didn't get him first of course.

***

Sterling sat up suddenly in her chair. The smell of ogre was strong but she couldn't work out where it was coming from. Then she heard Cassidy's strangled cry.

'Dammit!' she hissed. 'It's got into the building! It must have climbed up the fire escape when I dozed off.'

Grabbing an antique swordstick as the only weapon to hand, she ran upstairs. The door to Cassidy's room was hanging off its hinges and there was splintered wood everywhere.

'Holy shit!'

Cassidy was awake and backed up against the wall of his room with the ogre bearing down on him emitting a low gurgling noise from its throat. There was no time to lose.

'Hey, Fetch—you wanna play with me?' she yelled, standing up in the doorway clutching her swordstick. Slowly, the ogre turned its huge, hairless head towards Sterling, momentarily distracted from its intended victim.

'*V-a-m-p-i-r-e...*' it growled, furrowing its brow in dim recognition. As the ancient truth finally dawned in its tiny brain, the creature opened its jaws to expose a mouthful of yellow teeth as sharp as steak knives.

Sterling leapt out of the way to dodge its charge, but she was too late. The ogre had her pinned against the wall on the opposite side of the corridor and it wasn't about to let go.

'Fucking hell! Don't just sit there, Cassidy! Help me!'

'How?'

'Grab its neck!'

'Like hell I will.'

'Grab its fucking neck! Just do it!'

Summoning up his courage, Cassidy ran towards where Sterling was grappling with the ogre. The beast had its back to him, making it difficult to determine exactly where its thick, muscle-bound neck ended and its bald, bullet-shaped head began. Grimacing, he put his hands around the creature's neck and squeezed hard.

Sensing someone at his back, the ogre growled and turned his head, giving Sterling the opportunity to unsheathe the blade of her swordstick and strike at his torso. An anguished cry emerged from the ogre's mouth, followed by a high-pitched shriek as Sterling struck again and again through the monster's shabby brown overcoat and deep into its thick leathery hide. Unable to bear the pain any longer, the ogre turned tail and ran off back down the stairs with Sterling in hot pursuit. Cassidy followed her as she ran, finding it hard to keep up with the athletic vampire as she took the stairs three at a time in her determination to catch up with the creature and finish it off. When he eventually caught up with her, she was standing by an open fire exit door staring downwards into the alleyway below.

'I've lost him,' she said. 'He's gone down the fire escape. They're agile bastards for their size.'

'What the fuck was it?' said Cassidy, still in a state of fright.

'Like I said, it's an ogre. There used to be a lot more of them around centuries ago, before the human population expanded. A few, like the one we've just seen off, work as minders for men like your old friend Jimmy. Its handler should be around somewhere in the city, but I don't know where.'

'It's Tarrou…'

'Who?'

'Tarrou. He's a big black guy, Silver employs to do all his dirty work. The handler must be him.'

'Well it doesn't matter anyway. The thing's probably halfway home by now. They can move quite fast apparently. It's a pity though. I could have done with taking him out before we go down to Silver's place.'

***

'Did you sleep well?'

Cassidy put down his coffee mug and stared at the vampire standing in the kitchen doorway. She was wearing a grey bathrobe and her hair was shining wet. It was obvious that she'd just taken a shower even though she was still wearing her mirrored sunglasses.

'Not really.' It was the truth. The shock of wrestling with the ogre had left Cassidy in such a state of high alert that he feared his head would never touch the pillow in quite the same way again.

Sterling smiled and went over to the refrigerator. Taking out a clear polythene bag full of red liquid, she cracked open the seal and poured its contents into a wine glass.

'I hope that's not what I think it is,' said Cassidy.

'Isn't our National Health Service wonderful, Stuart. You have to pay a fortune for this in the States, but over here it's virtually free, providing you have all the right contacts.'

Cassidy knew what it was that she was drinking and looked away.

'Each to their own, Sterling.'

'Here, try a sip—it's organic.'

'No thanks. I'll stick to my coffee if you don't mind.'

Sterling tilted her head to one side, regarding him sympathetically. 'You did very well last night, Stuart... I'm proud of you. Most humans would have run a mile up against one of those things. You didn't. How come?'

Cassidy shrugged. 'It was nothing, Sterling; really it wasn't. I mean, you and me, we're like mates... aren't we?'

'I suppose we are, but I have to admit you're adapting amazingly well to the situation... for a human.'

Best break the news to him slowly, she thought. *He's had too much of a shock already. I've got to be gentle with him even if I don't feel like it.*

'What news is that?' said Cassidy, regarding the vampire strangely.

Sterling jerked her head back in surprise. She hadn't expected this so soon and was truly astounded.

'You can read my thoughts already, Stuart—I'm impressed.'

Cassidy coughed shyly. 'Yes, I know. It's been coming on for several days. At first I didn't know what was happening, but everything is much clearer now. I can see stuff too.'

'What sort of *stuff?*'

'Well, that strange fuzzy red haze around your head and shoulders for starters.'

'That's my aura, Stuart. All vampires have them. It should start appearing much sharper when your psychic skills improve. What else can you see?'

'All kinds of weird shit. Some of it is pretty damn scary. Like the big black dog I saw yesterday. It had glowing red eyes and vanished straight through a brick wall up by Skinner's place.'

'That was a Hell Hound, Stuart. They're one of the messengers of hell, in case you wanted to know. Anything else…?'

'Yes, as a matter of fact there is. I've seen the ghost of Claude Dubois. He told me what you did to him.'

Sterling smiled. 'If you said that to make me feel guilty, forget it. I don't do remorse.'

Cassidy took a mouthful of coffee and swallowed hard. 'Look, Sterling, it's not that I'm ungrateful or anything, but I'm starting to get a bit worried about my mental state. How can I stop all this shit going on inside my head?'

'You can't. It's part of your nature, Stuart. You're a Sensitive now whether you like it or not. Get used to it… *I had to.*'

Balling his fist, Cassidy thumped the table hard. 'But it's driving me nuts!'

'So? What do you want me to do about it? Give you a hug?'

The thought of being in a clinch with one of the Undead filled Cassidy with revulsion and he very quickly calmed down.

'That's better, Stuart. You've just got to learn how to control it, that's all. Anyway, you'd best take a shower. We've both got a long day ahead of us.'

'Oh… and what is it that we're doing? Remind me again.'

'We're going shopping.'

'What for?'

'A gun—what else!'

Fourteen

Maz took the gun out of a brand new Harrods shopping bag and slid it across the table towards Sterling. Neither said a word as she looked first at the gun and then at the grizzled old Jamaican gangster sitting opposite.

'That's not a Glock, Maz,' she murmured at last.

'I know.'

'But I ordered a Glock...'

'It's a Mauser pistol. It was all I could get at such short notice.'

'And the bullets...?'

'Yes, I managed to get my hands on a few of them. They're silver bullets like you asked for. You going after some *big game* then?'

Sterling ignored his remark and returned to the subject of the gun.

'How old is it?'

'It's a real antique, Sterling. Semi-automatic Mauser pistol, made in 1910—'

'Who the fuck do you think I am, Maz—Sherlock fucking Holmes? I wanted a Glock 17, not this fucking hand-cannon. It's about as discreet as a pork pie at a Jewish wedding.'

'But you didn't give me enough time. Glocks aren't that easy to come by these days. What do you want—*blood?*'

Cassidy raised his eyebrows at this remark, a gesture which had the effect of calming things down a little. All three had been in the front room of the small terraced house in Brixton for the better part of an hour discussing the deal. The pungent smell of ganja weed hanging in the air was by now the only thing preventing the negotiations from breaking down and turning ugly.

'Just try the weapon, that's all I'm saying,' said the Jamaican as he checked the safety mechanism and handed the gun over to Sterling. 'It isn't loaded.'

Cassidy instinctively ducked out of the way as Sterling took the Mauser and pulled the trigger: *Click – Click – Click – Click!* The slide went in and out with consummate ease, forcing Sterling to admit that maybe the old handgun wasn't such a bad deal after all.

'It feels okay, Maz. How many shots can I get off before I have to reload?'

'It's got a forward internal magazine that holds ten rounds.'

'What calibre?'

'This one is a 7.6 mm,' said the Jamaican with a smile.

'I wanted a nine,' the vampire replied firmly.

'Parabellum? No way. They're rare in this model and you don't get as many rounds in the magazine. Sorry.'

Sterling creased her brow in thought. 'Okay, let's see the bullets then.'

Reluctantly, Maz produced a small plastic bag and undid the knot he'd tied in the top. Carefully, he emptied the bullets out onto the table.

'These were all I could get in this calibre, Sterling. I tried all the usual places but there just weren't any available.'

One by one, Maz counted them out. There were what looked like four silver bullets and six ordinary rounds.

'Four? You could only get me four?'

'Sorry, Sterling. Ammunition like this is hard to come by. I bought them at a Steampunk convention in Surrey about two months ago.'

'A Steampunk convention…?'

'Yeah. You should try checking one out. They would be right up your street I would have thought.'

'Maz—'

'What?'

'Shut up!'

'Okay.'

Sterling looked across the table to where Cassidy was sitting and pointed to the leather shoulder bag she'd given him for safekeeping earlier in the day. Obligingly, Cassidy handed it over and placed both his hands on the table to show he wasn't packing a concealed weapon.

'Here, Maz,' she said, pulling two clear polythene bags out of the leather satchel, 'it's two kilos like we agreed. Check it out why don't you.'

Slowly, the old yardie reached out and took the packets. Then he eyeballed Sterling.

'This is cannabis. I asked for cocaine.'

'And I asked for a Glock, if you remember. Take it or leave it.'

'But—'

'There's no buts about it, Maz. It's a fair trade for that old barker you've just tried to fob me off with. You can have your coke if you answer my next question.'

'Oh... and what might that be?'

'Where can I find Linda Bailey?'

'Ha-ha-ha-haaaaaaa.' The elderly Jamaican laughed, showing ivory teeth against ebony lips. 'So that's what you want the gun for?'

'No Maz, it isn't. I just wanted to ask her a few questions, that's all.'

'Yeah, I bet. Hmm, well let's see, girlie. How long has it been since you last had dealings with Linda?'

'Since 2003—and don't call me *girlie,* okay?'

The Jamaican nodded. 'Hmm, that's a long time, Sterling. It may surprise you to learn that Linda isn't the same person you once knew.'

'How do you mean?'

'She works much higher up the food chain-these days.'

'How high?'

'The bitch runs most of the street crime across the city much like you did back in the day. Rumour has it she's got friends in high places. You know how it is in England.'

Sterling scowled. 'So, where does she hang out these days?'

'Jabberwock's.'

'What?'

'You remember. The Jabberwock nightclub in Kilburn. Been there a while she has. It used to be a punk venue back in the 1970s when Jack Malone had it. The place was standing empty for years until Linda took it over and themed it into a goth bar. It tends to attract a lot of gothic dykes from what I've heard.'

'That doesn't surprise me, Maz. What about the *real* undead?'

'Vampires? I wouldn't know, Sterling. The only duppy's I'm aware of are you, Linda and Jimmy Silver. Us Jamaicans don't associate with that sort of thing, if you know what I'm saying.'

'Very funny, Maz. What's the best time to find her?'

'I don't know that either. She has a manager who runs the place for her when she's not around. Today is Saturday though, so she could well be in residence with her latest chick. She sure knows how to pull the women does old Linda.'

'Thanks, Maz. I'll bear that in mind if I ever need some advice.'

'Don't mention it, Sterling. Always a pleasure to do business with you. Now, where's my gear?'

The vampire took another polythene bag out of her satchel. Handing it over to the Jamaican with a smile, she waited for his reaction.

'What the fuck?'

'It's half a kilo of powdered ecstasy tablets, Maz. I hope you don't mind, but you didn't get me the gun I wanted so it's not such a bad deal when you think about it.'

'But where can I get rid of that?'

'Oh, I'm sure you'll think of something. There's enough diz in that bag to fry the brains of every clubber in Manchester. Don't say I'm not good to you. I'm a regular Mary Poppins, I am.'

With that, Sterling put the Mauser pistol and ammunition into the satchel and gestured to Cassidy that it was time for them to go. As they made their way out of the front door of the house and walked towards where she'd parked her motorcycle, Sterling turned and waved back at Maz.

'That, Mr Cassidy, is how you do business around here. I knew Maz would try to fuck me over so I brought the ecstasy along just in case.'

'You drive a hard bargain, Sterling.'

'I'm pleased you think so, Stuart. It's how I've survived all these years. Now, let's get on to our next port of call. We haven't got much time.'

***

The afternoon light was fading fast by the time Sterling brought the huge motorcycle to a halt outside the *Black Dog* public house.

'We're here,' she said, dismounting from the bike and handing her leather shoulder bag over to Cassidy.

'Where's here?'

'Finchley. This pub is known locally as the Dog. I'm meeting someone here – well, two people to be exact. Follow me. I shan't be long.'

Together, they stood at the bar waiting to be served. Presently, a youngish looking bartender – a man – came over and asked them what it was they wanted.

'I'd like to speak with the owner please,' said Sterling, 'and I would also like a pint of Carling for my friend here.'

The man produced a clean glass from beneath the counter. 'Who shall I say it is?'

'Tell him it's Sterling. It's okay. Archie knows me.'

Serving Cassidy his drink, the bartender took Sterling's money then wandered off through a door behind the bar. In less than a minute, he returned. Lifting up the counter flap, he gestured Sterling through with a tilt of his head.

'Stay here and mind the satchel,' she said to Cassidy as she made her way through the gap. 'This shouldn't take long.'

Cassidy watched as she disappeared through the door. At a loss to know what to do with himself, he glanced around the room. Apart from the grey-haired man sitting by the window reading a newspaper, the place was virtually empty.

Empty bar, he thought. *Still, it's Saturday night. I expect the place should start to liven up soon.*

As the minutes ticked by, Cassidy became increasingly apprehensive. *What is she up to?* he wondered. *Buying more ammunition?*

His apprehension grew as he regarded the man silhouetted by the window in what was left of the afternoon twilight. He seemed familiar somehow. Now where had he seen that guy before?

Trying his best not to attract attention, Cassidy screwed up his eyes and took a closer look at the man. Realising now who it was, he stiffened.

This is a copper's bar! She's brought me to a police bar. What the fuck is going on? Am I being set up or what?

He was about to make his way quietly out of the pub when he thought better of it. There was nowhere he could run to and nowhere he could hide. If Sterling didn't track him down then Silver's pet ogre would. He'd simply run out of options.

No, it can't be the same bloke. Too much of a coincidence. Just act normally and pretend I haven't seen him. He probably won't remember who I am...

'What's up, Stuart? You look like you've just seen a ghost.'

It was Sterling. So absorbed he'd been with watching the man by the window that he hadn't seen her returning through the door brandishing a plain manila envelope in her right hand.

'Where have you been?' he said. 'You've been gone ages.'

'Just doing some business,' Sterling replied waving the envelope under Cassidy's nose.

'What kind of *business?*' Cassidy enquired suspiciously.

'Rent collecting, Stuart. The owner of this place was falling behind with his monthly payments so I had to pay him a visit.'

'He's paying you protection money?'

'Not me. I'm doing it for Shaun Tulloch. I owe him for what happened to his brother, Steve, back in 2003. He ended up getting himself shot and it was kind of my fault.'

Cassidy wasn't listening.

'See that middle-aged man sitting over there by the window, Sterling.'

'Uh-huh... What about him?'

'He's a copper, in case you were wondering.'

'Yes, I know. He's called, Lefarge... Inspector George Lefarge to be exact. He's one of the reasons why we're here.'

'He is?'

'Yes. I arranged a meeting with him earlier in the week. Does that shock you, Stuart?'

'Well, yes, it does a little. For one thing, he's a senior police officer, and for another, he's a raving loony.'

Cassidy looked over to where Lefarge was sitting. The casually dressed policeman looked away, not wishing to make eye contact.

'But he's a fucking loony,' whispered Cassidy in Sterling's ear. 'He barged into the room where I was being interviewed and did his nut in front of all the other officers. I'm telling you, he's not right in the head.'

'Probably stress related,' chuckled Sterling with a telling grin. 'A shot of whisky should do the trick. Bartender! A bottle of Scotch and two glasses if you please. I'm going to have a word with the inspector over there and we don't want to be disturbed.'

Cassidy was well into his third pint by the time Sterling returned, clutching a half empty whisky bottle in her hand. When he next looked, the policeman had gone.

'Where's Lefarge?' he asked.

'He left. There was no point in him drawing the matter out.'

'I don't follow you…'

'It's simple. Any charges laid against you will be dropped, Stuart. My terms were plain enough to Lefarge.'

'How do you mean?'

Sterling took a swig of whisky from the bottle and sat herself down on a barstool next to Cassidy. 'Me and Lefarge have come to an agreement, Stuart. Part of the deal involves getting you out of trouble plus a couple of other things I've been trying to sort out.'

'In return for what?'

'In return for me not stitching Lefarge up with his superiors on account of a couple of serious breaches of police protocol back in the 1990s. I also gave him some of Shaun Tulloch's money as a sweetener, but I can square that up with Shaun later if I have to.'

Cassidy had to admit that his friend's ability to handle the forces of law and order ran a whole lot deeper than his own and he felt truly humbled in her presence.

'That's great, Sterling. So, I'm off the hook then?'

'You are for the time being. Just don't go round bragging about it or you'll have every scrote in London banging on my door wanting the same. I'm not a frigging charity.'

'No, you're definitely not that, Sterling. But exactly *what* you are still remains a bit of a mystery to me. You don't seem to behave like others of your kind.'

'Well spotted, Cassidy. Let's just say that there are vampires like Linda Bailey and then there are vampires like me. Alexei Stanislavsky explained the difference to me many years ago when I met up with him one night.'

'The night you were at the party?'

'No, it was several years later—on the night I tried to commit suicide.'

'You mean you once tried to top yourself?'

'Uh-huh. It was shortly after Sharon was killed. Stanislavsky rescued me and took me to his house. It was then that he explained certain things to me about an ancient race of beings known to history as the Titans.'

'Titans…? I've heard of that name before. What were they?'

'The Titans were a race of humanity who lived a long time ago, Stuart. They were possessed of the power of telepathy and could also foretell future events, traits which some human Sensitives still possess to this day, albeit in a much-diluted form. I inherited these genes through my father's bloodline but my psychic abilities remained dormant until I became a vampire, which is when they kicked in along with everything else. You see, Stuart, it sometimes happens when a human Sensitive becomes a vampire the resultant mix produces a very fearsome creature indeed.'

'I wouldn't argue with you on that score, Sterling, but—'

The truth suddenly dawned in Cassidy's mind...

'But, you said that I was a Sensitive too...'

'Yeah, I did. Live with it, Stuart and count yourself lucky you're not a vampire like me. We might be fashionable in certain branches of literature these days, but that's where the fairy tale ends. The rest of the deal isn't so pleasant.'

Cassidy finished his lager and glanced at the pub clock. 'Time's getting on. What do we do now?'

'Now? Well now, I'm going to pay Linda a visit and you're going back to the warehouse for the night.'

'What about, Fetch?'

'The ogre? Oh, I shouldn't worry about him. Ogres are all cowards at heart, mostly used to preying on small children just like they did in the middle ages. If he knows I'm around, he won't be so keen on paying you a return visit.'

'Thanks. I'm pleased to hear it. So, how do I get back to Southwark then?'

'You take a taxi like everybody else. Here's some money to tide you over for the next few days. I might be gone for a while.'

'How long, Sterling?'

'Dunno. It all depends how I get on with Linda and what she's prepared to tell me about Silver's whereabouts. We've got a lot of catching up to do have me and Linda Bailey.'

Fifteen

It was night by the time Sterling reached the outskirts of Kilburn, North London. Halting her bike at a set of traffic lights, she felt for the Mauser pistol she'd concealed in the inside pocket of her jacket. Its presence felt reassuring in the circumstances, especially with that ogre still on the prowl.

But ravenous ogres weren't her only problem. Given what Maz had told her about Linda Bailey's rise in status among the rank and file of London's criminal elite, there was no telling how much muscle the woman could call on if she felt herself in any way threatened. This being the case, Linda would have to be tracked down and confronted in such a manner that she would be unable to summon any assistance when the trap was finally sprung.

And there was something else too...

Glancing to one side of the road and then the other, Sterling utterly failed to spot any familiar landmarks in a district of London that she'd once inhabited on an almost daily basis well over thirty years ago.

Just where the fuck was the Jabberwock Club...?

As the lights changed from red to green, she throttled her motorcycle and continued on her way, cruising at low speed so she could take a better look at the area. Yes, there were a few buildings she still recognised, but the shop fronts had all changed and the street furniture was totally different from how she remembered it all those years ago.

Nothing ever stays the same, she reminded herself. *This is what all vampires have to deal with in the end. I just wonder how old Silver manages to cope with it all? What's his secret...?*

More traffic lights. Another pause.

Gently turning the throttle, Sterling let the engine idle as she waited at the pedestrian crossing. *It's Kilburn High Road I want. Somewhere near the railway viaduct where the trains pass over. That's where I need to be.*

Five more minutes passed as Sterling cruised through the district searching for her visual clue. It wasn't long before she found it.

That's the railway bridge. The turn-off should be dead ahead. Here we go...

A thick mist covered the ground as she drove down the narrow side road towards her destination. After a while, the scenery changed and became more recognisable in spite of the poor visibility.

Not far now, she thought. *It's around here somewhere. I know it is.*

And suddenly, there it was. The Jabberwock Club appeared, looming out of the mist like some eerie phantom mirage. The neon sign may have changed and there were no familiar turnstiles at the entrance, but it was the same place all right, even down to the semi-circular archway above the front doors.

Fighting a wave of nostalgia, Sterling brought her bike to a halt at the kerb and took a closer look. There were two burly minders flanking the entrance to the club, one of whom was bald.

Patiently, she checked out the man's aura. Good, he was human and not an ogre as she'd first thought. Clearly, Linda wasn't expecting her, but it wouldn't do to just go barging into the club through the front door. The place was probably reserved for members only and Sterling didn't have a pass.

There's a back way in, she recalled. *Assuming it's still accessible, I can enter there without being noticed.*

Lifting her foot off the kerb, she drove off slowly in the direction of Paddington Cemetery without so much as a second glance from the two men guarding the doors. If they had noticed anything at all, they made no indication of it and just carried on chatting to one another in the intervals between checking out the groups of people arriving at the club.

The mist was closing in by the time Sterling found what it was that she was looking for. It was a narrow alleyway between two red brick buildings on the left-hand side of the road. The entrance to the alleyway was illuminated by a single old-fashioned street lamp that still burned with a welcoming orange glow.

It's still there after all these years, she thought. *Now, where can I park my bike?*

Finding a suitable place to leave her motorcycle, Sterling glanced up and down the road. Satisfying herself that she hadn't been observed, she entered the alleyway and was immediately swallowed up by the swirling mist and throbbing beat of the music coming from further up the lane. It wasn't long before she found herself standing in a small courtyard lit by a single security light that switched itself on as soon as it detected her presence.

Immediately to her left was a doorway. It was the rear entrance to the club and someone had left the door open.

Moving closer, she was just about to enter the building when she heard a low, growling sound coming from behind. Slowly turning round, she came face-to-face with the meanest looking pit-bull she had ever seen. The dog was secured by a single length of chain to a rusted iron ring set into the opposite wall. In spite of the chain, the dog could still reach where she was standing and she still had a few steps to go before she got to the open door. There was nothing else for it. She would have to show the slavering mutt who was boss before things got out of hand.

'Hey, Rover – come here, boy!' she said, slapping the front of her thighs with both hands in a welcoming manner.

The dog let out a rattling growl from the back of its throat and advanced slowly towards her. It was going to attack.

'Come here boy... just a little closer... yes, that's a good dog...'

Then, just as the pit-bull tensed itself to spring, Sterling removed her sunglasses and glared at the beast, allowing her aura to flare out and engulf the startled animal in impenetrable darkness. All at once, the dog began to whine piteously, finally rolling over onto its back in a surrender position while weeing itself profusely until Sterling replaced her sunglasses and patted the terrified dog on its belly to calm it down.

With the dog suitably neutralised, Sterling entered the club and carried on walking down a long service corridor until she encountered a set of swing doors. Now she knew exactly where she was. She wasn't far from Jack Malone's old office. Perhaps she would find Linda lurking inside. Well, anything was worth a try.

Suddenly, her thoughts were interrupted by the sound of footsteps approaching from behind the swing doors.

'Dammit! Someone's coming,' she hissed. 'I'd better hide—'

Too late. A man in black burst through the doors, almost knocking her over. It was one of the bouncers she'd seen earlier on manning the front entrance to the club. Evidently, he was on his way to relieve himself in the staff toilets.

'Oi! Where do you think you're going? He exclaimed, surprised to see her standing there in the passageway.

'Who? Me? Oh, I just got lost, that's all.'

Unconvinced, the man grabbed her by the shoulder of her jacket and made to escort her off the premises.

'Don't do that!' she said firmly.

The bouncer ignored her and began dragging her along the corridor towards the rear entrance of the building where she'd just entered.

Wrenching herself free of his grasp, she turned on him and removed her mirror-shades just like she'd done with the dog. Then she stared directly into his eyes.

Whatever the startled bouncer saw when he met her gaze, it didn't bear thinking about. Stupified with terror, the man backed up against the wall, his mouth opening in a silent scream.

As Sterling closed in on him, she uttered a simple set of commands. 'You will turn around and return through the doors from whence you came. You will re-join your friend at the front entrance and forget that you ever saw me here. Is that understood?'

Deep in shock, the bouncer nodded and turned slowly towards the doors. As Sterling watched him leave, she noticed the CCTV camera set up high in the ceiling void of the corridor. Had it recorded the event she wondered? Perhaps, but all anyone monitoring the screen would have seen would have been the man backing up against the wall then turning round to go back the way he'd came. Sterling herself hardly ever showed up on CCTV. Vampires usually didn't.

Humming a tune, she followed closely behind the hypnotised bouncer as he made his way back through the swing doors and into the main part of the club. Just before they parted company, Sterling replaced her sunglasses then checked another door on her right to see if it was open. *This used to be Jack's office*, she thought, turning on the light switch and looking inside. *No sign of Linda though. I hope she hasn't decided to take the night off.*

Switching off the light and closing the door, Sterling continued on down the corridor until it branched off to the left and right where an ascending staircase snaked its way up into the shadows of the first-floor landing.

'It's to the left,' she murmured. 'I need to go left here.'

Following the sound of the throbbing music, she finally emerged into the main dancehall where a familiar sight met her eyes. Sure, it wasn't the same place she remembered from all those years ago, but Linda hadn't altered it so radically as to cause it to lose all semblance of its former glory. The dance floor was still there, along with all the old Victorian opera boxes that were arranged at first-floor level all around the walls of the main hall. Yes, it was all still very much recognisable as the

Jabberwock Club of old, unless of course you took into account the regular clientele who now inhabited it. They had definitely changed.

It was getting on for ten o' clock and the place was already beginning to fill up with all manner of goths and punks from the Greater London area. Scanning the club for any sign of Linda Bailey she failed to locate her. There was simply no sign of her whatsoever. Just the mingling crowds of urban goths and faux vampires intent on having a good night out, totally oblivious to the fact that they were actually sharing the club with a real member of the Undead who could quite easily have driven any one of them completely insane with a single, protracted stare. Well, they weren't to know, were they? But where the fuck was Linda Bailey?

Glancing up, Sterling allowed her gaze to travel around the walls, casually scanning the Victorian opera boxes that dated back to the time when the place had been a theatre. Most were empty, though there were a few that were occupied, and it was to one of these in particular that her attention was now drawn.

Two figures, both of them women, were plainly visible, seated together chatting to each other in the theatre box. One of them had the unmistakable hairstyle of Linda Bailey.

'She hasn't changed,' muttered Sterling to herself. 'I wonder who her pretty young friend is?'

Without further hesitation, Sterling left the noisy dance hall and returned the way she'd come, only this time the staircase leading up to the first-floor was immediately in front of her. The stairs were quite steep and there was a violet fluorescent strip-light illuminating her way as she climbed up towards the landing.

Now she knew exactly where she was and where Linda could be found. Box number five. But would the door be locked? She hoped not, but if it was then she'd just have to kick it open anyway. Here goes...

'Aaaagh!!'

Linda let out a cry of alarm as the door flew open to reveal her worst nightmare standing there as plain as day. The young woman sitting at the table with her glanced first at Sterling and then back to Linda for some explanation.

'Don't worry, darling,' said Linda to her friend, 'it's nothing I can't handle.'

'Scat!' exclaimed Sterling, looking at the startled girl. 'Me and your meal ticket have got some catching up to do.'

The young lady frowned at this remark and was just about to pick up her glass of champagne and hurl it into Sterling's face when Linda caught her arm.

'No! Leave this to me, Denise. You go down to the office and wait for me there. We shan't be long.'

The woman glared angrily at Sterling as she got up from the table and prepared to leave. Standing to one side, Sterling allowed her to pass through the door and out of the room before she herself walked over to where Linda was seated. Pulling up a chair, she sat herself down and waited for Linda's reaction.

'Why are you here, Sterling?'

It was a simple enough question and quite honestly asked. Christ, but the little butch dyke hadn't changed at all, thought Sterling as she regarded Linda sitting opposite in her city-gent pinstripe suit, white collar and tie. Her face was almost feline in shape, with the same scheming eyes heavily accented in kohl and black mascara, while her hair was cropped quite short down the centre where it was dyed blond, except for two sections above her ears which she'd dyed black and then had lacquered so they stood up on either side of her head like the pointed ears of a wildcat. This, coupled with the screaming gash of red lipstick across her mouth gave off the impression that the woman who wore this alarming mask had wilfully ravaged a great natural beauty to attract attention to herself and spit in the face of convention.

'Don't try anything stupid,' exclaimed Sterling, pulling her gun out of her pocket and sliding it under the table until its muzzle made contact with Linda's right knee. 'These bullets are silver, but then you'd know all about that, wouldn't you, Linda.'

'I don't know what you mean,' replied the terrified nightclub owner as she took a sip of champagne from her glass.

'Then allow me to jog your memory, Linda. It was in Naples, back in December 2003. You and Jimmy Silver had me gunned down in the Piazza Garibaldi – remember?'

'I haven't got a clue what you're talking about, Sterling. Here, try some of this champagne why don't you? You can ring for another bottle if you like—'

'Put the phone down, Linda.'

Reluctantly, Linda withdrew her hand from her mobile phone just as the device rang with an incoming call.

'Don't answer that!'

'But it might be important, Sterling.'

'It can wait.'

The phone went silent as whoever it was on the other end had given up and rang off. Pressing the barrel of the gun closer to Linda's knee, Sterling continued with her interrogation.

'So, where were we? Ah yes – the Piazza Garibaldi. There I was, crossing the square in front of the railway station when these two geezers drive up behind me on a motor scooter and it's like, *Blam! Blam! Blam!* and I'm out of the picture. All very convenient in the circumstances, wouldn't you say?'

Linda stared down at the table. Her phone rang again. Eight times it rang and then fell silent once more. 'What do you want?' she said, looking across at Sterling.

'I want to know where Jimmy Silver lives, that's all.'

'And then I can go…?'

'I'll think about it.'

Linda went quiet for a moment as she considered her situation. She knew that betraying her boss meant instant retribution if he ever found out. But equally, with Silver out of the way, she would be relatively free to pursue her own interests in the capital without him demanding a percentage. It was worth a try.

'I don't know where he lives, Sterling. He never told me. But I can point you in the right direction.'

'Point away, Linda. I'm listening.'

'Well, I know that Silver sometimes has dealings with a PR company based in the Oxford Street area. The company is owned by a man called Howard Sackville who was into the business when most of his contemporaries at public school were still filling out their application forms for university. A pillar of the British establishment, he operates his concierge service largely for the benefit of the old power elite and wealthy newcomers from abroad. Naturally, some of the latter include a few of Jimmy Silver's friends – usually those from Italy, if you get my drift.'

'What's this company called?'

'It's called the Sackville Agency. It's likely they would have Silver's address on file.'

'Can you get it for me?'

'No way. My face is too well known. They would tell, Silver and then he would start asking questions. I can't do it, Sterling – please...'

'Very well, Linda. I'll have to think of something myself, but in the meantime, you're going to keep your mouth shut. Understood?'

Linda nodded rapidly, only too relieved to be off the hook for a while. She was even more relieved when Sterling retracted the gun covering her knee and began backing out of the theatre box towards the door.

'I'm going now, Linda, but remember this. You breathe one word of the meeting we've just had to anyone and I will return, and when I do, all this cosy little world you've built for yourself is going to crumble into dust... and that includes your pretty little girlfriend as well.'

***

He didn't like being here.

It wasn't that the old warehouse was particularly unpleasant, thought Cassidy as he paced up and down trying to keep warm. No, it was the fact that the place was so damn cold, and the tiny three-bar electric heater he'd found earlier on in the day wasn't doing very much to improve the situation.

Despairing of ever feeling warm again, he was just about to go into the kitchen to brew himself yet another steaming hot mug of tea when he thought he heard a noise in the street outside.

That's a motorcycle engine, he thought. *Sterling must be back already. I'm sure she said she might be gone for a couple of days. Strange...*

The only window in the room was set quite high up in the wall. Grabbing a chair, he carried it over to where the window was situated and clambered up onto its seat to take a better look down into the street below.

Damn! A steadily thickening mist outside made it virtually impossible for him to see. It was then that he heard the tell-tale sound of the warehouse doors opening and guessed it must be his friend returning from whatever business it was that she'd been up to.

Then he heard something else.

It was the sound of a second motorcycle engine revving, followed by another and then another. From where he was standing he could just about make out the main beams of several motorcycle headlamps shining through the fog. One, two, three, four, five, six, seven. There were a total of seven bikes out there in the lane. What the fuck was going on?

Cassidy listened as the sound of the engines grew louder. They were powerful machines and they caused the whole building to vibrate with their noise. Then, one by one, he heard the engines fall silent followed by the clatter of the outside door closing and the sound of footsteps coming up the stairs.

Now he could hear voices. They were men's voices and they were getting closer. There wasn't a moment to lose. Without further hesitation, Cassidy got down from the chair and ran across the room to hide himself behind a large folding screen just in time before the motorcycle gang entered the room.

'Sterling—it's us!' shouted one of the men upon entering the chamber.

'Looks like she's not around, Joe,' observed a second member of the gang, clasping himself against the cold.

'Just like her,' the man called Joe replied. 'Best get settled in for the night and make ourselves a brew. The kitchen's over there, Spike. You can do the honours.'

Cassidy watched through a gap in the screen as Spike wandered off into the kitchen to make tea. Then he turned his attention back to the men gathered in the centre of the room.

They're Hells Angels, he thought, regarding the insignia on the back of their jackets. *They're the same blokes that Sterling and Skinner were talking about. Christ, but they all look well over fifty. What the fuck can they do?*

'What's this place then?' enquired another member of the pack as he gazed up at the antique chandelier hanging from the ceiling.

'You mean you've never been here before?' answered Joe, not a little surprised.

'No. Never,' the man replied, mesmerised by the ornate light fitting suspended above his head. 'What exactly are we here for again – remind me?'

Joe Rackham exchanged glances with the rest of the group and breathed heavily through his nose.

'I received a message from Skinner telling me to meet him here. It's got something to do with the job we've got planned.'

'So, where is he then?' asked the man gruffly.

'He said he might be a bit late. He's gone to collect a couple of people he knows.'

'Oh… right. And who's this woman who calls herself, Sterling? What's she got to do with it all?'

'Sterling is a mate of his. This here warehouse is her headquarters. It's also where I've got our gear stashed. Come on, let's take a look.'

Walking over to the far end of the room, Joe found what it was that he was looking for.

'This is it boys,' he said, lifting a section of black plastic sheeting from the stacked wooden pallet and rummaging through the polythene bags beneath.

'There's a couple of kilos missing, boss,' declared one of the more observant members of the group.

'Not to worry, Gordon,' replied Joe. 'I expect Sterling has taken some of it to bargain with. In any case, it's not the gear we should be concerned about. It's what's underneath that's more important.'

Moving aside some of the polythene bags, Joe reached inside the stack.

'Ah, here they are,' he exclaimed, removing a small cloth sack from the middle of the pile and pulling the red drawstring open at the top. Then he emptied the contents of the sack out into the palm of his hand.

'Diamonds, boss?' said the man called Gordon, open-mouthed with astonishment.

'Yeah, and not just ordinary diamonds either. These here little gemstones are called brilliants and they're worth well over thirty grand each.'

Gordon picked up one of the stones from Joe's outstretched palm and examined it carefully.

'Looks okay to me – where'd you get them from, boss?'

'They're part of the haul from the Hatton Garden diamond robbery a few weeks back. You remember – it was all over the newspapers.'

'So, what are they doing here?'

'One of Sterling's mates had a hand in cracking the safe-deposit boxes during the robbery. It was a bloke called Orlando. He owed her for some favours she'd done him in the past and she owed me likewise, so this is my share.'

'Why show them to us then?'

'Because you all get a couple of them each as payment for the job we're about to do.'

'And what is this job exactly?' exclaimed another member of the gang, who up until this moment had been silent. His nickname was Keg, and he was well over six foot five inches tall with a beard and belly to match.

Joe swallowed hard. 'There's no better way of putting this,' he said, letting his gaze roll around the assembled group of bikers. 'We're going after Jimmy Silver.'

There was a short pause, vaguely reminiscent of the moment before a wolf pack strikes. And then:

'Fuck off!' said Gordon Dyer bluntly.

'Yeah. Count me out as well,' added Ronnie Frinton. 'I didn't join the Hells Angels so I could end up committing suicide. I've got a wife and kids to think about.'

'So have I,' said Joe, 'but just think what you could do with ninety grand.'

'Buy myself an ornamental gravestone?'

'Listen up,' Joe declared, trying to bring the impromptu meeting to some sort of order. 'If we plan this thing properly, nobody needs to get hurt.'

'That's what they said about D-Day.'

'All right. All right. If any one of you wishes to pull out of the job now then you're perfectly within your rights to do so, but remember this. Whoever pulls out now forfeits their share of the diamonds to the rest of the gang, is that understood?'

There was another pause, followed by murmurs of consent as the maths kicked in.

'Okay, we'll do it,' said Gordon. 'But if any one of us gets themselves killed in the process then the ninety grand goes to their missus or nearest living relatives, and I don't mean the raw diamonds either. You'll have to cash them in first.'

Joe nodded. 'It's agreed then. The price of the diamonds and a percentage of whatever I can get for these here drugs out on the street. It won't be as much as you think though. This sort of shit doesn't fetch as much as it used to. There's talk of the government legalising it as well.'

The men indicated their agreement just as Spike returned from the kitchen with some bad news.

'There ain't enough mugs to go round, boss. What should I do?'

'We'll just have to take turns then.'

'Right, but there's something else an'all.'

'What's that, Spike?'

'It looks like someone's made themselves a brew shortly before we arrived. The water left over in the kettle was still warm.'

'Yeah,' added Ronnie, 'and that electric heater over there was still on when we entered the room, not to mention the lights. If you ask me, there's someone else in the building.'

Cassidy's heart sank. What should he do – reveal himself now and explain who he was, or should he just wait things out behind the screen and hope the men didn't find him? It didn't seem like he had much of a choice, and he was just about to step out from his cover when fate intervened in the form of a large antique pot-stand which he accidentally brushed up against causing the large ceramic pot it was supporting to fall to the floor with a crash.

The startled bikers exchanged glances as Gordon Dyer pulled out a sawn-off shotgun from the customised pocket of his biker jacket and pointed it at the screen. 'Come out with your hands behind your head,' he snarled as the others looked on.

'Don't shoot,' implored Cassidy stepping out from behind the screen with both his hands raised. 'I'm a mate of Jerry Skinner's.'

'Who's this scrote?' said Gordon, looking at Joe. 'I've never seen him before.'

'Yeah – what's your name?' added Spike, still holding the electric kettle in his hand.

'Stuart – it's Stuart Cassidy. It's okay. I'm not armed.'

'I'm pleased to hear it,' said Joe laconically. 'What are you doing here?'

'I was with Sterling earlier on. We went to see this guy called Maz and she bought a gun off him.'

'Uh-huh – I'm hearing you. Go on.'

'When we left Maz's place, she told me to wait here while she attended to some other business. She said she would be a while.'

'What's a while?'

'A couple of days, I think. She wasn't very specific.'

'A couple of days?' echoed Gordon, lowering his shotgun. 'You mean we've got to stay in this dump for two whole days?'

Cassidy nodded. 'I think that's what she said.'

Joe regarded Cassidy thoughtfully. 'What's your part in all of this?' he said. 'How come you know Sterling?'

It took the better part of ten minutes for Cassidy to explain everything that had happened to him up to the point when he'd arrived back at the warehouse. When he had finished speaking, Joe casually took him to one side:

'Breathe so much as a single word about those diamonds to anyone outside of this room and you're going to wish that fucking ogre really had ripped your head off, is that clear?'

Cassidy nodded. 'Crystal.'

'Good. Now, what I suggest is that we all sit ourselves down around that table over there and have ourselves a game of poker. Then, when we're done, we can all doss down on the floor over there and get ourselves a bit of sleep. It looks like it's going to be a long night.'

***

Sterling brought her motorcycle to a halt near the Victoria Embankment. Only the other day, some stupid twat had gone and thrown themselves onto the underground line and there was still a smell of roast pork hanging in the air and a ghost in the road.

London was full of ghosts, she thought as she waved the suicide's spirit away with a sweep of her hand. You couldn't drive half a mile through the city without crashing through one.

A policeman walked by, interested to know who it was that was perched half-standing there on a motorcycle in the middle of the street.

'Is everything all right, miss?' he said in a curiously old-fashioned sort of way.

She was just about to answer in the affirmative when something about him caught her eye. Yes, he was a policeman, but not the sort of copper that had been seen in the capital for many a long year. For one thing, he wore a black, elbow-length cape around his shoulders secured by a silver chain around his neck; and for another, he sported a thick, brown moustache over his top lip, reminiscent of the sort that had last been in fashion during the Victorian era.

Another ghost, she thought, bidding the spirit depart into the ether from whence he'd come. As she watched the spectral police officer gradually dissolve back into the mist, she experienced a brief moment of reflection;

London... My eyes are full of your history. Downriver or upriver, it's all the same to me. Downriver is Bank Underground Station where the tunnel passes through one of the old plague pits. There's plenty of ghosts down there. Sometimes the stink of the ancient dead rises up through the ground just to remind the living what it was built on... London is full of ghosts...

It was time to move on.

Finding a suitable spot to park her bike, she made her way towards the nearest Tube station to find a place to sleep for the night among the ranks of homeless people who were gathered there for warmth. She would not be returning to the warehouse just yet she reasoned with a smile.

***

Cassidy yawned. The poker game had gone on much longer than he had anticipated. By now, it was around three o'clock in the morning and there was still no sign of the survivors giving up.

'I'm going to make some tea,' said Spike, tired of watching the game.

'I'll join you,' replied Sub, the only member of the gang who actually resembled the classic image of a 1970's biker. Long, greasy hair and a thin moustache, he had earned his nickname on account of the almost continual diet of fastfood he seemed to exist on, not to mention the almost terminal quantities of cannabis resin he had consumed over the years and which had left him with a permanently psychotic stare to rival that of Charlie Manson.

Joe watched them leave the room and then began arranging his cards in order. He was just about to play his hand when he heard a noise. Cassidy and the others heard it too. A low, chanting sound was coming from somewhere deep inside the building.

'What the fuck is that?' exclaimed Ronnie, getting up from his seat and listening hard.

Joe put his cards down. 'That's Latin, Ronnie. Didn't they teach you anything at school?'

'No, boss. I went to a comprehensive.'

'Right, well I'm an old grammar school kid and I'm telling you that that there sound is Latin.'

'Yeah, but where's it coming from?'

'It's coming from the back stairs,' put in Cassidy nervously. 'Something's got into the building.'

'What do you mean, *something?*' said Joe, looking across the table at him.

Cassidy didn't like to answer, given all that had happened to him since he'd met Sterling.

'It's growing louder,' exclaimed Ronnie.

'It's coming from over there,' said Gordon, nodding his head in the direction of a large tapestry cloth that hung on the far wall. The cloth began to twitch, as if something – or someone, was trying to pull it aside and enter the room. As the chanting grew in volume, Gordon pulled out his shotgun. 'Show yourself!' he yelled, pointing the gun at the wall-cloth.

'Hey, slow down, kiddo,' said Ronnie, grabbing Gordon by the arm. 'We don't know who it is yet...'

The words died on his lips when the tapestry cloth was suddenly drawn aside to reveal the figure of a man clothed almost entirely in black and wearing a priest's biretta on his head. Slowly, the dark apparition began walking towards the poker table still chanting in Latin and clutching a long silver dagger in its raised hand: *'Transfiguratum in angelum lucis,'* the man babbled almost incoherently, *'cum tota malignorum spiritum.'*

'Fucking hell, it's a Catholic priest with a nine-inch bade!' spluttered Whiskey Pete, the only American present among the group who were seated around the table.

'Antiquus inimicus et homicida,' the priest rambled on, his eyes wide open and staring wildly ahead as if he had worked himself up into some kind of a trance.

'What are we gonna do, boss?' exclaimed Gordon, barely able to restrain himself from pulling the trigger.

The matter was taken out of his hands when Sub returned from the kitchen with Spike and saw what was happening. In an instant, he reached into his trouser pocket and drew out a large spanner-wrench, hitting the priest on the back of his head with an almighty thwack!

The priest fell to the floor, his black biretta rolling aside to reveal a head of neatly trimmed ginger hair.

'Christ, don't hit him again!' yelled Joe, as Sub stood over the man preparing to give him another whack with the spanner. A miserable childhood spent in a church-run orphanage had left him with an almost pathological hatred of Catholic priests that verged on the homicidal.

'Yeah, leave it out, Sub,' said Spike. 'We don't want a body on our hands.'

'I don't care. I'll do for the cunt anyway!' was all, Sub said in response as he raised his spanner to deliver the final blow.

'That's enough!' Spike countered, grabbing his friend by the wrist. 'Besides, we need to know what he's doing here.'

'Uh-h-h-h...' moaned the priest, raising himself up on his elbows before Spike and Sub helped him to his feet and escorted him over to the table where they promptly sat him down in a vacant chair.

'Where is she?' the priest murmured, rubbing the back of his skull with the palm of his hand. He was a youngish-looking man with a long face and prominent ears that stuck out from the side of his head at an angle.

'Where is who?' enquired Joe, taking on the role of interrogator.

'The vampire—,' replied the priest, '—the one I was sent to exorcise and destroy.'

Joe glanced around the table, feigning surprise. He alone among all the gang knew the truth about Sterling and he wasn't about to let on. Quickly, he changed tack.

'What's your name, priest?'

'It's Dominic Kennedy. Father Dominic Kennedy. I'm from Ireland.'

'Who sent you?'

'It was Cardinal Streffan. He sent me on the orders of the Vatican.'

'Fuck me, we've got ourselves a right loony here, boss,' exclaimed Gordon, chipping in. 'What are we going to do with him?'

Joe looked at Gordon, then turned to the priest once again. 'Well, I'm afraid you've come to the wrong place, Father. There aren't any vampires here; only my Hells Angels, so maybe you were thinking of exorcising them perhaps?'

'No, no. It was definitely a vampire I was sent to deal with. I've got it all written down in this letter here…'

Fumbling around in his cassock, Father Dominic pulled out a crumpled piece of paper.

'This is a letter from Rome written to Cardinal Streffan telling him all about it.'

Joe took the letter. 'It's in Italian,' he said, running his eye swiftly down the page.

'I know—'

'Then read it to me, Father.'

'I can't. I don't know Italian either, but Cardinal Streffan does and he said it was a matter of the greatest urgency.'

Joe handed the letter back to the priest.

'So, why come here then?'

'Because, Cardinal Streffan said this place was the vampire's lair – the one who calls herself, Sterling.'

There were murmurs around the table which Joe quickly silenced with a glance before turning back to Father Dominic.

'The only Sterling I know is a woman who I have always had dealings with, and I can assure you that she is no vampire. As a matter of fact, she's ten times worse.'

The priest stiffened, his mouth opening in shock. Vampires really did exist, he thought. Cardinal Streffan hadn't been kidding after all. The silver dagger he'd been supplied with was real. The flask of holy water in his hip pocket – that was real too. There really was a department of the Vatican that dealt with demons and vampires. Maybe even Jesus was real as well...

Joe raised an eyebrow, sensing that the priest wasn't at all convinced by what he'd just said. Catholic priests were trained to detect liars, much in the same way as police detectives and psychiatrists were. One way or another, it was only a matter of time before someone else in a black cassock and biretta caught up with Sterling and stamped her card. He would have to think of something fast.

'Father Dominic,' he said.

'Yes...?'

'You might be advised to stay here for the rest of the night. The weather outside is pretty bad and we wouldn't want you catching a chill, would we. Why don't you just pull up a chair and sit yourself down. I think you've got a bit of explaining to do.'

Sixteen

It was Sunday morning and the streets of the capital were practically deserted as Sterling drove her motorcycle down through Piccadilly and on towards the fashionable district of Mayfair and the Noyland hotel where she had her next appointment.

Sterling was irritable. She'd just spent a cold and miserable night dossing down outside an underground station and hadn't had much in the way of sleep. Still, she wouldn't be doing that again if everything went according to plan. Tonight, she would be living it up in one of London's top hotels and all at someone else's expense.

It wouldn't be the first time she'd been to the Noyland. Way back in the 1970s when she'd worked as a prostitute, she had paid the place enough visits to familiarise herself with all of the protocols necessary to gain entry to the establishment without having to go through the tedious ritual of actually having to book a room. Now, all of that experience was about to come in useful once more in enabling her to gain an audience with one of the people she most needed to talk to at this present moment in time.

'Would, Cardinal Streffan be in residence?' she enquired, addressing the concierge behind the reception desk.

For a luxury hotel, the Noyland was a cosy, old fashioned sort of a place. Just the kind of hotel where you'd expect a senior member of the Catholic Church to be staying if they happened to be visiting London for any length of time.

'Who should I say is calling?' replied the man behind the desk, not entirely convinced by Sterling's attempt at bluffing her way into the hotel.

'Tell him it's Julie,' she replied coyly. 'He's expecting me.'

Picking up the phone, the concierge dialled a number and waited. A brief conversation ensued, during which time the man kept glancing up at her suspiciously.

'Send her up anyway,' she heard the man on the other end of the line say before whoever it was rang off abruptly, causing the man behind the desk to shake his head in disbelief.

'Cardinal Streffan's room is on the third floor,' he said, putting down the receiver and looking at Sterling. 'He's staying in the Surrey Suite. It's room number twelve.'

The carpet felt soft beneath her feet as she made her way along the third floor corridor. Counting off the numbers, she came to the door she wanted and noticed that it had been left slightly open. Uncertain as to what she should do, she knocked three times on the door and waited.

'Enter,' came a voice from within. It was an authoritative voice with a southern Irish accent, but scarcely audible above the sound of a Mozart symphony playing from a speaker system somewhere in the room.

'Bless me, Father for I have sinned,' was all she said as she made her entrance on the unsuspecting Divine who was seated on a plush armchair facing the door.

'You!' exclaimed the cardinal, almost spilling his glass of champagne all over the elegant carpet.

'Were you expecting someone else, Your Eminence?' replied Sterling with a vicious smile.

'Get out! Get out! You little fecker,' spluttered the middle-aged cleric, clutching desperately at the silver crucifix around his neck. Every inch a cardinal, down to his broad scarlet sash and episcopal ring, Patrick Streffan was still in a state of shock when Sterling advanced slowly towards him without once lifting her gaze.

'Oh, come now, Patrick. That's no way to greet an old friend. Why don't you offer me a glass of champagne and some of that coke you've got lined up on the coffee table over there? You know how much I like it.'

'You can feck off now, you little goblin or I'll—'

'Or you'll do what—call for room service? I don't think so,' replied Sterling, sitting herself down in an armchair opposite and taking an enormous pinch of cocaine from the table. As she did so, Cardinal Streffan eyed her warily.

'What have you done to him, you murdering bitch?' he said, composing himself once more.

'Who?'

'Father Dominic, you lying bastard! Is he all right?'

'Oh, him. I had a tip-off you'd put him on my tail. I expect he's okay – assuming Joe knows how to handle his boys that is.'

'Well, he'd fucking better be,' replied Streffan, not entirely convinced. 'Anyway, what is it you're wanting?'

'Just a few requests, Your Eminence.'

'And what might they be?'

'Well, you can get the Vatican off my case for starters. It's not the middle ages, in case you hadn't noticed.'

'That wasn't my decision, Sterling. It was the Order of Exorcist who ordered the hit on you. I just attended to the details.'

'All the same, Patrick, you're not without some influence in the corridors of power. You could put in a good word for me with the Curia. After all, it was Jimmy Silver who compromised them to do the hit in the first place – the *Italian connection,* if you know what I mean.'

The cardinal frowned. 'I'll see what I can do, but I can't promise anything mind you. Irish influence is a bit thin on the ground in Rome at the moment, what with all that trouble in the press and all.'

'I'm not surprised, Patrick,' said Sterling, taking a look around the room. 'Were you expecting visitors?'

'All right, all right,' the cardinal flustered. 'What else do you want?'

Sterling ran her tongue along the edge of her lip. 'The Book of Vampires, cardinal. I want the Incunabulum.'

The elderly clergyman sat back in astonishment. 'How in god's name do you expect me to lay my hands on that infernal tome? There hasn't been a copy in print since 1501. I doubt if there are more than three copies left in the whole world!'

'What about the Vatican archives, Patrick? Surely you must have enough influence to blag your way in there?'

'I suppose I could,' replied Streffan thoughtfully, 'but there isn't a copy available at the moment because—'

The cardinal halted in mid-sentence, realising what he was about to say.

'Because of what?' enquired Sterling patiently.

'Because the book is out on permanent loan.'

'Oh, it is, is it? And who to, exactly?'

The cardinal looked away, momentarily dropping his crucifix. 'Look, there's no way I can get you that damn book, Sterling. It's more than my life is worth.'

'No matter. You've answered my question anyway. But there is something else you could do for me.'

'Such as what?'

'I need a one-gallon container full of holy water from St Peter's in Rome.'

'You what?'

'A gallon of holy water from St Peter's. Is that too much to ask?'

'I... I can't.'

'Oh, come now, Cardinal Streffan. You can do better than that.'

'No, I won't do it... *It's unholy.*'

'Well, in that case you won't mind me contacting the press about that embarrassing little incident in Norfolk back in 1989 when you were still a priest, will you?'

Streffan fell silent, glaring across the room at her.

'When do you want it?' he said angrily.

'Within three days, Patrick. You can send it on a plane by courier if you have to. Just say it's for *business purposes.*'

'Where do you want it delivered – the warehouse?'

Sterling nodded. 'Yes, you can send it there. Oh, and just before I go, Patrick, there's one more thing you can do for me.'

'What's that?'

'I need a decent room for a couple of nights. How about booking me one here? I'm sure your expenses can stretch to it.'

Seventeen

The concierge barely recognised the woman who deposited her room keys at the reception desk before walking through the front doors of the hotel and out onto the street outside. Yes, she had the same black hair and sunglasses he had witnessed when she'd first arrived, but that was as far as it went. Everything else about her was different, down to the expensive high-heeled designer shoes she wore on her feet. Armani jacket, leather handbag, matching skirt and complimentary blouse – all high-end fashion-house couture, and not a hair out of place. Why the sudden change, he wondered, before his phone rang and he was once again thrust into the minutiae of running a hotel.

Incredible, thought Sterling as she paused to admire her reflection in a shop window before flagging down a passing taxi. *Debbie and Orlando have really put themselves out for me this time. I wonder where they nicked all these clothes from?*

'Where to, miss?' said the driver of the cab, turning round in his seat.

'The Sackville Agency please,' replied Sterling, 'and make it quick if you can. I have an appointment at ten and don't want to be late.'

As the cab drove off, she relaxed in the back seat, casually noting the route the driver was taking. It was Monday morning and the traffic was heavy. She might have been quicker walking, but not in heels.

'Come far, miss?' said the driver, making polite conversation.

'From Chelmsford,' she replied. 'I'm an art dealer.'

Secretly, Sterling scanned his thoughts and smiled. Her disguise had worked. She had been travelling around with the designer clothes in the panniers of her motorcycle for several days now and was concerned that her new image might not be accepted. Now, the driver of the black London taxi had allayed those fears with his total belief that she was who she claimed to be – Francesca Harrington, the art dealer from Chelmsford. Let's hope the same deception would work on the staff of the Sackville Agency when she finally arrived. Well, anything was worth a try.

***

'My name is Francesca Harrington,' said Sterling, introducing herself to the svelte, young twenty-something at the reception desk of the Howard Sackville Agency. 'I have an appointment to see Howard at ten.'

'You're the fine art dealer…?' enquired the girl behind the desk.

'Yes,' replied Sterling, crisply.

'Please take a seat over there by the fountain. Someone will be down presently. Would you like a coffee while you're waiting?'

'No thanks. I had one at my hotel earlier on.'

The girl nodded and returned to her work, oblivious of the fact that she was now sharing her space with a seasoned predator. Her face was completely immobile as she checked her computer screen. *She's Botoxed herself up to the eyeballs,* thought Sterling. *Anorexic too, by the look of it. What a world...*

It was a full twenty minutes before she heard the sound of someone coming down the staircase. That someone was a tall, elegant woman with long blond hair and a straight nose.

'You are, Francesca Harrington?' the woman said with a faux smile and a heavy Polish accent.

Sterling nodded and rose to her feet.

'Good,' replied the woman. 'Howard will see you now. Come this way please.'

Not the first floor but the third it was before they reached a spacious landing where the blond woman turned down a short corridor that had a large mahogany door at the end of it. There was a shiny, brass nameplate on the door which read, Howard Sackville in big, bold letters. The woman knocked softly.

'Yes...' came a voice from within.

'I've brought Francesca Harrington to see you, Mr Sackville.'

'Just a moment,' came the voice.

There was a click as a hidden electronic device unlocked the door from inside. Evidently, Howard wasn't taking any chances given the reputation of some of his clients.

Just before they entered the room, Sterling felt around in her handbag. Good, she thought. The gun was still there. It would come in handy if the man panicked.

Opening the door, the blond lady ushered Sterling in and then departed without a word, gently closing the door behind her as she left. To Sterling's relief, the door did not lock as it closed, satisfying her mind that she would not be trapped inside the office if she needed to make a quick getaway. Smooth and by the numbers was how she liked to operate, and the same could probably be said for Howard Sackville now that she got a closer look at him seated there behind his office desk.

Charismatic and sophisticated, it was impossible not to be seduced by his broad smile and disarming manner that practically oozed optimism like a fairy tale with a happy ending.

'Please take a seat, Miss Harrington,' he beamed. 'I won't be a moment.'

Sterling looked on as Howard's gaze darted between his Rolex watch, mobile phone and computer screen before it eventually came to rest on a smart, leather-bound notebook embossed with his initials in swanky gold lettering.

'Ah, here it is,' he exclaimed, adjusting his half-moon reading glasses to a more comfortable position before scanning down the page. Christ, but he was about as top-drawer as they came, thought Sterling as he read on. A regular, "Mr Establishment" if ever there was one, his neatly trimmed brown hair possessed the kind of parting you only acquired if you'd done serious time in one of Britain's top public schools.

'I see you are connected with the art world, Miss Harrington,' he said at length, raising his gaze from his notebook. 'My son is into that sort of thing. He works at the Tate Modern, you know.'

Sterling's heart sank. She hadn't bargained on anyone in the field of business and public relations knowing anything at all about museums and art galleries. Now, she was confronted by someone who had got his foot well and truly wedged in the front door of one of the most prestigious public galleries in England. She was going to have to improvise.

'I'm more into historical collections myself,' she responded, hoping this would deflect any suspicions on his part.

'Any particular period?' enquired Howard, genuinely interested.

I'll have to give that one the swerve, thought Sterling, grasping for any scrap of leverage she could get. 'The eighteenth century!' she declared, almost yelling out the phrase in desperation.

'Ah, the Whig Supremacy. Then you must admire the work of Thomas Gainsborough, I shouldn't wonder.'

'Yes, him.'

'Indeed. A damn fine portrait painter, but not half as good as, Allan Ramsay, wouldn't you say?'

'Not in the same league,' replied Sterling, hoping this would satisfy the man and convince him she was genuine. He had a shrewd face, with a mouth that wore a sly smile. A thin, upturned nose, separated eyes that were set just a tad too close together. Wearing his well-pressed black suit, Howard Sackville looked more like a senior, Crown Court barrister than a savvy PR guru with a passing interest in art history. Taking off his reading glasses, he cleared his throat and turned to face her.

'So, what can I do for you, Miss Harrington?'

Sterling was out of her depth and she knew it. What she said now would have to be general and not very specific or Howard was going to smell a rat.

'Well, it's a couple of things actually. I'm putting on an exhibition at my gallery in Chelmsford and I'm going to need some sponsorship pretty quickly.'

'Hmm, I see,' said Howard. 'Have you tried Lottery funding?'

Sterling shook her head. 'No, I haven't.'

Howard Sackville raised an eyebrow. He was genuinely surprised she hadn't already considered this line of approach and regarded her quizzically.

'The National Lottery is usually the first port of call in these matters,' he replied, his right leg jogging up and down in nervous agitation. 'I'm not an expert in this sort of thing, but my son knows a bit about it. He might be able to help you if you give him a call.'

I'm losing him, she thought. *He's beginning to waver. Best fuck him over quickly before his foot hits the panic button.*

'Thank you, Howard. I'll do that if you would be so good as to give me his contact number.'

'No need, Miss Harrington. Just call the Tate Gallery and mention my name. They'll put you straight through.'

Christ, but was there no end to this geezer's connections? pondered Sterling, remembering the gun in her handbag. It was time to close in for the kill.

'Thank you, Howard. That would be very helpful. Now, if it's not too much trouble, I was wondering if you could help me out with another of my little problems.'

'And what might that be?' he beamed, not expecting what was going to happen next.

'You can give me Jimmy Silver's address,' she said coldly, pulling out her gun and pointing it directly into his face.

Howard's mouth opened like the void of a doughnut as his hands automatically raised themselves in shock. It was funny how they always did that, she thought before pressing home her advantage.

'Silver's address. I want it – now!'

'Who are you?' said Howard, sheepishly, his hands still raised.

'That's none of your business. Just give me Silver's address and you get to live.'

Sterling looked on as Howard reluctantly typed on his keyboard and looked at the screen. There was a short interval before the relevant window came up, providing him with access to his client list.

'There,' he said, turning the screen in her direction.

'Write it down on a piece of paper,' Sterling demanded, 'and don't try anything stupid.'

Tearing a sheet out of his precious notebook, Howard hastily scribbled out the details. 'If you ever find Silver you must tell him that I did this under duress, is that understood?'

'I think he'll realise that, Howard, don't you? Now lie on the floor face down and put your hands behind your back while I cuff and gag you. Don't worry. I dare say your PA will be up presently to see if you are okay. Now, I must be on my way. I have some urgent business to attend to. Goodbye—'

***

She was getting closer. He sensed her presence like a spider checking the strands of its web. How could he sleep with the knowledge she was on the prowl? How could he have been so stupid as to ignore anything so lethal?

At first, he'd refused to believe that she had escaped from her tomb on the island. He'd been careful. Taken all the necessary precautions. Left nothing to chance. But chance had intervened and now she was on his trail.

Even from the relative safety of his lair there was no mistaking the manner of her steady encroachment. Slow, deliberate and predatory, Sterling was a thing of terrible beauty, just like the vampire mother who had created her. Such a pity she would have to be destroyed.

That fool, Cassidy was still with her. Considering his close proximity to her, he had adapted quite well for a human, still managing to retain some scraps of free will within his soul. Perhaps she was just being kind to him.

Heaving a sigh, Silver rose from the antique carved chair in his study and reached for the bell-rope. Presently, a tall black man entered the room.

'Lock all the doors and windows, Tarrou. I've had some bad news from London.'

'Sterling?'

'Yes. I fear she's stolen a march on us.'

'What are we going to do?'

'Best get in touch with the Outlaws. I hear she's bringing some friends with her. They're Hells Angels, apparently.'

Eighteen

'That must be them now,' exclaimed Ronnie, hearing the sound of a car engine in the street outside.

'About fucking time,' replied Joe. 'You'd better go down and let them in. I don't think Skinner has a key for this place.'

The others watched as Ronnie padded off downstairs to unlock the doors of the warehouse. It wasn't long before he returned holding a large cardboard box sealed with official-looking parcel tape.

'Where's Skinner and Debbie?' enquired Joe with a puzzled expression.

'It wasn't them, boss. Just a courier with a parcel delivery for this address.'

Joe glanced first at the parcel then looked at the other men in the room. 'Get down!' he yelled, throwing himself to the floor.

'What's up, boss?' said Ronnie, still holding the box.

'Ronnie, just put the fucking box down on the table and get on the floor.'

Shrugging his shoulders, Ronnie walked over to the table and did what he was told. Pretty soon, everyone present in the main room of the warehouse were lying face down, flat on the floor, holding their breath.

'What's the problem?' said Cassidy, who was closest to Joe.

'It's a fucking bomb,' Joe whispered in reply.

'How do you know?'

'Because, Silver's tried it before…'

'No, I don't mean that. What I mean is; how do you know it's a bomb?'

'…Because it's the sort of thing, Silver would do if he knew we were here.' Joe answered, his nose pressed flat against the carpet.

'But he doesn't,' put in Cassidy, gamely. *'No one knows we're here except for Sterling and Skinner.'*

'Okay,' replied Joe. 'If you're so damn certain that parcel sitting there on the table isn't a bomb, then you go over and open it. Or perhaps, Father Dominic might care to volunteer?'

'Feck that! You can count me out! I'm not ready to meet my maker just yet.'

'Oh, really, Father?' said Joe, 'I would have thought you were the most qualified of us all for that sort of thing?'

'Yeah,' added Spike. 'Can't you go and pray over it or something.'

'Feck off! No way!'

The room went quiet for a while as the men considered what best to do.

'It's not ticking,' observed Spike, speaking into the silence.

'Modern bombs don't tick,' mumbled Joe, his face still pressed to the floor.

More silence followed, during which time, Cassidy decided to take a brief review of his life so far. If he ever got out of this mess alive, he thought, he would definitely turn over a new leaf and start all over again. A life of crime was no longer an option. Look where it had got him – lying face down on the floor of a disused warehouse in South London with a gang of renegade bikers for company. He was about to make a pact with himself to go straight when another member of the gang spoke out. It was Gordon Dyer—

'We can't stay here on the floor all day. I'm going over to take a look at it.'

'Be careful,' said Spike. 'It might be booby trapped.'

Breathing slowly and rhythmically, Gordon approached the box on the table. Checking for wires, he carefully removed the delivery note from its plastic envelope and began reading.

'Hey boss,' he said at length.

'What?' inquired, Joe.

'This note. It says this here parcel is from St Peter's in Rome.'

'It's what—?'

'The box – it's from the Vatican.'

'What's the Pope doing sending us a fucking banger?' exclaimed Sub, raising his head from the floor.

'Let me see that,' demanded Joe, getting up and walking over to where Gordon was standing with the note in his hand. Scanning the letter briefly, he turned to Father Dominic who was still lying on the carpet. 'What do you make of this?' he said, gesturing for the priest to follow him.

Reluctantly, the priest rose to his feet and wandered over to the table. Taking the letter in his hand, he examined it thoughtfully.

'They're St Peter's keys all right,' he declared, pointing to the gold-embossed logo at the head of the delivery note. 'No doubt about it. This box has come from Rome.'

'I wonder what it is?' remarked Cassidy as he joined the trio around the table.

'There's only one way to find out,' bellowed Keg, his enormous bulk casting a shadow over the proceedings as he approached the group. 'Let's open it up.'

'Be careful—'

Too late. Keg's large hands tore into the parcel like a terrier dog with an attitude problem. Within no time at all, a translucent, white object swathed in bubblewrap and polystyrene bits emerged from the scattered remains of the cardboard box.

'It's a plastic container,' observed Keg triumphantly as he removed the last of the bubblewrap.

'Yes, and the stopper's got something attached to it,' added Spike.

Sure enough, the plastic screw-top container was sealed with an old-fashioned red wax seal bearing the same motif that Joe had witnessed on the covering letter.

'I think I know what it is,' said Dominic, picking up the translucent container and giving it a shake.

'What is it?' inquired Joe.

'It's holy water – about a gallon of it.'

'It's fucking what?'

'Holy water – and don't swear!' the priest snapped irritably, putting the container back down on the table as reverently as he could.

Another interval of silence came on as the men stood around the table trying to figure out all that this impromptu delivery from the Vatican might imply. It wasn't long before Gordon spoke up.

'What does Sterling want with a gallon of holy water, boss?'

'Yes,' exclaimed the priest, 'what does a vampire want with holy water? That's usually my part of the job.'

At first, no one even blinked at the mention of the V word. Only, Joe and Stuart Cassidy looked at one another knowingly, while the others just stared blankly at the priest and then back to the container without so much as a syllable passing their lips. Then, Gordon stared hard at Joe.

'Joe—'

'Yeah?'

'Just what the fuck have you got us into this time?'

***

Sterling sighed as she laid out the clothes on the bed of her hotel room. She would not be needing the persona of Francesca Harrington again for a very long time but was loathe to part with the disguise. There was something about the image of the confidant young art dealer that reminded her very much of herself when she'd been Julie Kent all those years ago. Still, she also liked the image of the biker-chick that she'd recently adopted, complete with the scuffed, leather jacket and the biker boots. She wasn't going to part with them in a hurry.

Now, where had she put that map?

She'd purchased an old Ordnance Survey chart shortly after her visit to the Sackville Agency. It was a map of the south coast showing the area between the towns of Hastings and Folkestone. According to Howard Sackville, Silver's address was located near a place called Lower Storpington, but she'd been unable to find it on any modern road atlas that was available in the shops. Then, quite by chance, she'd stumbled across an old OS map in a second-hand bookshop on the Charing Cross road. Nothing on the map made very much sense, and some of the roads depicted in green and purple ink probably didn't exist anymore, but at least it showed the village of Lower Storpington together with its ancient church and the old apple orchards which had once inhabited the area.

Pouring over the map, Sterling tried to work out how the road networks of the twenty-first century might correspond with those of the 1920s shown on the chart. From what she remembered, roads were always a bit thin on the ground in that part of Kent, and thinner still on the ancient chart she was now reading. Maybe, Skinner could work it all out for her when she returned to him with the news. He was good at that sort of thing.

Almost two days had elapsed since her meeting with Cardinal Streffan. That should have been ample time for her parcel from the Vatican to arrive. Smiling, she donned her leather jacket and checked her pistol. It was time to go.

***

'What kept you?'

It was Joe Rackham who asked the question as Skinner entered the room together with Debbie and Orlando.

'Car wouldn't start,' replied Skinner. 'The alternator was on the blink, and decent mechanics are hard to come by in my neck of the woods.'

'Oh, right – but it's okay now, isn't it?'

'Sound as a pound. A mate of Debbie's fixed it. Needed a new battery as well.'

Joe nodded, then looked at Debbie and the man who was with her. 'You must be, Orlando,' he observed. 'I've heard a lot about you. You're one of the best safe-breakers in the business, or so I've been told.'

'He is *the* best,' chipped in Debbie, as Orlando and Joe shook hands. 'My, but this old warehouse hasn't changed much over the years, has it Orlando?'

'Looks about the same as it always was,' the man replied, looking around. 'Who's that bloke over there?' he added, pointing at Cassidy.

'He's called Stuart Cassidy,' answered Joe. 'He's a new mate of Sterling's. Don't worry, he's *one of the chaps,* aren't you, Stuart?'

Cassidy nodded, not quite sure what to say under the circumstances. Orlando smiled warmly then turned to look at Father Dominic who was standing close by.

'What's that priest doing here?' he said warily.

'Yeah, boss,' exclaimed Gordon, 'tell him why the priest is here. I'm sure we all want to know.'

'It's okay,' put in Orlando. 'I think I can guess.'

The room went quiet as the truth slowly sank in.

'Tell me it isn't true, boss,' was all Gordon said, breaking the silence. 'Tell me, Sterling isn't a vampire.'

'Why don't you ask her yourself,' exclaimed Debbie who was standing over by the window. 'This is her arriving now.'

Father Dominic crossed himself and muttered a few words under his breath as Sterling appeared in the doorway. Then, she began walking across the floor of the warehouse in a series of long, lazy strides, just to make her presence felt.

Christ, but she loves a dramatic entrance, thought Skinner observing the reactions of the other gang members as she drew closer. Not one, but three of the men reached for concealed weapons, ready to use them at a moment's notice if they deemed it necessary.

Reaching the table, Sterling smiled at each of the men in turn, with the exception of the priest.

'I see my holy water has arrived safe and sound,' she said, gesturing at the plastic container on the table. 'Cardinal Streffan certainly knows how to pull a few strings in Rome.'

'You dirty fucking bastard!' spluttered Dominic, reaching for his rosary. 'You'll burn in hell for this!'

'Aw, get over yourself, padre,' replied Sterling, forcing him down into a nearby chair with a push. 'It's all in a good cause.'

'Like what?'

'Like mine. Now, shut up and sit down. We've got some serious business to discuss and I don't want you sticking your shiny crucifix in where it's not wanted, okay?'

Reluctantly, the priest obliged her by sitting tight-lipped in his seat as she opened the proceedings. Cassidy too, remained silent, anxious to know what else Sterling had in store for him. If he managed to survive over the next twenty-four hours, then he was determined to take the first train out of London and make a new life for himself in Cornwall. It was the only option he felt he had left in the circumstances.

'Spike—' said Joe, 'go and make us all a pot of tea or something; I think this is going to be a long session.'

'Okay,' answered Spike, pottering off to the kitchen with a clutch of empty mugs in his hands. When he returned, most of the gang were gathered around the table with Sterling seated at its head, flanked by Joe, Skinner and Cassidy who were seated on either side of her. Everyone else had to make do with whatever else was available to sit on, including several old crates and a couple of cardboard boxes that happened to be lying around.

'I take it that Joe has briefed you all about the reason why we are here,' said Sterling, bringing the meeting to order.

The gang nodded solemnly, but only Gordon answered her.

'Yeah, we're going on a suicide mission to deal with Jimmy Silver, or so I've been led to believe.'

Cassidy and Skinner cringed, knowing only too well that Sterling's sense of humour was paper thin at the best of times, and at the worst, practically non-existent. Silent and apprehensive, they waited for her response.

Her response was to light up a cigarette and wait for Gordon's words to sink in. 'Yes,' she said after a suitable interval, 'we're going after Silver, and if any one of you feel you're not up to the task then you'd better leave now, is that clear?'

More sombre nodding followed, during which time, Sterling brought out the Ordnance Survey map from her inside jacket pocket together with the Mauser pistol she had concealed there.

'Fuck me! Where'd you get that cannon from?' exclaimed Ronnie Frinton, pawing at the weapon in fascination.

'None of your business,' she snapped, opening up the map and spreading it out on the table where everyone could see it. Only Debbie and Orlando had a problem viewing the old chart and had to move round so they were looking at it over Cassidy and Skinner's shoulders.

'This is a map of the south coast,' announced Sterling. 'Cassidy here, told me that Silver's residence was located somewhere near the sea, and I have since had it confirmed that he lives close to the village of Lower Storpington, at a place called Martello Towers.'

'Sounds like Silver's address,' said Skinner. 'A real toff's place – reclusive and yet ostentatious all at the same time. Where is it on the map? I can't see it?'

'It's not shown on the map, Jerry. That's probably why Silver chose it for his headquarters in the first place. This chart dates back to the 1920s which may have been when he first moved there. It's not on any subsequent maps either, and neither is the village of Storpington. In fact, it wouldn't surprise me if Silver had the location of the village obliterated from the Ordnance Survey system shortly after he moved in. Masonic influence, I shouldn't wonder,'

'Ah yes, the Ancient Order of Stonecutters; they're about as persistent as you vampires, eh, Sterling?'

'And just as lethal if they want to be, Skinner. Just remember this all of you. Silver has been around for a whole lot longer than any one of us sitting here in this room. There's no telling what forces he might call upon if he feels himself to be threatened in any way. Surprise is our only weapon – and talking of weapons, what exactly have we got? Come on boys; lay them out on the table. I want to see them.'

Hands reached into pockets and sleeves, as knives, guns and improvised weapons were drawn out and laid on the table on top of the map. Joe obliged everyone by producing a Webley revolver which was almost as old as Sterling's own handgun, while Spike pulled out a knife from the inside of his motorcycle boot. Other instruments of death soon followed, including

Gordon Dyer's shotgun and the lethal spanner-wrench carried by Sub, so that pretty soon the table top came to resemble the interior of a police station incident room on weapons amnesty day.

'That's quite a collection,' observed Sterling, casting her eyes over the table. 'And what have you brought to the party, Jerry?'

Up until now, Jerry Skinner had been reluctant to show his hand in the weapons' poker game. Now, he reached down into his coat pocket and produced the most archaic specimen of handgun that anyone had ever seen.

'What the fuck do you call that?!' exclaimed Joe, utterly gobsmacked by what Skinner was holding in his hand.

'It's called a Saint Etienne,' Skinner declared proudly. 'French army service revolver made in 1878. I don't normally pack a gun so it was all I could get hold of.'

'Did you get it from Maz?' enquired Sterling with a scowl.

'No, I bought it off a bloke called Peckham Charlie. It didn't cost much either.'

'That's probably because it'll blow your fucking hand off,' declared Joe sarcastically.

'No it won't,' replied Skinner with confidence.

'How do you know?'

'Because it hasn't got any bullets in it, that's why. Nothing I could get would fit in the chamber. I can only use it to threaten with.'

Sniggers broke out all around the table which Sterling quickly suppressed with a snarl. Both she and Skinner went back a long way and she wasn't going to see him belittled in front of her.

'That's quite enough, boys,' she said tetchily, 'there'll be plenty of time for snide remarks when the job is over. In any case, Cassidy wants to say something. Stuart, the floor is all yours. What is it you have to say?'

Cassidy cleared his throat to speak. 'From what I remember of my car ride down to Silver's house, we drove down a long cinder track for the last part of the journey. I remember someone stopping the car and getting out to open the gate before we proceeded on down the track for about a quarter of a mile or so. Shortly after that, we arrived at Silver's place where my blindfold was removed. I guess Silver's house must lie some distance off the road near Storpington village and not in the actual village itself.'

'Good,' said Sterling. 'That's just the sort of information I need. We'll be driving down to the south coast tomorrow, setting off in the morning and arriving sometime in the early afternoon. What I suggest is that we hole up in the village pub for a few hours until Debbie and Orlando have located the gate and cinder track leading to Martello Towers. That way, we won't attract any attention.'

'Why don't we just ask directions?' interrupted Gordon, reclaiming his shotgun from the table. Sterling sensed his apprehension and immediately telegraphed it to Joe before replying:

'We could, but I don't think it would work. Silver's most likely paid the locals off or put a glamour on them. Either way, he's part of the local landowning establishment so nobody would dare say a word against him. No, we'll have to rely on Debbie and Orlando here to do a bit of scouting around the neighbourhood in the car. We can't risk asking anyone in the pub. The landlord and his cronies would only get suspicious and raise the alarm. They would also be able to stand as witnesses if the matter ever came to court.'

'Nice one, Sterling,' confided Skinner. 'You still haven't lost your touch.'

'Thanks, Jerry – I'm please you think so. Now, has anyone else got any more questions?'

'Yes… I have,' responded Father Dominic, still clutching his rosary. 'What am I going to do? I haven't got any weapons to speak of and I'm only allowed to use violence in self-defence. I would be a liability.'

'Oh, I shouldn't worry too much about that, Father,' replied Sterling with a mischievous grin. 'In fact, if the truth were known, you probably have the most powerful weapon of us all at your command.'

'And what might that be?' said the priest, dumbfounded.

'Why, your faith of course, Father Dominic. Your faith.'

Nineteen

'So, this is Lower Storpington,' exclaimed Cassidy, getting off the bike and stretching his legs.

'That's what it said on the sign as we came in,' replied Sterling, glancing around.

'Not much of a village then. More of a large hamlet really, but at least it's got a pub. It's called The Square and Compass in case you hadn't noticed. Looks like you were right about the Masonic influence, Sterling. This place practically reeks of it.'

She wasn't listening. The journey down from London had taken longer than she had anticipated and several members of the gang had yet to arrive.

'What's happened to Spike?' she said, turning to Joe.

'He had a bit of trouble with his Yamaha near Ashford and had to pull in. Spark plugs, more than likely. Don't worry. He's fairly handy when it comes to engines so he shouldn't be too long.'

Sterling gave a curt nod. 'And the car? Where's Debbie, Orlando, Skinner and the priest?'

'Dunno. We got separated on the motorway, but at least they've got your map and a Sat Nav on board, so I expect they'll find their way here soon enough. Anyway, here's Spike now. We can ask him if he's seen them.'

The gang watched as Spike brought his sputtering machine to a halt outside the inn. Switching off the engine, he removed his helmet and brushed his hair back over his head.

'That was close,' he said with an expression of relief on his face.

'What was close?' asked Joe.

'A gang of Outlaws. About five of them, riding some expensive-looking bikes. They turned off back there at the crossroads heading in the direction of Hastings.'

'So?'

'They were wearing their colours, boss...'

'That doesn't mean anything. We haven't had a beef with the Outlaws in years, so what is there to worry about?'

'I'm not sure, Joe. They usually stick to their own turf up in the Midlands and Nottinghamshire. I don't know what they're doing down here.'

'Ships that pass in the night, Spike. Blow it out of your arse – it's probably nothing.'

'If you say so, boss, but it's a bit strange all the same.'

'I agree,' put in Gordon. 'We'd best be on our guard.'

Sterling listened but made no immediate comment. If the Outlaws gave them any trouble, she would deal with the situation as she knew best. Until then, it was better to put the matter out of her mind. At the moment, her little battle group had other problems. 'Let's get into the pub,' she said. 'We can wait for Skinner and the others there. It'll be dark soon and I don't want to waste any more time.'

They could tell they weren't welcome almost as soon as they walked inside. The pub had the sort of interior which seemed to resist change with a grudge. In fact, it was so archaic that Queen Victoria would have felt at home there. Low ceiling rafters and a shifty-looking landlord with a Dickensian moustache, the place looked as if it hadn't had a makeover since 1898.

'It's just like something out of a Christmas card,' declared Gordon, casting his eyes over the room. 'Let's grab ourselves a table over there. Mine's a lager for whoever's buying.'

'No alcohol,' said Sterling firmly. 'Soft drinks only. We might have a long wait of it here and I don't want any of you getting yourselves spannered before the job. You can all have a Jack Daniel's before we leave, but only one mind you.'

The men nodded. 'Looks like it's on top,' muttered Spike in Gordon's ear. 'I'm glad I brought my knife along with me.'

'Same goes for my shotgun,' whispered Gordon, nudging Spike's arm. 'Take a look at the landlord. He's been watching us like a hawk ever since we came in.'

The landlord glanced down as Sterling and Joe approached the bar. As they drew nearer, he looked up and made eye contact. 'And what will you be having?' he asked with the kind of smile that wouldn't have looked out of place in a 1970's Hammer horror film.

'Lime and soda with ice for me—,' said Joe, '—and the same all round?' he continued, turning to the others.

'I'll have a coke,' exclaimed Whiskey Pete, sitting down at the table by the fireside. 'Me too,' said Keg, towering above the others. 'I can't be doing with lime and soda.'

'Come far?' enquired the landlord as he prepared the drinks, helped by his bartender.

'From London,' replied Sterling, scanning his aura. *He's human,* she thought. *Silver hasn't turned him yet. Maybe the whole village is clean. Either that or he's covering his tracks well.*

'What part of London?' the landlord continued, seeming to probe her further.

'Blackheath,' put in Joe. He was lying of course. Any mention of Harlow in connection with a gang of Hells Angels would have alerted Silver to their presence in the village. The innkeeper may just have been making polite conversation, but Joe wasn't taking any chances. Paying for the drinks, he took his change, then both he and Sterling wandered over to the table where the rest of the gang were seated waiting for Skinner to arrive in the car. As they waited, Spike and Sub played a game of dominoes, while the others chatted among themselves, casting occasional glances at the bar to make sure they weren't being overheard.

'So, you think we can pull this job off?' said Gordon, confiding in Joe.

Joe sensed his associate was nervous and quickly moved to calm his fears. 'I don't see why not,' he said confidently. 'What's your opinion on the matter, Sterling?'

The vampire sipped her drink slowly. 'If we maintain the element of surprise, then Silver won't know what's hit him.'

'How do you know that?' continued Gordon, edgily. 'This is Silver's manor after all. We don't know what muscle he's got to call on. Even that twat over there behind the bar could be in his pocket for all we know.'

'Don't you think I haven't taken the matter into consideration already,' she snapped, bearing her teeth at him.

'Fuck me, it's true! You really are a vampire!' exclaimed Gordon, sitting back in his chair with shock.

'Did you think I was kidding?' Sterling growled, baring her fangs once more. She was about to pull off her sunglasses and reveal her eyes when Joe stopped her. 'No, Sterling! Not here. Not now—'

Cassidy nodded in agreement and Gordon noticed the gesture.

'What's it got to do with you, Cassidy. I should have capped you when I had the chance.'

'That's enough!' hissed Joe, glancing over his shoulder then back to Gordon. 'We need to keep this thing together— understood?'

'Fuck this. I'm going outside for a breath of air,' Gordon replied before getting up from his seat and storming out of the pub.

'Follow him, Joe,' said Sterling sharply. 'I think he's beginning to crack.'

Joe nodded and ordered Keg to follow Gordon out of the room and keep an eye on him. Satisfied the situation was under control, the rest of the gang settled back and continued their vigil by the fireside. There was no way Gordon was going to try anything stupid with a beast like Keg breathing down his neck.

'Okay, so what's the plan?' enquired Ronnie, turning to Joe.

Joe looked at Sterling and then back to Ronnie. 'Well, first we have to find Silver's exact location. We'll need Debbie and Orlando to do that.'

'And then?'

'And then, we break into Silver's place after dark and settle the fucker's hash for good.'

'You mean we're going to do him?'

'Yes,' cut in Sterling, 'I thought you already knew that.'

'I... I did, but...'

'But what?'

'Well, it's like Gordon said, what if Silver's got loads of back-up with him?'

'That's why I've brought you lot down here, Ronnie... Oh, and four silver bullets as well.'

The middle of Ronnie's brow creased upwards in a furrow as the truth began to dawn. 'Is Jimmy Silver one of them too, boss?' he murmured, his gaze flickering momentarily in Sterling's direction.

Joe nodded slowly, a gesture that was confirmed when Cassidy added: 'Welcome to hell, Ronnie. I didn't know what Jimmy was either until Sterling told me. Just think of it as a learning experience and you'll be fine. Anyway, I think I can hear a car coming. I'll just go outside and take a look. Won't be long.'

Heads were turned and necks were craned in the direction of the window as Cassidy walked to the door. A bitterly cold wind blew in as he opened it, causing the flames in the fireplace to weave and twist around the burning logs in the grate. Pretty soon, he returned with the news.

'It's them,' he proclaimed, popping his head round the door. 'They're just getting some stuff out of the boot.'

'Good,' replied Sterling. 'There's a few things I need to see to. You stay here with the boys, while me and Joe go outside and have a word with them. Tell Keg to bring Gordon back inside. We don't want him catching cold as well.'

Skinner and Orlando were out of the car when Sterling and Joe appeared. 'You're late,' she said. 'What happened?'

'We got lost,' replied Skinner. 'The old map you gave us wasn't very accurate and the car's Sat Nav managed to lead us to the wrong village. Debbie managed to work it all out though, so we made it in the end. Not too late, are we?'

'Almost,' said Joe. 'We were beginning to get worried. Anyway, you've brought the stuff with you, I hope?'

'Yes. A couple of two-way radios and a pair of infrared binoculars like you said. I got them from a mate of mine I used to be in the army with. They're old kit left over from the Cold War, but they still work.'

'And what about the holy water?' enquired Sterling, glancing into the boot of the car. 'Where's that?'

'It's with Father Dominic in the back seat,' replied Skinner. 'He wouldn't let it out of his sight for some reason.'

Sterling looked in the side window. Instinctively, the priest turned away. He was sitting hunched up with the plastic container on his knees and he wasn't about to part with it easily.

'Ah-h-h, but isn't that sweet,' she said, regarding the priest with a smile. 'He's looking after my holy water for me.'

'What are you planning on doing with it, you fucking bitch?' exclaimed Dominic, looking at her through the half-open window.

'You'll see when we get to Silver's place, Father. Talking of which, isn't it about time you set off in the car with Skinner and the others to search for Martello Towers?'

'Not necessary,' cut in Debbie, stepping out of the front passenger door with a grin. 'We passed it earlier on when we were driving around trying to make sense of your map.'

'Where is it?'

'About two miles down the road in that direction,' replied the young shoplifter, making a backward gesture with her thumb.

'You certain of that?'

'As sure as I can be. It's got the name, Martello Towers written in white paint on a bit of plywood attached to a five-bar gate, so I reckon it must be the place.'

'Excellent!' complimented Sterling. 'Then it's about time I bought us all that shot of Jack Daniels I promised. I think we're going to need it.'

***

'That's the entrance.'

'Where?'

'Straight up ahead to the right.'

It was Debbie talking to Skinner who was driving. Cassidy was sitting in the back seat squeezed up between Father Dominic and Orlando. They'd been driving down the road for about fifteen minutes with the rest of the gang following on behind on their motorcycles.

'Slow down,' exclaimed Debbie, raising her hand.

'What's up?' said Skinner lifting his foot off the accelerator and gearing down.

'There's some headlights up ahead. Looks like they're coming our way.'

'So?'

'I don't know. Just a hunch I guess. Looks like they're turning into the lane where we want to be. The gate must have been left open for them, whoever they are.'

Skinner and the others watched as a long, black stretch limo accompanied by five motorcycle outriders negotiated the turning and slunk off down the lane without indicating.

'Fuck me,' declared Skinner, 'that was some car. You reckon it was Silver?'

'Could be. We'd best pull over here and have a word with Sterling. Flash your hazards and warn the others we're stopping.'

'I can smell the sea, boss,' said Spike, removing his helmet. 'We must be near the coast.'

'Yeah, you're right,' observed Joe thoughtfully. 'Just a minute. I'm going to have a word with Skinner and ask him why we've stopped.'

Joe walked toward the car with Sterling. As they approached, Skinner wound down the driver's window. 'What's the problem?' he asked.

'Black limousine. Turned in up ahead. They were flanked by five bikers. Looks like an escort.'

'This is the place then?'

'Debbie thinks so.'

'What do *you* think, Skinner?' asked Sterling, cutting in. It was dark and the branches of the trees that lined either side of the road were black against the winter sky.

'I reckon it could be. Looks different in the dark though.'

'What about the bikers?'

'They're heavy. Silver's called in some muscle by the look of it.'

'Outlaws?'

'More than likely. I only counted five of them but there may well be more in the area.'

'What do we do?'

Sterling thought for a moment, carefully examining the situation. Just then, another car came down the road in the same direction and turned into the lane.

'Looks like quite a party,' observed Joe, following the path of the second limousine with his gaze.

'I wasn't expecting this,' replied Sterling, with a look of concern.

'So, how do you want to handle it then?'

'We follow them in,' said the vampire at last. 'That way we won't attract any attention. If Silver's got any of his spotters in the grounds, they'll just think we're another convoy approaching and ignore us. Come on, let's go. What have we got to lose?'

***

'Good evening, Clarice,' said Silver as the tall, aristocratic woman with dark hair and a crimson evening gown entered the hallway of his elegant mansion. 'I do hope you had a pleasant journey down from London.'

'Tedious – and I could have done without the motorcycle escort.'

'Do accept my apologies,' Silver replied, 'but one can't be too careful these days. There's been a spate of carjackings in the neighbourhood recently and I didn't want you taking any chances.'

'Highway robbers, Jimmy? I remember seeing one hanged once. Can't do that anymore, can we?'

'Indeed not, Clarice. Please allow me to take your coat. I do so enjoy these little annual get-togethers of our club, don't you?'

'I was here at the founding, Jimmy. I couldn't very well miss the bicentennial and neither could my partner, Lady Cora... and here she comes now.'

'Ah, still together after all these years,' oozed Silver warmly as he regarded the smaller of the two patrician ladies who had just entered the hallway from outside. 'Please allow me to take your wrap, Lady Cora. Drinks are being served in the reception room. I'm just going to welcome some of the other guests, then we can all have a proper chat later.'

The two women nodded and walked off down the hall arm in arm with each other. Their flesh was deathly pale in marked contrast to the vibrant colour of their gowns. Exactly how old these two women were was anyone's guess, but they couldn't have been much under two hundred years of age at a conservative estimate. Silver watched as they made their way into the reception room where a small crowd had already gathered. *Still as young as ever,* he thought. *They both chose to be what they are... Didn't want the party to stop, I suppose. Well, who can blame them...*

***

'I don't remember this,' exclaimed Cassidy, stepping out of the car.

'Sand dunes,' observed Joe. 'We're lost.'

'Can't be,' put in Sterling, looking at Debbie. 'You're sure that this was the right gate we went through back there?'

'I'm certain of it. There was a monkey puzzle tree to the left as we entered. It's the same tree we saw when we were driving around looking for the village earlier on – no doubt about it.'

'Then we'll just have to keep searching until we find Silver's place. It can't be that far surely.'

'Being dark doesn't help,' remarked Sub. 'I can't see a bleeding thing up ahead.'

Just then, Sterling remembered the infrared binoculars they'd brought. 'Debbie,' she said, 'climb up to the top of one of those sand dunes and scan the woods with these binoculars. Something's bound to show up.'

'Okay. Will do—'

As Debbie ascended the dunes, the sound of several motorcycle engines could be heard coming from somewhere off in the distance. Since the gang's own engines were either idling or turned off completely, it was more than apparent that the noise was coming from another gang of bikers, and whoever it was, they were closing in fast.

'It's the Outlaws!' exclaimed Spike. 'Looks like they've turned back on us.'

'Dammit,' growled Joe. 'Quick – hide the bikes now! We can take them on as they come round the bend.'

***

'Quite a gathering this year, Silver old chap. You've done us proud again I see.'

It was Sir Roger Bullivant who spoke. Both he and Silver were standing talking beside the ornate marble fireplace in Silver's reception room as the other guests mingled.

'I'm pleased you think so, Roger. Unfortunately, I was unable to contact Count Anzo this year.'

'Oh really. What's the problem? He was always a regular visitor to these little shindigs of yours.'

'Some left-wing anarchists caught up with him in Vienna and I'm afraid he's...'

'Dead?'

'Yes. Decapitated with a silver machete. Nasty business. You can see why I have to employ so much security down here on the south coast.'

'Indeed. A fellow can't be too careful these days. I blame the French Revolution myself. Gave the underclass too many ideas above their station in my opinion.'

'Mmm, yes. Highly regrettable, but unfortunately it's the world we all have to live in now. Anyway, how is the banking industry these days, Roger?'

'Mustn't grumble, Silver. I've made a small fortune this year. Closed down over two hundred branches in England alone and we've got more planned for next spring.'

'So I've heard. Some of my tenants were complaining that they have to make a fifteen-mile round trip just to access their bank.'

'Can't they use the village post office?'

'No, they can't. That's been closed down as well.'

'Too bad. I expect they'll adapt over time. This wine is excellent by the way, Silver. What is it?'

'It's a claret. Special import via my wine merchant. Can you guess its origin?'

'Hmm,' soothed Roger, savouring the dark aroma of the wine as he swirled it around in his glass. 'Is it a Burgundian?'

'Bravo! I knew you would get it. Oh, and here comes Cora and Clarice, looking as beautiful as ever—'

'Sir Roger,' announced Clarice, introducing herself with a smile. 'How are you doing these days? Always a pleasure to see you.'

'The pleasure is mine, your ladyship; oh, and of course your lovely wife, Cora. I remember when we first met at one of the Duchess of Devonshire's parties in London back in 1750. You turned up dressed as a rather handsome young boy I seem to recall.'

'Yes – three-cornered hat, fancy waistcoat and knee breeches. I turned quite a few heads that night I can tell you.'

'How can I forget. Ye gods! But how I yearn for those times.'

'Reminiscence doesn't become you, Roger. You don't look a day over forty... but pray tell me... how old is it that you are *exactly?*'

Bending towards her, Roger whispered conspiratorially into Clarice's ear and her eyes opened wide with surprise; *'No-o-o,* surely not? That would make you almost as old as Uncle Felix.'

'You're probably right, Clarice, but don't let on that I was around when old King Charles was still on the throne. It doesn't do to brag about one's survival skills.'

'So, you would remember the Great Fire of London then?'

'Remember it? I bloody well started it! Biggest insurance scam in history. How do you think I got so damn rich in the first place? Of course, I've made and lost several fortunes since then, but that's all water under the bridge. The banking industry is where I do business now. Bloody marvellous it is!'

Spontaneous laughter erupted from the little group gathered around the fireplace as Roger continued to amuse them all with his historical anecdotes. He was just about to give a graphic account of his vigorous opposition to the extension of the right to vote when another guest entered the room and walked over to where they were all standing.

'Hugo!' exclaimed Silver. 'I'm so glad you could make it. Do take a glass of wine and mingle. Roger was just entertaining us with one of his old stories.'

'Not his opposition to the vote again?' said Hugo, a bluff, well-proportioned man with a whisper of grey around his temples.

'Shame he didn't succeed,' put in Clarice, banging her wine glass down on the mantelpiece with a smack.

'Clarice!' admonished Silver wryly, 'we all live in a democracy now. Things have changed a lot since our day.'

'More's the pity,' she continued with venom. 'They'll be demanding eternal life next!'

'I'm sure that privilege shall always remain ours and ours alone, dear heart,' replied Silver with a gleam. 'Would you care for some more wine?'

Clarice took another goblet of Riesling from the servitor and sipped it irritably. It was clear to everyone gathered around the fireplace that something was bothering her and they wondered what it could be.

'Well', continued Silver, turning to Hugo once more, 'I hear you've moved into the property business recently. Had any luck?'

'Can't complain,' Hugo replied, smiling at his host. 'I bought three low-rise apartment blocks in South London last year and forced the existing tenants out by hiking up their rents. Sold the lot for a cool twenty million, without so much as a whimper of protest from the local council.'

'Ah, that old trick. I used to do a bit of that myself back in the 1840s. It's good to know some things don't change in this country of ours—'

Silver was about to amuse everyone with one of his Victorian anecdotes when his words were cut short by the sound of several loud cracks and bangs that seemed to have their origins coming from somewhere outside in the grounds.

'What was that?' exclaimed Hugo in surprise.

'Oh, it's probably just one of my groundsmen out shooting pheasants on the estate,' Silver responded, taking a sip of wine.

'What! – at this time of the night?' put in Hugo, who happened to be quite a keen sportsman himself. 'Seems to me like you've got poachers, Jimmy—'

-DRR-R-R-R... DRR-R-R-R-R... DRR-R-R-R-R-R-R-R...

'—And do your groundsmen usually shoot with automatic weapons? That sounded very much like a machine pistol to me, Silver old chap.'

'It's nothing, Hugo, I can assure you... Ah, but here comes Tarrou now. It must be time to begin our meal.'

'Dinner will be served in approximately ten minutes time, Sir James,' announced the tall, well-manicured Nigerian with exquisite diction. 'Shall I light the candles now?'

'Yes, if you would be so kind, Tarrou. Thank you.'

Silver waited for his henchman to depart before tapping on his wineglass to bring the room to order.

'Before we all repair to the dining room,' he said, 'I have a couple of important announcements that I wish to make... As some of you may be aware, our dear friend and associate, Count Anzo, passed away this year, the victim of a cowardly and brutal attack by a gang of anarchists while he was in the process of taking his annual holiday in Vienna. Rest assured, that my agents in that city will be making vigorous enquiries among the population in an effort to track down these miscreants, and when they finally do, then I can promise you that whoever it was who was responsible for Count Anzo's murder will be most summarily and brutally dealt with!'

Having delivered the first part of his address, Silver waited for the murmuring in the room to die down before broaching his next piece of news.

'On a lighter note, my friends, you should be made aware that we shall be entertaining a special mystery guest at our table this evening – one who is not entirely a stranger to our ranks, but who has lately been absent for quite some time. I shall not reveal to you as yet who this mystery guest is, save to assure you that her appearance here tonight should prove quite a surprise to you all. Now, when you have all finished with your introductions, pray follow me into the dining room where a sumptuous feast awaits our pleasure.'

***

Debbie looked down in horror at the scene below

From her vantage point behind the crest of the sand dunes, she watched as the gun battle raged on between the two rival gangs of bikers, neither side giving any ground or backing down to the other. Earlier on in the fight, Joe had ordered Skinner to take Cassidy, Orlando and the priest to a place of safety while he and Gordon Dyer held the Outlaws off with their revolver and shotgun. Now, as the bullets whined over their heads, they weren't too sure they could keep up their suppressing fire long enough for Spike, Sterling and Sub to get round the back of their opponents and do what they had to do.

'There were only five of them a moment ago,' said Gordon, breaking his shotgun open to reload. 'Where'd those other two fuckers come from?'

Joe wasn't listening. Ramming another six bullets into the chamber of his Webley, he aimed a shot into the darkness, the old revolver pulling to the side as he fired. Then it was Gordon's turn, his shotgun blast tearing a yellow gash through the night as he discharged his weapon at something moving between the dunes. Almost immediately, there was a yell and he saw what looked like a pair of boots with legs attached to them flailing in the air as the man went down.

'I think I've hit someone, Joe. Over there, between the dunes. That leaves six of the bas—'

An incoming round struck one of the parked bikes and bounced off its front forks with a moan. Joe felt the breath of its path on his cheek just before it hit.

'That was fucking close,' he exclaimed. 'I hope Sterling wades in and finishes the job soon. I think I'm running out of ammunition.'

DRR-R-R-R... DRR-R-R-R-R... DRR-R-R-R-R-R...

'There goes that machine-pistol again, Joe. Looks like Santa's brought someone a Mac-10 for Christmas!'

Again, Joe wasn't listening, all his attention now being focussed on the gun battle going on around him. 'Where's Whiskey Pete?' he said. 'Has somebody stamped his card, or what?'

'Dunno, Joe. I last saw him and Keg moving off in Sterling's direction about five minutes ago. He said he was going to deal with that machine gunner, but obviously he hasn't.'

'Well, I hope he gets a move on. This old Webley of mine is fucking crap in a fire fight...'

Debbie flinched as another stray round whizzed over her head. More accustomed to blagging the wealthier shops and boutiques of London's West End, she'd decided that suicide missions weren't exactly her cup of tea and was almost on the point of making a run for it when something caught her eye. Bringing up her binoculars, she scanned the battle scene. In spite of all the chaos and confusion, she could just about make out the figure of Whiskey Pete and another man she took to be Keg edging their way on all fours towards where she'd last seen the guy with the machine-pistol letting off his rounds—

DRR-R-R... DRR-R-R-R... DRR-R-R-R-R...!

There it came again. A relentless barrage of hot lead describing an arc of fire roughly in the direction of where Joe and

Gordon's muzzle flashes were coming from, pinning both men down so neither of them could move. But where were Sterling and the others? In vain, she panned her binoculars to the left and right of the battlefront but saw nothing except a terrified rabbit as it scuttled across the road in an effort to escape the noise. *I know exactly how you feel,* she thought. *I want to be out of here as well.*

Turning round, Debbie scanned the area below where she'd last seen Jerry Skinner and the car. Peering through her binoculars, she could see the shape of the vehicle silhouetted against the sand along with four figures crouching down behind it. *That must be Skinner, along with Orlando, Cassidy and the priest,* she reasoned. *They're pinned down too. What the hell can I do?'*

It was then that she had a bright idea. Without pausing to think about it, she rolled away from the crest of the dune and began running down its sandy flanks towards the car where her four companions were taking cover. If this plan of hers didn't get them out of the mess they were all in then she couldn't think of anything else that would...

'Why don't Whiskey Pete and Keg get a move on,' exclaimed Sub. 'That guy with the machine-pistol needs taking out.'

'I reckon he's firing a Scorpion, myself,' added, Spike, nudging Sterling in the arm where she lay. 'Why don't you go over there and put one in his napper with that Mauser pistol of yours. I've heard vampires can see better in the dark.'

'Not funny, Spike,' replied Sterling. 'In any case, he's got himself too well concealed and I can't get his range. Just leave it up to Keg and Whiskey Pete. I'm sure they both know what they're doing.'

'Yeah, but according to the movies, real vampires can only be killed by silver bullets and stuff like that.'

'So, what are you saying, Spike?'

'So, why don't you just walk over there and do to him whatever it is that vampires do?'

'Because I've been shot by a machine-pistol before, Spike, and I don't want a repeat performance. In any case, how do I know he's not packing silver ammunition?'

'Uh – oh, right. I see what you mean. So, we wait until he has to reload and then Pete and Keg move in?'

'They won't even have to do that, assuming they can see him.'

'How do you mean?'

'Pete's got a grenade on him.'

'Fuck me! No way. He didn't tell me that!'

'Well he has, so shut up and keep your head down. It's only a matter of time before he gets the opportunity to use it. Ronnie's been shadowing that machine gunner as well, so one of them's bound to get lucky sooner or later.'

'Hello – it's me!'

Cassidy almost jumped out of his skin when he discovered the little blond shoplifter crouching down beside him behind the car.

'Debbie, what the fuck were you thinking of running down the dunes like that? You could have got yourself killed.'

'No way – I'm too quick for them. Ain't that right, Skinner?'

'What are you doing down here, Debbs?' was all Skinner said in reply. 'I thought Sterling told you to keep watch up there on the dunes with the binoculars.'

'I was, but I've had an idea.'

'Oh yeah – like what?'

'Like turning on your effing car lights in the direction of that twat with the machine gun over there. That way we can render him temporarily blind and pick him out for Pete and Keg to deal with.'

'You think it will work?'

'Have you got any better suggestions, Jerry? At least it's better than just sitting here on our arses waiting to be picked off. Wait a moment while I call Sterling on the two-way radio, then you can get in the car and turn the headlights up to full blast. That should do the trick...'

'Who was that on the radio?' Spike whispered, still keeping his head down among the dunes with Sterling and Sub.

'It was Debbie,' replied Sterling, looking in the direction where she'd last heard the rattle of machine gun fire. It was evident she was waiting for something to happen.

'I can't see a damn thing over there,' declared Sub.

'Me neither,' echoed Spike. 'Maybe that geezer with the machine-pistol's changed his position and he's creeping up behind us even as we speak.'

'Oh, I shouldn't worry about that,' put in Sterling without bothering to look over her shoulder.

'Why?'

'You'll see in a moment. Just keep your eyes on that pine tree over there. That's where I last saw his muzzle flash.'

Everyone tensed, lying flat on the ground as the moments ticked by. All around them was silence, except for the sound of waves breaking on the shore and the rhythmic pulse of their beating hearts. Just then, Sterling's two-way radio crackled into life once more, giving away their position like a pointing finger.

'Damn!' hissed Spike. 'That's torn it. He'll spot us for certain this time.'

'Get ready,' said Sterling, ignoring him. 'One... two... three... *now!*'

Suddenly, the whole scene lit up as the car's headlights raked the area with their beams, catching anyone who was in an exposed position in their glare.

'Throw your grenade, Whiskey!' yelled Sterling. 'Throw your fucking grenade at the pine tree! Just do it!'

Watching from his car window, Skinner saw Whiskey Pete rise up from a depression in the sand and throw something in the direction of the nearest tree. Two or three seconds passed and then there was a deafening boom followed by total silence. The machine gun chatter had stopped, but still no one moved.

'You reckon it's done for him?' said Keg.

'No,' replied Pete, 'but he's out of it. That was a stun-grenade I threw at him and it's hit him almost square on.'

More time passed and still nothing moved out there on the beach. Then suddenly, and to everyone's surprise, men began rising up out of the sand with their hands raised high above their heads.

'They're surrendering,' declared Gordon. 'We've won—'

'Careful,' warned Joe. 'I've only counted four so far. There were six of them, remember.'

Gordon looked on as another two of the men appeared out of the sand. Now, Whiskey Pete and Keg got up and walked towards the surrendering men, followed by Sterling, Spike and Sub. Of Ronnie Frinton there was no sign.

'Where'd you lot come from?' said Spike addressing one of the Outlaws who he took to be their leader. Sterling said nothing, but watched the six men intently.

'We're from Birmingham,' the man answered gruffly, a short, stocky individual with greying hair and a bad soul. Another man was standing beside him. He had only one hand raised and the other was hovering behind his leader's back.

'How's your machine gunner?' enquired Sub, pointing to one of the men who was having trouble standing up and in need of support from his comrades.

'I guess he'll live,' replied the Outlaw's chief, 'but he won't be hearing all that well for a while. Silver said nothing about you lot being here.'

'He wouldn't,' put in Sterling, still keeping her eyes on the man at his side. She knew what he was about to do and tensed herself in readiness to block him. Then, just as the man made to pull a gun out from the back of his leader's trouser belt, there was a flash of steel in the air and a knife buried itself in his right shoulder causing him to drop his weapon. Sterling spun round to see Ronnie Frinton standing about two metres behind her with a broad smile on his face. 'Nice one, Ronnie,' she said. 'You beat me to it.' The wounded man stared at Ronnie in disbelief, then very slowly sank to the ground as his knees gave way beneath him in shock.

'That was stupid of you,' said Joe, walking over to join the crowd. Behind him came Gordon, levelling his shotgun at the Outlaws to cover Joe. Their leader just shrugged and looked away.

'So, what are we gonna do with them, boss?' enquired Gordon.

'I don't rightly know. What do you think?'

Gordon wasn't sure and looked to Sterling. 'Might as well let them go,' she said coolly. 'They won't be giving us any more trouble in that state. Take their guns off them and send them on their way. I've still got matters to settle with Silver—'

As Gordon led the men away to their bikes, Sterling looked at Joe. 'That was too easy,' she confided in a low voice so the others wouldn't hear. 'What do you think?'

'I'm not sure. I mean, they put up a pretty convincing fight of it.'

'Yes, Joe... *convincing* – but not convincing enough in my opinion. That guy with the machine-pistol could easily have taken us all out. Why didn't he?'

Joe thought for a moment. 'You reckon it was some kind of a trick?'

'Could be. It's almost as if Silver is drawing us all into his lair like a spider luring flies into its web.'

'A trap?'

'Possibly. He already knows what we're capable of, so he's not taking any chances.'

Just then, there came a loud whistle followed by a shout of triumph. It was Spike returning with his captured prize. 'Look what I've found,' he announced with glee. 'It's a Scorpion machine-pistol and it's still got a full clip of ammunition in the magazine. I could take on all of hell with this.'

'You may well have to,' declared Skinner arriving with Debbie, Orlando and the priest. Cassidy followed on behind, looking decidedly unhappy with the way things were turning out.

'How do you mean?' answered Spike, his expression turning sallow.

'Oh, nothing. Just an observation, that's all.'

'Well, keep it that way,' snapped Sterling, not wanting the others spooked out too early in the game. Both she and Skinner knew from bitter experience what they could be walking into and realised that some of them might not be coming back.

'So, what's the plan then?' enquired Joe, rubbing his hands together with enthusiasm. Buoyed up by the victory of his gang over the Outlaws, he was just about ready for anything.

'First, we do a reconnaissance of the grounds and locate the position of Silver's house,' the vampire replied, checking her pistol before turning to young Debbie. 'What could you see from your position on top of the dunes, Debbs?'

'Silver's place ain't that far, Sterling. It's about a third of a mile down the road from here.'

'Good. You stay here in the car with Orlando and Father Dominic while the rest of us walk on ahead and approach the house on foot.'

'Wait a minute!' exclaimed Cassidy, more than a little alarmed. 'You mean to say I'm going as well?'

'I don't see why not,' Sterling answered with a smile. 'You used to be one of Silver's men, so you might as well be present when I kill him.'

***

It wasn't at all what they were expecting.

For one thing, the front door was standing wide open beneath the canopied portico, and for another, all the house lights were on, accompanied by the sound of a Mozart symphony being played from somewhere deep inside the building.

'This is too easy,' remarked Joe as they approached the house. A small fleet of limousines stood on either side of the portico. Cassidy counted nine in total, including Silver's own BMW saloon parked up against the ivy-festooned garden wall. Evidently, some kind of a meeting was in progress.

Spike squinted up at the main security light. 'I'm not having that in my eyes,' he said, and moved round until he stood at a different angle to the door and several paces away from where Joe was standing with Sterling and the rest of the gang.

'How are we going to do this, Sterling?' asked Cassidy nervously.

'Simple. We split up into two separate groups as we enter the house. You follow me together with Joe and Skinner, and we make for wherever the noise is coming from. I have a feeling Silver is hosting one of his famous supper parties in the dining room.'

'And, like we're invited too…?'

'No, but I've a feeling plenty of other people have been, judging by all those motors parked up in the driveway.'

'What—you mean, people like you, Sterling?'

'Yes,' the vampire replied sharply, 'people like me. I hope that doesn't worry you, Stuart, because it sure as hell worries me.'

Cassidy tensed and swallowed hard. Things were not turning out quite the way he had expected. In his mind, he had believed that Sterling was going to hit the place with a full-on assault using Spike with his newly acquired machine-pistol to rake all the rooms with suppressing fire while she went in hard with her Mauser and shot Silver dead. Instead, what he was now confronted with was a plan to infiltrate the house by stealth in which he was about to play the starring role. The very thought of it horrified him and he quickly made to change her mind.

'Should we be doing this, Sterling?' he said... 'I mean, wouldn't it be better to get Spike to clear the place out first?'

'What, and risk losing the only element of surprise we have left? I don't think so, Stuart. In any case, we'll have Spike and the others at our backs to make sure we're not attacked from behind. Who knows what manner of creatures could be lurking inside this old house.'

'Such as what?' enquired Ronnie, apprehensively.

'Oh, you wouldn't believe it if I told you, Ronaldo. I've seen some pretty scary things in my time – things that are best not talked about even in jest.'

'You mean like in all those, H.P. Lovecraft stories an' that?'

'Yes, I think you've hit the nail right on the head there, Ronnie.'

'Uh-huh... I see. Well, in that case I'm not going in the house then, am I?'

'So, you'd prefer to stay out here on your own and take your chances with whatever Silver's got prowling around in these grounds then, would you?'

Ronnie thought for a moment, carefully weighing up his chances of survival. 'Okay,' he said reluctantly, 'I'll follow you all in, but I'm not too happy about it.'

'Neither am I,' said Joe, 'but what option do we have? Silver's fucked us over so I reckon we owe him one.'

'Pretty much my sentiments as well,' added Skinner. 'I've been wanting to leave my boot up his arse for a long time, and now I've got my chance. Come on, let's do the cunt!'

Sterling and Joe entered the house ahead of all the others and took a look round. The massive interior of the mansion was dark and gloomy in spite of all the lights being on and seemed to consist, for the most part, of a series of architectural impossibilities designed to confuse the onlooker and introduce into the mind of any intruder an intense feeling of dread and despair. Apart from the sound of the Mozart symphony coming from somewhere up the hallway, there didn't appear to be anyone around.

'We split up here,' she said in a low voice. 'Spike, you go with Whiskey Pete and the others and reconnoitre the place while I go on ahead with Skinner, Joe and Cassidy. Once we've secured the hall, a couple of you can venture upstairs and see whatever is lurking up there. If the place is clear, come back down and follow us up the hallway. We should have found what it is we're looking for by then.'

'How will we know?'

'From the sound of gunfire more than likely,' the vampire replied. 'Now, no more questions you lot. We need to take Silver by surprise.'

As they set off down the hall, Cassidy was gripped by a strong sense of foreboding. The house just wasn't quite how he remembered it from his last visit. For one thing, the hallway had seemed a whole lot shorter than he recalled and it had opened out into a conservatory on the right-hand side situated almost immediately opposite the main staircase to the left. The staircase was still there, that much was true, but everything else seemed oddly out of place somehow and of the conservatory there was no sign.

'What's up, Cassidy?' enquired Joe, 'you don't look very happy. Is something the matter?'

'Not really, it's just that I don't remember being here, that's all...'

'How do you mean?'

'The hallway—it's changed.'

'It's your perception of it that's at fault, Stuart. The last time you were here, you probably didn't take everything in. It's human selective memory at work, I shouldn't wonder.'

'Where'd you learn a phrase like that, Joe?' put in Skinner, not a little surprised by his friend's use of language.

'What phrase?'

'*Selective memory*... Where'd you pick that up from then?'

'At university,' answered Joe as if it were common knowledge.

'You never told me you'd been to university. When was that?'

'Early 1980s. I took a BA degree in human psychology. The working class could still do things like that back then.'

'Well, fuck me, Joe; you never told me that before. Hey, Sterling, Joe sez he's been to university.'

'So have I, Skinner. I studied music apparently. Now, shut up. We're getting closer...'

'There it goes again,' announced Spike, sensing the vibration of the floor beneath his feet. 'It does that every time we walk through a door.'

'It's your imagination,' said Keg. 'I can't feel a thing.'

'That's cos your feet are so big,' replied Sub. 'This floor is definitely vibrating. I can feel it too.'

Spike and his group seemed to have been wandering through the house for ages without having encountered anything remotely dangerous or even marginally threatening. Now, the prospect of a vibrating floor did not seem to worry them unduly and they soon resumed their journey down the hallway as if nothing had happened.

'Where's Sterling and Joe?' said Gordon, looking puzzled.

'I don't know,' answered Spike. 'I thought I saw them going up the hallway only a few minutes ago.'

'A few minutes? According to my watch it's almost midnight, which means we've been wandering around inside this house for well over three hours!'

'That's impossible... Hey, Ronnie; what time do you make it? Gordon here says it's close to midnight.'

'He's right, Spike. That's what my watch says as well – five minutes to twelve to be exact.'

Spike scratched his chin, perplexed. 'Looks like we've lost them,' he said. 'We must have taken a wrong turning somewhere.'

'How?' exclaimed Gordon. 'It's just one long corridor for fuck's sake! You can't make a wrong turning—'

'Shhh! Keep your voices down,' said Ronnie. 'This is supposed to be a stealth-operation, remember.'

'What's in here?' remarked Whiskey Pete, pointing at a door immediately to his right. 'We haven't tried this door yet.'

Opening the door, the group were met by the sound of running water and the pungent aroma of dense tropical foliage. 'It's a conservatory,' said Keg, running his fingers gently over the leaves of a giant fern. 'Looks like old Silver's a plant lover.'

Cautiously, they made their way into the room. The night sky was black and visible above their heads through the conservatory windows.

'There's that vibration again,' said Ronnie. 'It happens every time we walk into a room... Odd thing that.'

Now, there was complete silence as the men infiltrated the conservatory, ever alert for danger and expecting to be attacked at any moment. When at last they'd satisfied themselves that the place was secure, Spike had a word with Gordon.

'There's nothing here,' he said. 'It looks like the place is clear. Let's go back down the hallway and see if we can find Sterling and her mob.'

With a nod of agreement, Gordon led the others out of the room and into the corridor, only too pleased to be back in the main body of the house once more. Stepping across the threshold, he hesitated and waited for the vibration that Ronnie had mentioned. Nothing happened, and it was only when he finally walked into the hallway that he noticed something was horribly wrong.

'What's happened to the hall?' he exclaimed in alarm, looking slowly up and down the corridor. Spike looked too and drew in his breath at what he saw. Whereas before, there had been a reasonably well lit passageway with the promise of more beyond, there was now only a blank wall of coffered oak panelling blocking their path and still no sign of Sterling. In the space of less than three seconds, Spike assessed the situation and came to the conclusion that they were now all hopelessly lost.

'I don't understand it,' he said. 'It's the same door we used before but the hallway's changed. How come?'

'I think I know,' answered Ronnie, kneeling down and examining the doorframe. 'There's a couple of infrared sensors embedded in the wood down there. They must get triggered every time we cross the threshold.'

'So...?'

'So, I remember when I was a kid watching a TV series called The Avengers where this woman called Emma Peel gets trapped in an old house where all the rooms keep moving around on rollers that get triggered every time she goes through a door. It was all done to confuse her and drive her barmy.'

'Oh, yeah... I remember that episode too. It was called "The House That Jack Built" and went out in 1965 it did.'

'Fucking hell, are you that old, Spikey?' said Keg with a laugh.

'It was a 1980s repeat I watched,' replied Spike, curtly.

'I'm pleased to hear it. So, what are we going to do then?'

Spike thought hard before glancing back into the room. 'Let's double back into the conservatory and see if there's another way out. Maybe we can catch up with Joe and Sterling before they locate Silver. I wonder how they're doing...?'

***

'This must be the dining room,' whispered Joe, hardly daring to breathe.

'Well, it's where the music seems to be coming from so I guess it must be,' Skinner replied softly. 'What do you think, Sterling?'

'It's Mozart... Wolfgang Amadeus Mozart,' was all the vampire said in response.

'You what?' hissed Joe, trying to keep his voice down.

'Mozart – Silver's playing Mozart on his sound-system. It's the Jupiter symphony, if I'm not mistaken. I remember it from when I...' –she corrected herself – 'from when Julie Kent was a music student. It was her favourite piece I seem to recall...' *Damn it! Silver's trying to get inside my head already. I must block him... I've got to block him...*

Nice try, Sterling, came an all-too familiar voice exploding deep within her brain. *Stir any memories does it?*

'Get out! Get out!'

'You all right, Sterl?'

It was Cassidy who spoke, and he looked concerned.

'Yes, yes; I'm okay. It's just a migraine, that's all.'

'I didn't know vampires got migraines?'

'Well they do, so shut the fuck up, right!'

'Okay—understood,' Cassidy answered, turning his attention to an oil painting that was hanging on the wall opposite the dining room door. 'Hey, that's Caroline Westvale,' he exclaimed, pointing to the portrait.

'Yeah, and you'll be joining her if you don't keep your trap shut. Now, be quiet will you, I'm trying to think—'

Think all you want, dear heart, came Silver's voice again. *It won't do you any good when we finally clash...*

Shit! thought Sterling; *he's going to make a psychic duel of it. I'm not equipped to fight him that way—*

'Why don't we just walk in shooting,' exclaimed Joe, breaking the vampire's train of thought. 'I can use my revolver to cause a distraction while you close in for the kill with your silver bullets.'

'I don't think it's going to be like that, Joe. In any case, we need Spike and his machine-pistol to keep their heads down. We still don't know how many people Silver's got in there—assuming they are people, that is.'

'Where is Spike anyway?' cut in Skinner. 'I thought he was tailing us up the hall with the rest of the gang.'

'I don't know,' replied Sterling with a note of anxiety in her voice. 'I could have sworn I saw him only a moment ago, but now it's almost midnight and...'

The vampire stalled in mid-sentence. Something had caught her attention. It was the handle of the dining room door slowly turning as if some invisible hand were guiding it in its course. The others noticed it too and looked on silently as the large, brass doorknob kept on turning around until it finally reached full lock and stopped.

Skinner glanced first at Joe and then to Sterling. 'What do you think?' he said, seeking some reassurance. But the words had scarcely left his mouth when there came a creaking sound and the door slowly began to open.

'I think…' the vampire said, hesitantly, '…I think we can go in now, boys. Jimmy Silver just invited us to his party.'

Twenty

From deep within the dining room came the sound of laughter.

Sterling knew that laugh. She'd last heard it at a party in London, over thirty years ago.

'I'm coming for you, you bastard!' she whispered under her breath, her fingers closing on the butt of her gun. 'I'm gonna make you pay for what you did.'

'Steady on, kid,' said Skinner. 'Don't lose it now. We're all counting on you.'

'Don't worry. I'm more together now than I've been in years. How about you?'

'Me? I'm fine—just fine,' Skinner replied, his sweaty palm gripping the handle of his Saint Etienne revolver as if it were the very last thing on earth. Joe was covering him with his Webley, which at least had some bullets left in it, while Cassidy followed on behind, hardly daring to breathe as the dining room door opened further to reveal the scene within.

Not one, but many voices were engaged in the convivial merriment of the hour as the sound of the Mozart symphony played on above the chatter of the guests seated on either side of the long rectangular dining table. Cassidy counted sixteen in total, with the seventeenth, who he guessed must be Jimmy Silver, sitting in the shadows at the far end of the table.

'Are they all…?'

Sterling nodded. 'Yes, Stuart; every one of them, including that cunt seated at the far end. Do you believe me now?'

Cassidy was about to reply when his psychic vision kicked in and he saw exactly what it was that Sterling was seeing.

It was a horrible sight. Mummified corpses, dressed in the finest of bespoke suits and evening gowns were seated around the table chattering with each other or taking pieces of food into their mouths with elegant, bony fingers. Most of them still possessed enough skin to cover their bones, although it was as stiff and as yellow as parchment. The ones who still had their faces were the worst; their lips pulled back in the parody of a smile irrespective of whatever mood they happened to be in at the time.

Walking further into the room, Sterling paused to take in the ghastly scene. She'd never got used to it in all the years she'd possessed the vision to see. Cassidy too, was uncomfortable with what he was now witnessing, as one by one, all of the guests turned their black, empty eye sockets in Sterling's direction and began talking among themselves.

'It's her; it's really her!' hissed one of the cadavers, dressed in a sequined gown and seated next to a similarly attired female corpse who was about to take a mouthful of champagne from a crystal glass.

'Settle down, Cora,' replied her skeletal partner, placing a hand on the woman's bony knee. 'Silver always likes to spring a little surprise at these events of his. You should know that by now.'

Sterling tensed as one of the dead things wearing a dark dinner jacket and trousers got up from its seat and offered her a cigarette.

'Miss Sterling. Delighted to make your acquaintance. I hear you are quite a legend among our kind, or so I've been led to believe.'

Cassidy's vision shimmered, and the walking corpse returned to normal, becoming none other than a prominent Tory MP who he recalled having seen several times before in the tabloid newspapers. He did not look out of place among the ranks of the Undead, Cassidy thought, and neither did another of the, by now, fully-fleshed guests dressed in the latest Italian fashion, his eyes obscured by designer sunglasses just like Sterling's. Presumably, this individual was a representative of the notorious Camorra clan who Silver was rumoured to play host to.

The man said something in Italian, his manner anxious. He rubbed his hands together, watching Silver expectantly.

'Yes. I can see that she's here,' the shadowy figure seated at the far end of the table snapped. 'Tarrou, if you would be so kind…'

Sterling flinched as she heard the door slam shut behind her. Then she whirled round only to be confronted by the tall, African man aiming a heavy calibre pistol directly at her chest.

'They're special bullets,' was all Tarrou said as he gestured for her to walk forward into the dining room along with her accomplices. 'Don't think of doing anything stupid. Your own guns won't work inside this room. Mr Silver's put a glamour on the place. Only our own weapons are any good inside here.'

The chattering voices became silent as Sterling walked towards the table, still clutching the Mauser pistol in her hand. The guests all looked normal now she was no longer seeing them with the vision of the Undead. It could have been a supper party anywhere in England were it not for the long black candles arranged at intervals among the diners, their eerie blue flames burning tall and bright in the stagnant air. Overhead, the room was spanned by a beautiful stained-glass ceiling of Victorian design, while beyond that lay the bleak December sky, ebony black and thick with stars.

'You must forgive Tarrou,' apologised Silver. 'He can be very abrupt when it comes to matters of security. Unlike ourselves, he has no control over his psychic abilities and relies on me to provide the necessary medication to calm the voices inside his head.'

'How humanitarian of you, Jimmy.'

Silver raised an eyebrow. 'Yes, isn't it. Even vampires have their weaknesses I suppose. Would you care for a glass of champagne?'

'No thanks.'

Cassidy, who was standing beside Sterling, desperately wanted to make a run for it but found the mental duel that was now developing between the two alpha vampires so fascinating that he wouldn't have moved even if he thought the room was on fire. Joe and Skinner were likewise rooted to the spot, powerless to do anything but watch as the arcane psychic chess game unfolded before their eyes.

'Were you surprised when you received my letter, Sterling?' enquired Silver with a smile. 'Do say yes, it would flatter me so.'

'Yes, I guess I was surprised. How did you know where to find me?'

'Did you think I would be so foolish as to neglect to keep myself informed of your whereabouts? I've had you watched ever since you set foot back in England. Your killing of those three Camorra men and the presence of the single black rose you left with their bodies was all it took to finally convince me that you'd escaped from the island. That *is* why you left the roses there, wasn't it?'

'Maybe.'

'I thought so. You see, there are a great many things I know about you my dear. Like the fact that you've teamed up with that sad loser Cassidy over there. He used to be one of my men... but I suppose you know about that already.'

'I do.'

Silver cleared his throat before continuing.

'Then it would interest me to know, dear heart, exactly who it is that you work for?'

'I don't know what you're talking about.'

'Oh, come now, Sterling. Surely you're not that ignorant! Your escape from the island cannot have been of your own making. You must have had some assistance... from an Adept perhaps?'

'If you mean, Alexei Stanislavsky then I'm afraid you're mistaken. Stanislavsky died years ago. My escape was entirely of my own making. Some construction workers accidentally crashed their bulldozer into the tomb. Their actions broke the magic circle you'd had placed around my coffin. That's all.'

'Then who is your clan master? You must have a clan master, surely?'

'I don't have one.'

Silver looked genuinely perplexed. His voice became distant and remote, as if he were thinking aloud.

'What was Virginia thinking of spawning a creature like her... I should have disposed of her body more thoroughly while I still had the chance....Getting careless in my old age I suppose...' Glancing up, he noticed the puzzled expression on Sterling's face, and his sardonic smile returned.

'What you must understand, my dear, is that all vampires like yourself have a clan master. You are far too young to be operating all on your own. It simply wouldn't do to have hundreds of the Undead running loose and taking matters into their own hands. Why, even I was in fief to a clan master once, but now it is I who rule the roost—at least in England anyway.'

'I have no clan master, Jimmy. I'm my own master.'

Voices were raised in protest at this remark. Such a thing had never happened before within living memory. Sterling had broken all the rules and stepped out of line... and at a dinner party too.

'Slap her down, Silver,' bellowed Hugo. 'The bitch has issued you a challenge.'

'Yes, slap her down,' snarled Clarice, a little the worse for drink. 'Bloody underclass think they can say anything they like these days. Teach her a fucking lesson she won't forget!'

'Common as dirt,' added Cora, wrinkling her nose as her hand dropped to touch something concealed at her waist.

Someone's come prepared, thought Sterling. *That's a dagger she's got down there...*

Silver raised a hand for silence and the room became still. Looking down the length of the table, he regarded Sterling with a mixture of surprise and amused contempt.

'What is it you're after, girl – a shot at the title or just a seat beside the band?'

Sterling shook her head, not quite sure what he meant.

'I mean, what is it that you want? Is it revenge or something else perhaps, hmm?'

Again, Silver arched an eyebrow. She hated it when he did that.

'As you know, Sterling, we vampires have a strict pecking order... a hierarchy if you like, that mimics what little remains of our aristocratic culture.'

'What are you saying, Jimmy?'

'Saying? Why, isn't it obvious, my dear? What I'm saying is that *you're not one of us.* You never were. You're just Julie Kent the music student from Chelmsford.'

'That's right, Jimmy,' put in Clarice. 'You tell her straight. She's just a fucking peasant. Always has been and always will be.'

'Dead for over three hundred years and she's still a snob,' muttered Cassidy to himself. 'Some things never change in this country.'

'Shut up,' snapped Sterling angrily. 'This is going to get bad. Real bad.'

None of the guests spoke as they all waited for Silver to continue with his dressing down. But, just as he was about to

279

open his mouth to deliver another salvo, there came the muffled sound of gunfire issuing from somewhere deep inside the house.

'That was Gordon's shotgun going off,' declared Joe. 'Looks like the others are in trouble.'

Sterling said nothing but just kept on staring at Silver who was still seated beyond the tapering candles at the end of the table. There followed another series of muffled bangs and then the sound of someone shouting. Then everything went silent.

'I think your boys have just encountered one of my minders,' exclaimed Silver at last. 'He's called Fetch and he doesn't take very kindly to intruders. Ogres are territorial creatures at heart. Quite like vampires in many ways, wouldn't you say, Sterling... or should I call you Julie?'

'That was a bit below the belt,' observed Skinner. 'Is that the best you've got?'

Silver ignored this remark and kept on with his relentless baiting of Sterling.

'Anyway, every dominant vampire like myself eventually comes to have a following; namely, those members of the Undead who are subservient to him and to whom they must all pledge their allegiance. Isn't that right, Hugo?'

Hugo nodded reluctantly. He hated to admit his own weakness but felt he had no choice. Silver's will was far too strong.

Sterling glanced up and down the length of the dining room table. 'You mean all these revenants here are actually nothing more than your obedient creatures, Jimmy?'

'Correct! The size and quality of an alpha-vampire's following automatically determines their social status in the world of the Undead… and the power of their will. Don't look so surprised, child. What did you expect?'

'Are you saying that I'm weak then?'

'Quite the contrary, Sterling. At first, I thought you were acting under orders, but now I can see that you are quite alone… apart from your human associates of course. You know, it can take a vampire several decades to break free from their master and assert their own authority, but you practically did it overnight. I've only ever had it happen to me once before and that was with Caroline Westvale.'

'Which is why you left her marooned in Venice surrounded by water just like me?'

'Precisely. England is a small country. It wouldn't do to have too much competition around. Virginia Cavendish was becoming a problem as well until you dealt with her. Thank you for that.'

'It was a pleasure.'

'Sarcasm becomes you, my dear. But I would not be so bold if I were in your shoes.'

'Oh, and why is that?'

'Because by now, my creature, Fetch will have slaughtered your comrades and disposed of their bodies. I need not tell you how an ogre deals with human remains. It really doesn't bear thinking about.'

***

'Is it dead?'

'I don't know, Spike,' replied Gordon, his hands still trembling with shock. 'I emptied my shotgun into its chest about six times before the thing went down, so I guess it must be.'

'Go take a closer look then.'

'No way. You can if you want to, but I'm not going anywhere near that thing, dead or alive.'

With a gesture of his hand, Spike indicated for Sub to go over to where the ogre's body lay on the floor of the conservatory. Reluctantly, Sub approached the beast and gently nudged it with the toe of his motorcycle boot. There was no reaction.

Relieved, Sub turned to Spike and the others. 'I reckon it's dead.'

'Thank fuck for that,' exclaimed Keg. 'It nearly had you there, Gordon.'

'Yeah, tell me about it. I've only got two cartridges left.'

'You should have put a bullet in its napper,' said Spike. 'A head shot is usually the only way to make sure.'

'You think I should do it now?' replied Gordon angrily.

'Mmm... maybe not. I reckon you've just about done for it. Now all that remains is to find our way out of this damn moving labyrinth and locate Sterling. I don't know about you lot, but this here conservatory of Silver's looks a whole lot bigger than it did the first time we entered it. What do you think, Sub?'

There was no answer, only a yell of surprise as Sub felt a huge hand wrap itself slowly around his left ankle. Next thing he knew, the creature had sunk its long, yellow teeth deep into the leather of his motorcycle boot causing him to emit an ear-piercing shriek as the ogre's jaws closed on his leg.

'Get it off! Get it off me! It's got my fucking leg!'

'Jesus effing Christ, the thing's still alive!' exclaimed Ronnie, pulling out his knife and stabbing the creature repeatedly in the head. It did no good, only serving to enrage the nightmare cryptid even further. Ignoring the motorcycle boot, the beast rose up and turned on Ronnie, sweeping aside his blade with a deft movement of its paw. Then, just as it was about to crush him in a bear hug, Keg moved in and punched it hard in the face. Keg was a large man, almost as big as the ogre itself, but he was no match. It only took a second for the snarling troglodyte to rally before it came at him with a deep resonant growl, ready to tear out his throat.

Again, Ronnie lunged at the beast with his knife, but the blade just snapped off in its thick rubbery hide and stayed there embedded in the creature's right shoulder without so much as a glimmer of pain showing on its hideous face.

'It's no good,' he shouted, backing away. 'Let's get out of here!'

'And go where?' replied Sub, breathing hard. 'The hallway's sealed off. We'd never make it out of the house.'

'Stand clear,' yelled Spike, levelling his machine-pistol at the ogre's head. 'Here, chew on this, you cunt!' he snarled, pulling the trigger.

Instantly, the creature's huge bald head exploded, spraying everyone with pieces of brain and bone fragments. Nobody spoke, only looking on in amazement as the body slithered to the floor with a sibilant thump. Of the head, nothing remained except for the stump of its neck and a section of the lower jaw bone. Everything else was gone, atomised to a bloody pulp that slowly dripped from the green foliage of the conservatory plantings or ran down the faces of the bikers gathered around.

'Shouldn't you have been wearing safety goggles for that sort of thing?' said Gordon, half-jokingly.

Spike ignored him, checking the ammunition he had left in his magazine. 'I've emptied half the box at it. Let's get out of here and see what's happened to the others. I think I saw an exit up ahead through those giant ferns. Come on, let's take a look.'

***

Sterling felt the rage boiling up inside her. The knowledge that most of her companions were probably dead wasn't helping, nor was the gloating image of Silver seated smiling at the end of the table.

'They're only human,' he said. 'Their lives were short anyway. Why mourn their passing?'

'They were my friends,' replied Sterling with a tremor in her voice.

Silver laughed at this, and Sterling's vision wavered as she shifted spectrum, causing his image to warp and twist in the candlelight. Now, his flesh withered until it came to resemble the wrinkled skin of a dead thing as his features slowly sank back into his skull like melting snow. The smell that emanated from him was truly appalling, but no one else seated around the table seemed to mind.

Sterling sensed the awesome power that dwelt within that living corpse and knew what damage it could do once it was unleashed. She'd never forgotten the clash she'd had with Baron Von Geisenheim all those years ago, but back then she'd had some support from Alexei Stanislavsky to help her out. This time, the fight would be between her and Silver alone.

'You know, there's one thing that I don't understand,' said Silver, his features gradually resuming their normal appearance.

'What's that?'

'How you managed to make your escape from the island, of course. Vampires usually can't cross large bodies of water without some assistance. Who helped you?'

'I did it alone.'

'Impossible! None have ever done that without...' Silver paused, not wanting to reveal any more than he should.

Sterling was genuinely surprised. She'd not expected him to show his hand so early on in the proceedings. This would have weakened his will—but only by a fraction.

'Without what?' she enquired, half-realising what it might be that Silver wished to conceal.

He has the Incunabulum, she thought, *but where is he hiding it?*

Lifting her gaze, she looked up. Overhead, she could see that the dining room possessed a glass ceiling which revealed the night sky beyond. Secretly, she implored the heavens for guidance but no answer came. Perhaps, God no longer listened to creatures like her who lacked a soul. Julie Kent was dead.

Silver's expression changed. He was no longer certain what he was dealing with. Before, he had been confident in the fact that he'd baited his trap well and it was only a matter of time until Sterling's will cracked. Now, he wasn't so sure.

It was true that what he saw standing there in front of him was definitely Sterling. Her appearance may have changed over the years and she was no longer the hybrid goth-punk he'd known back in the 1970s, but it was her all right, down to the black leather jacket and mirrored sunglasses.

Sunglasses...?

Why the shades? he thought. Was she becoming allergic to sunlight already? It happened with some—usually the older ones. He himself no longer enjoyed the sun on his face and had recently taken to venturing indoors around midday to avoid its glare. But, Sterling was young. A mere stripling in fact. Surely, she wasn't old enough to have developed the affliction? No, it wasn't possible.

Silver's lips twisted into a cruel smile.

'So, we finally meet after all these years,' he said, his handsome, debonair features now fixed firmly back into place once more. 'I must say, I didn't recognise you at first. Do you know how many young women I have disposed of over the years, my dear? Did you expect me to remember *you* among all the multitude?'

'I... *She* was called Julie Kent. London 1977.'

Silver nodded. 'Ah yes; young Julie Kent, the music student Virginia took a fancy to! I remember dumping your body in the sea afterwards but somehow it managed to get washed up on a beach. Careless of me.'

'Cut the crap, Jimmy! You know who I am and why I'm here.'

Silver sighed, making a towering gesture with his hands. 'Yes, yes, I know. You are here to kill me, aren't you? But tell me, my dear, what exactly would my death prove?'

'That I'm not like you—'

Suppressed giggles broke out around the table. The others were enjoying this little duel, all the more because Sterling seemed to be in such obvious denial of what it was that she had become.

'Burn the witch!' someone shouted in jest, and the rest of the party joined in with the chant, banging their palms down on the table with a steady, rhythmic beat. Silver allowed their enthusiasm to build for a while before silencing it with a sweep of his hand.

'I must apologise for the rudeness of my guests, Sterling. They were born in a different time to yourself, and lack the customary refinements of our modern age. However, I am sure you must appreciate the reason for their rough humour.'

'No, I don't, Jimmy... or should I say, *Sir James*. Pray enlighten me.'

Silver smiled and studied his fingernails. 'If as you say you are not like me, then how is it that you have survived? *How do you feed?*'

'I—I have my ways.'

'Sure you do. We all do. But are you telling me that you have never savoured the blood of the innocent?'

'No—!'

'What—*never?*'

Sterling thought back. The rapist truck driver she'd torn apart. The dodgy Chinaman she'd wasted in Soho. The teenage psychotic she'd killed in Highgate Cemetery. All of her victims had been hardened criminals and a threat to her in one way or another. No, there were no innocents among their number. But then—

He's trying to catch me off-guard, she thought. *He's engaging my mind in an ethical dilemma in order to distract me and weaken my will.*

'No, Jimmy. They all had it coming.'

Silver smiled a low, cunning smile and Sterling fought the urge to tear it from his lips.

'How many?' he enquired with a smirk.

'None of your business.'

'Ha!' Silver exclaimed, the smile widening to reveal his sharp yellow fangs. 'And you say you're not like me. The hypocrisy!'

'I'm not one of your kind!'

'That's what they all say,' replied Silver in a mocking, sing-song voice. 'Oh, it couldn't possibly be me, could it? I'm such a sweet little girl.'

'Shut up! I'm not like the others.'

'That is true, after a fashion. If only Linda Bailey had turned out half as good as you. But I suppose that's what I get for working with poor material. Still, it's a pity to have to destroy something as unique as yourself. You remind me so much of my dear Caroline.'

She was in trouble. She sensed it with every fibre of her being. Silver possessed the Incunabulum, and what was more, he knew how to use it. What secrets it contained she could not even begin to fathom, but none of them would be very pleasant if she knew Jimmy Silver and what he was capable of.

He was inside her head in an instant, striking this way and that like a rattlesnake on amphetamines. She moaned as his will crashed into hers, ransacking her mind for anything it could latch on to. As the pressure mounted inside her skull, she swayed a little on her feet and Cassidy caught her by the arm in case she fell.

'No, Cassidy! Don't touch me! He'll kill you! Let go.'

As Cassidy relaxed his grip, he felt a trickle of warm liquid run down his top lip. Even a momentary contact with Silver's mind had caused him to have a massive nosebleed.

'Why fight it, child?' she heard a voice say deep within her brain. 'Is this how you treat your grandfather?'

Quickly, she spat the thought back at him. 'You're not my grandfather!'

Impressed with her ability, Silver withdrew his will temporarily and sat back in his chair.

'That was exhilarating, my dear. Almost evenly matched I would say, but you still have a lot to learn.'

'Such as what?'

'Your psychic barrier wouldn't have lasted. You're not skilled enough for that.'

'That's your opinion.'

'It is a fact. Your will lacks focus... and skill.'

Silver tilted his head to one side. 'When I heard that you'd returned to England I couldn't believe it. At first I thought you were just some new kid on the block. Some chancer from Europe, trying their luck in fresh pastures, so to speak. I had originally planned to find out who your master was and deal with them accordingly. But when it became apparent who you were, I had another idea.'

'Which was?'

'To offer you a contract.'

A murmur now arose among the guests. This had never happened before. What on earth was Silver thinking of negotiating with a peasant.

'What kind of a *contract?*'

Silver reached into his jacket pocket and pulled out a small parchment scroll tied with a length of scarlet ribbon.

'A contract to work for me, of course. Now that I've lost Cassidy here, I need another agent to represent my interests in London. Someone like yourself to compliment Linda Bailey.'

'Did she tell you I was coming here?'

'No, as a matter of fact it was Cardinal Streffan who informed me. He has the protection of the Vatican by the way, so don't go churning your oats with him. They'll just send the boys round anyway... and it won't be Father Dominic who pays you a visit next time.'

Was this a veiled threat, she wondered? Years ago, she had regarded religion as nothing more than a fairytale; a myth conjured up by power-hungry plutocrats, intent on manipulating the infantile minds of the masses. Tell a big enough lie and everyone believes you in the end. It was the oldest con trick in the book—but that was before she'd become a vampire.

Of course, the current wave of fundamentalism that was sweeping across the world was just that. A massive con trick aimed at getting people to do precisely what you wanted them to do. But the Catholic Church had had its origins in a much older world. What secrets had it managed to accrue over the last two thousand years? What was the true source of its power?

She would not yield.

'Screw your fucking contract! I'm not working with Linda Bailey!'

Silver sniffed. 'Too bad. There is much I could have taught you if only you'd had the patience and humility to learn. Personally, I find your attachment to whatever remains of your humanity rather touching if not a little misguided. Mankind is a flawed vessel. Doesn't the Bible teach us that?'

'It also says that we are capable of redemption.'

'We...?' Silver shook his head slowly. 'No, Sterling. You cannot retain that illusion any longer and you know it. Why not surrender now and be done? Here, take the contract and sign it. It's my final offer.'

One could have heard a pin drop, so close and silent had the room become. As the tension mounted, the flames of the tall, black candles successively dimmed then brightened once again as if all the energy had been momentarily drained out of them and then restored by some malevolent unseen intelligence.

'And what do I get in return for learning at your feet, Silver?'

'You get to live, Sterling... and you become like all my friends here.'

'Go to hell!'

Silver let out a sigh. 'Very well then. You leave me with no alternative.'

Now things moved fast as Sterling felt his will lock with her mind once more like a giant squid seizing on its prey.

'Why are you fighting, my child? There is no denying me. I am your creator. I made you what you are and I can unmake you just as quickly again. Perhaps I will dispose of your body properly this time when I have finished with your mind.'

Then it came. The relentless pressure of his will penetrating her consciousness. The temptation to surrender was intense, but she knew that if she did surrender, it would be the end.

Slow breaths. Nice and slow, she thought. *Block him. Block him. Concentrate...*

Sensing her resistance, Silver moved in closer, seeking to gain whatever purchase he could inside her skull.

'Beautiful!' he said. 'Such defiance in one so young. You remind me so much of myself when I was your age. Angry, volatile and defiant. Quite the young Napoleon in many ways.'

Like a mouse caught in the coils of a python, she felt his will closing in around her, encircling her mind in an all-embracing stranglehold from which there was no possibility of escape.

Sterling closed her eyes and saw the spirit of Julie Kent standing in front of her dressed in the punk fashion of her era. Her clothes were dripping wet and she was sobbing in huge uncontrollable gulps. The expression on her face was one of utter despair and regret. Regret that she had been so stupid as to attend the party in London that night back in 1977, and despair that she would never live to become the person she had most wanted to become. Julie Kent, the famous concert pianist.

'Bastard!' she exclaimed.

Then she saw another figure standing close by Julie, resting a comforting hand on her shoulder. It was none other than the long-dead Alexei Stanislavsky in spirit form and he looked concerned.

'Thirty years! You've been waiting over thirty years to pay him back for what he did to you! Take my advice before it's too late, Sterling. Remove your sunglasses. Do it now!'

In an instant, Sterling knew what this impromptu message from the spirit world might mean. Raising her hand, she reached for her sunglasses and tried to remove them but found her arm rendered stiff and heavy with the effort.

He's blocking me. Silver's blocking me. What is he afraid of
?

With a supreme effort of will, she tried raising her hand once again and this time it worked, enabling her to grasp the sunglasses with the tip of her thumb and forefinger and tear them off before Silver had a chance to stop her.

'Aieee-e-e-e-e-e-e-e-e-e!'

A piercing shriek tore through the room causing all heads to turn in the direction of the noise. It was Clarice who had screamed. She was clutching her partner's arm so hard that her fingernails dug deep into Cora's flesh.

'Her eyes!' Clarice yelled. 'They're crimson! She's been to hell! She's one of Lucifer's own!'

Sterling smiled. She knew she'd won. None of the other vampires in the room, Silver included, had actually been to hell except for herself. She alone among them all had spoken to Lucifer on first name terms when she'd visited the Underworld on the outskirts of Naples all those years ago. It was Lucifer himself who had bestowed his blessing upon her for having returned the magical amulet to Hades on behalf of the Satanic Congress. No one could touch her now. Not Silver. Not Virginia. Not Linda Bailey. Not anyone. She was now free to roam at will in the world and woe betide anyone who contested her authority to do so. She relished seeing the expression on Linda's face when she finally returned to London with the news—Sterling, Queen of the Damned. Well how about that!

She began to laugh, and the tears rolled down her cheeks; an action which angered Silver even more, causing him to break contact with her mind.

'Cora! Use your dagger! Kill the bitch now!' he yelled, spitting out his words with venom.

Immediately, Clarice removed her hand from Cora's arm, allowing her partner to reach for the weapon—a nine-inch long, silver-bladed poignard that was concealed within the folds of her gown. Then, with a hatred bordering on the psychotic, Cora advanced on Sterling, brandishing the dagger in her clenched fist ready to strike.

Sterling realised her gun was useless, but she had another trick up her sleeve as she threw down her sunglasses and plucked a small packet of incense out from the side pocket of her motorcycle jacket. Reaching over to one of the burning candles, she sprinkled the precious incense onto its flame with the words: 'Azrael—Come! I command you to appear!'

There was a moment when nothing happened and then the glass ceiling above the dining room suddenly shattered and imploded into a million pieces accompanied by the hurricane sound of beating wings as a huge black shadow quickly descended on the startled guests, shrouding them all in darkness. Then there followed another blood-curdling scream, followed by the sound of machine gun fire and splintering wood before everything became still once more and the shadow departed with a sinister hiss.

The smell was appalling. It was the unmistakable stench of decay and it was coming from where Cora had been standing only a few seconds before. Clarice looked down, scarcely believing what she saw. Then she let out a hollow moan that quickly transformed itself into a wail of sorrow. Of her lover, Cora, nothing remained except for a shrunken corpse utterly devoid of its flesh save for a few tattered fragments of sinew that still clung to the major joints of the upper and lower body. Cora had suddenly aged two centuries and died where she'd stood, the silver dagger still clenched in her shrivelled hand.

Clarice was beyond tears. Her partner of over two hundred years was now reduced to nothing more than a freak-show mannequin of the kind she remembered gawping at in all the country fairs of her childhood. Even Sterling found it touching the way Clarice cradled her dead lover in her arms, rocking the withered corpse to and fro in her grief.

'Oh, Sterling, what have you done? What have you done?' she said, her sibilant voice cracked and hesitant with emotion.

'I don't know, Clarice. What have I done? You tell me.'

Clarice narrowed her eyes in anger. 'They'll never forgive you for this! For as long as you live, no vampire in the land will ever lift a finger to help you, you can be sure of that!'

'England isn't the world, Clarice. It just thinks it is. You people just need to get over yourselves, that's all.'

'You invoked the Angel of Death, Sterling! You showed them all how small they are.'

'Yeah, well I reckon I've done you fuckers a favour then. Isn't that right everybody?'

No one replied. All the guests' faces were downcast in sombre moods of reflection. Death had dominion over them all and now they knew it.

'Hey, where's Jimmy Silver?' exclaimed Cassidy, still shaken by the events of the last few seconds.

Sterling glanced up the table to where Silver had been seated. There was no sign of him; just an empty, vacant chair where he'd last been seen. Then she turned round and looked at Tarrou. The tall, black man now lay sprawled on the floor in a pool of his own blood. Spike was standing over him grasping his machine-pistol in both hands. 'That was a lucky shot,' he declared. 'Straight through the fucking door as well.'

'Where's your boss?' Sterling said to the dying African.

'He's gone... gone below,' whispered Tarrou with some effort. 'There's a secret door over there behind the folding screen... It leads down to a tunnel. The tunnel runs for miles... don't know where to though... The door is solid steel... It can't be blown—'

'He's right,' said Joe who had wandered over to the screen and looked behind. 'The door is reinforced steel. You'd need a tank round to blow it open.'

Sterling grimaced then looked at the other vampires seated around the table.

'You lot! Get out of here now! Scat!'

'But where can we go?' protested Hugo. 'It's one o' clock in the morning.'

'You've all got limos, haven't you?'

Hugo nodded.

'Well fucking well use 'em then! I've got business to attend to.'

One by one, the ghouls trooped out of the shattered room, only Clarice stopping to enquire what was to be done with her partner's body.

'Leave her to me, Clarice,' said Sterling. 'She's going to be cremated.'

'How do you mean?'

'Stick around long enough and you'll find out the hard way—Now move!'

With Silver's guests departed, the rest of the gang, Keg, Sub, Ronnie, Gordon and Whiskey Pete stepped through the door into the dining room and took their places beside Spike. Satisfying herself that all was well, Sterling pulled out her two-way radio and spoke into the mouthpiece.

'Debbie, bring Orlando and Father Dominic over here pronto. They've got some work to do.'

The radio crackled, *'Okay',* then closed.

'That was Debbie,' said Sterling turning to Cassidy. 'The others should be here soon. Now, tell me where Silver keeps all his valuables.'

'I don't rightly know,' Cassidy replied. 'Like I said, I've only ever been here once before.'

'Does he have a wall safe; a secret hidey hole; anything like that?'

'Well, we could try the study…'

'Lead the way,' commanded Sterling, replacing her sunglasses. 'Spike, you stay here in the hallway and wait for

Debbie and the others to arrive. We'll be waiting for them in Silver's study.'

**

'Hmm... I think I heard another click,' said Orlando, his left ear pressed against the cold steel door of the wall-safe. 'This thing is Victorian... I doubt if there'll be many surprises.'

'Can you hurry it up?' said Sterling.

'Nope. The main thing is the sequence... Aha! That's it! Now for the mortice lock.'

Searching inside a small canvas tool bag, Orlando selected one of several skeleton keys and probed the lock. It wasn't long before the key turned, but the door refused to open.

'Try making two turns to the left and one turn to the right,' said Debbie. 'It usually works on these old ones.'

Orlando nodded and turned the key accordingly. 'Voila!' he exclaimed, smiling at Sterling. 'The safe is now well and truly cracked. It's all yours.'

Looking inside, Sterling examined the interior of the safe. Then, reaching in, she drew out a thick wad of high-denomination banknotes.

'Who wants some?' she exclaimed, handing the money round. 'There's more where this lot came from.'

The gifts were gladly accepted by everyone in Joe's gang with the exception of Father Dominic.

'I... I can't,' he said with a note of regret.

'Why not?'

'Because I'm a Catholic priest, that's why.'

'Taken a vow of poverty, have you?'

The others laughed, apart from Cassidy who remained silent.

'It's not that,' replied Dominic. 'It's the fact that the money's most likely come from the proceeds of crime. I can't accept it... I'm a man of God.'

'Will you say that when I ask you to set fire to this house?' said Sterling, archly.

'What do you mean?'

'You'll see. Go get the holy water out of the car and bring it into the house. I'll tell you what to do with it in a moment.'

Turning to Cassidy, she handed him a bundle of banknotes. 'Here, Stuart,' she said. 'This is the twenty grand that Silver owed you. You can count it if you like.'

Cassidy took the money and riffled through the notes with his fingers. 'What about you, Sterling? What do you get out of all of this?'

'Oh, I think I've already found what I came for,' she replied, reaching back inside the safe and drawing out an old leather-bound book.

'What's that?'

'It's the Incunabulum. I knew Silver would have it somewhere.'

'A book...? You mean all of this was about a fucking book?'

'It's no ordinary book, Stuart. The Incunabulum is a grimoire written solely for the use of vampires. It's an instruction manual if you like.'

'It's written in Latin,' said Cassidy, taking the book and turning over a few pages.

'I realise that. We vampires are fluent in most languages without the need to be taught. It's called Talking in Tongues, in case you wanted to know.'

Just then, Father Dominic returned with the holy water. 'What do you want me to do with this?' he said, putting the plastic container down on the floor.

'Follow me,' said Sterling. 'I want you to splash it all over the ground floor of the house. The rest of you can leave. We'll join you presently when we've finished in here. Come, Dominic—we've got some work to do.'

The others looked on at a safe distance from the house. It was cold and dark, and an owl hooted somewhere off in the woods to the right. For a time, nothing happened, and then Sterling emerged from the front door with the priest. They were both running.

'Shield your eyes!' she yelled. 'It's going to blow!'

A steady blue flame showed in the windows of the house and grew in intensity until it seemed that the very walls of the building could no longer contain it. Then, just when they thought it was all over, there came a loud, roaring sound as the whole house was suddenly consumed in sacred fire in less time than it took to fry an egg.

'Jeezus Christ!' exclaimed Dominic. 'I've never seen holy water do that before!'

'Oh, ye of little faith,' replied Sterling with a smile. 'Come on you lot. Let's get back to London. I reckon we're finished here.'

***

Sterling stood in the lane outside the London warehouse with Cassidy and Skinner. The others had all received their rewards by now and had departed one by one, with the exception of Joe who was loading something into the back of Skinner's car.

'I need some of this coke to trade,' he said. 'The Californians are still wild about the loss of their memory stick and I won't be able to pay them off until I can find a suitable buyer for the diamonds.'

'You can post some of those diamonds by airmail,' said Skinner. 'I've heard it done.'

'I doubt if you'll need to bother,' put in Sterling, gesturing them both to look up the road. A vehicle was approaching and it had a flashing blue light on its roof.

'Fuck me, it's the coppers!' exclaimed Joe. 'What are we going to do?'

'Don't worry, I'll handle this,' Sterling replied, walking over to the car as it pulled alongside. As the police vehicle came to a halt, Cassidy recognised a familiar face staring out of the rear passenger window. It was Inspector George Lefarge and he looked decidedly pissed off.

'Hello there, Hooky,' she said, leaning into the window as it slowly wound down. 'Have you brought me what I asked for?'

Lefarge said nothing, but reached inside his coat pocket and handed her a small brown package.

'That it?' she enquired, unfamiliar with modern computer technology.

'It's the memory stick you asked for,' replied Lefarge. 'You can't even begin to imagine what strings I had to pull to get it for you. I hope you're fucking satisfied!'

'What about Stuart Cassidy?'

'All charges against Cassidy have been dropped. His case is closed.'

'Thanks, Hooky,' she said, accepting the package in her hand. 'Always a pleasure to do business with you.'

'Don't think this is over,' Lefarge answered dryly. 'There's always the next time in my line of business.' And with that warning, he wound up the window and the car drove off down the lane and into a new day.

Sterling looked on as the car diminished into the distance, then she turned to Joe Rackham.

'There you are, Joe,' she said, handing him the package. 'It's the memory stick you wanted.'

Joe was overcome with joy and high-fived Skinner with a mighty slap of his hand. 'Looks like we're in the clear, Jerry, thanks to Count Dracula here!'

'All's well that ends well,' added Cassidy, touching Sterling on the shoulder of her motorcycle jacket. 'You're a real diamond you are!'

'I know,' was all she said in reply. 'I know.'

Epilogue

The others had gone now, leaving Sterling alone in the warehouse with her memories. Some of her memories were good and some of them were bad, but at least they were a home of sorts.

She went into the kitchen to roll herself a joint, then climbed upstairs and walked out onto the flat roof to get some air. It was the hour before dawn and everything was still and dark except for the sound of river traffic on the Thames and the soft, drizzling rain on her face. Taking a draw on her joint, she looked out across the city and remembered the old times. London had changed a lot since the days of her youth, but she hadn't—at least, not in any physical sense. That was the problem with being one of the Undead. The world changed around you but the memories never went away.

Sensing a breeze on the back of her head, she turned. The lynch mob had arrived from the spirit world. They usually did around this time of the year.

They were all there... all of her victims, back from the dead to haunt her with their dark, accusing eyes. The truck driver; the teenage boy she'd killed in the graveyard; Rosa Korsch; Claude Dubois, and a good many more; all of them with the same accusing stare.

Sterling walked forward and the spirits allowed her to pass between them. As she did so, she looked them all in the eye one by one. 'You brought this all on yourselves,' she said. 'I never asked for this, but you did.'

Then she looked at Claude Dubois and spoke.

'You probably think these raindrops on my face are tears, Claude. Well, don't you believe it mate! Don't you fucking *believe* it!'